Henry Edward Manning

The Vatican council and its definitions

a pastoral letter to the clergy

Henry Edward Manning

The Vatican council and its definitions
a pastoral letter to the clergy

ISBN/EAN: 9783741189852

Manufactured in Europe, USA, Canada, Australia, Japa

Cover: Foto ©Andreas Hilbeck / pixelio.de

Manufactured and distributed by brebook publishing software
(www.brebook.com)

Henry Edward Manning

The Vatican council and its definitions

CONTENTS.

CHAPTER I.

The World and the Council.

CHAPTER II.

The Two Constitutions.

.(8)

CHAPTER III.

The Terminology of the Doctrine of Infallibility.

CHAPTER IV.

Scientific History of the Catholic Rule of Faith.

CHAPTER V.

Result of the Definition.

APPENDIX.

THE VATICAN COUNCIL

AND

ITS DEFINITIONS.

—◦◦◦—

CHAPTER I.

THE WORLD AND THE COUNCIL.

REVEREND AND DEAR BRETHREN.

From the opening of the Council until the close of the Fourth Public Session, when leave was given to the Bishops to return for a time to their flocks, I thought it my duty to keep silent. It was not indeed easy to refrain from contradicting the manifold errors and falsehoods by which the Council has been assailed. But it seemed for many reasons to be a higher duty, to wait until the work in which we were engaged should be accomplished. That time is now happily come; and the obligation which would have hitherto forbidden the utterance of much that I might have desired to say, has been by supreme authority removed.

To you, therefore, Reverend and dear Brethren, I at once proceed to make known in mere outline the chief events of this first period of the Council of the Vatican.

I shall confine what I have to say to the three

following heads:—First, to a narrative of certain facts external to the Council, but affecting the estimate of its character and acts; secondly, to an appreciation of the internal spirit and action of the Council; and thirdly, to a brief statement of the two dogmatic Constitutions published in its third and fourth Sessions. .

First, as to the external history of the Council. As yet, no narrative, or official account of its proceedings, has been possible. The whole world, Catholic and Protestant, has been therefore compelled to depend chiefly upon newspapers. And as these powerfully preoccupy and prejudice the minds of men, I thought it my duty, during the eight months in which I was a close and constant witness of the procedure and acts of the Council, to keep pace with the histories and representations made by the press in Italy, Germany, France, and England. This, by the watchful care of others in England and in Rome, I was enabled to do. In answer to an inquiry from this country as to what was to be believed respecting the Council, I considered it my duty to reply: " Read carefully the correspondence from Rome published in England, believe the reverse, and you will not be far from the truth." I am sorry to be compelled to say that this is, above all, true of our own journals. Whether the amusing blunders and persistent misrepresentations were to be charged to the account of ill will, or of want of common knowledge, it was often not easy to say. Two things, however, were obvious. The journals of Catholic countries, perverse and hostile as they might be, rarely if ever made themselves ridiculous. They wrote with

great bitterness and animosity: but with a point
which showed that they understood what they
were perverting; and that they had obtained their
knowledge from sources which could only have
been opened to them by violation of duty. Their
narratives of events which were passing under my
own eyes, day by day, were so near the truth, and
yet so far from it, so literally accurate, but so absolutely false, that for the first time I learned to understand Paolo Sarpi's " History of the Council of
Trent;" and foresaw how, perhaps from among
nominal Catholics, another Paolo Sarpi will arise
to write the History of the Council of the Vatican.
But none of this applies to our own country. I am
the less disposed to charge these misrepresentations, in the case of English correspondents, to the
account of ill will, though they abundantly showed
the inborn animosity of an anti-Catholic tradition,
because neither correspondents nor journalists ever
willingly expose themselves to be laughed at. I
therefore put it down to the obvious reason that
when English Protestants undertake to write of an
Œcumenical Council of the Catholic Church, nothing less than a miracle could preserve them from
making themselves ridiculous. This, I am sorry
to know, for the fair name of our country, has been
the effect produced by English newspapers upon
foreign countries. Latterly, however, they seemed
to have learned prudence, and to have relied no
longer on correspondents who, hardly knowing the
name, nature, use, or purpose of anything about
which they had to write, were at the mercy of such
informants as English travelers meet at a table-
d'hôte in Rome. Then appeared paragraphs with-

1*

out date or place, duly translated, as we discovered
by comparing them, from Italian and German
newspapers. They were less amusing, but they
were even more misleading. By way of preface, I
will give the estimate of two distinguished Bishops, who are beyond suspicion, as to the truthful-
ness of one notorious journal.

Of all the foreign sources from which the English newspapers drew their inspiration, the chief,
perhaps, was the "Augsburg Gazette." This paper
has many titles to special consideration. The infamous matter of Janus first appeared in it under
the form of articles. During the Council, it had in
Rome at least one English contributor. Its letters
on the Council have been translated into English
and published by a Protestant bookseller, in a volume by Quirinus.

I refrain from giving my own estimate of the
book, until I have first given the judgment of a
distinguished Bishop of Germany, one of the minority opposed to the definition, whose cause the
"Augsburg Gazette" professed to serve.

Bishop Von Ketteler, of Mayence, publicly pro-
tested against "the systematic dishonesty of the
correspondent of the 'Augsburg Gazette.'" "It
is a pure invention," he adds, "that the Bishops
named in that journal declared that Döllinger rep-
resented, as to the substance of the question (of infallibility), the opinions of a majority of the German
Bishops." And this, he said, "is not an isolated
error, but part of a system which consists in the
daring attempt to publish false news, with the object of deceiving the German public, according to
a plan concerted beforehand." ..... "It will be

necessary one day to expose in all their nakedness and abject mendacity the articles of the 'Augsburg Gazette.' They will present a formidable and lasting testimony to the extent of injustice of which party men, who affect the semblance of superior education, have been guilty against the Church."* Again, at a later date, the Bishop of Mayence found it necessary to address to his Diocese another public protest against the inventions of the "Augsburg Gazette," "The 'Augsburg Gazette,'" he says, "hardly ever pronounces my name without appending to it a falsehood." "It would have been easy for us to prove that every Roman letter of the 'Augsburg Gazette' contains gross perversions and untruths. Whoever is conversant with the state of things here, and reads these letters, cannot doubt an instant that these errors are voluntary, and are part of a concerted system designed to deceive the public. If time fails me to correct publicly this uninterrupted series of falsehoods, it is impossible for me to keep silence when an attempt is made, with so much perfidy, to misrepresent my own convictions." †

---

* The Vatican, March 4, 1870, p. 145.

† The Vatican, June 17, 1870, p. 319. "The Archbishop of Cologne has condemned a pretended Catholic Journal in which the dogma of the Infallibility is attacked, and the proceedings of the Council misrepresented and vilified. The sentence of the Archbishop on this matter derives the greater weight from the fact of his having, as he states, formed part of the minority in the memorable vote of July 13. The Archbishop says : ' The clergy of this Diocese are aware that a weekly paper, the " Rheinischer Merkur," constantly attacks, in an odious manner, and with ignoble weapons, the Holy Church, in the person of its lawful chiefs the Pope and the Bishops, and in its highest representative the Œcumenical Council ; so that men's minds are disturbed, and the hearts of the

Again, Bishop Hefele, commenting on the Roman correspondents of the "Augsburg Gazette" says: "It is evident that there are people, not Bishops, but having relations with the Council, who are not restrained by duty and conscience." *

---

faithful alienated from the Church. It also openly advocates the abolition, by the secular authority, of the Church's liberty and independence. I therefore hold it to be my duty, in discharge of my pastoral office, to expose the anti-Catholic character of the said paper; not because I regard it as of any greater importance than those other more noisy organs of the press which are the exponents of hatred against religion, but simply because the paper above-named pretends to be Catholic. It is on that account that, as Catholic Bishop of this city, I feel called upon to denounce the falsehood of the assumption of the name of Catholic by a journal which is laboring to overthrow the unity of the Church by separating Catholics from that rock on which she is founded. This declaration is also due from me to those my Right Reverend Brethren in the Episcopate who belonged with me to the minority in the Council. The journal in question assumes to be the exponent of the sentiments of that minority, but it never was in any way, directly or indirectly, recognized by it or any of its members; it has been, on the contrary, repeatedly blamed and denounced. Wherefore I exhort all the Reverend Clergy of the Archdiocese to be mindful of their duty as sons of the Catholic Church; and not countenance in any way whatsoever, either by taking it in or reading it, the journal above-named, which outrages our holy Mother. rejects her authority, and desires to see her enslaved. I also exhort you on all fitting occasions to warn your flocks of the dangerous and anti Catholic character of that journal, so that they may be dissuaded from buying or reading it, and may escape being deluded by its errors. I had resolved to order an instruction to be given from the pulpit upon the more recent decisions of the Council, and especially upon the infallible teaching of the Pope, and to explain therein the true sense of the dogma; and thus to remove the prejudices that have been raised against it, as if it were a novel doctrine or one in contradiction to the end of the Church's constitution, or to sound reason; and to meet generally the objections raised against the validity of the Council's decision.' "

* The Vatican, March 4, 1870, p. 145.

We had reason to believe that the names of these people, both German and English, were well known to us.

Now the testimony of the Bishop of Mayence, as to the falsehoods of these correspondents respecting Rome and Germany, I can confirm by my testimony as to their treatment of matters relating to Rome and England. I do not think there is a mention of my own name without, as the Bishop of Mayence says, the appendage of a falsehood. The whole tissue of the correspondence is false. Even the truths it narrates are falsified; and through this discolored medium the English people, by the help of Quirinus and the "Saturday Review," gaze and are misled.

To relieve this graver aspect of the subject, I will add a few livelier exploits of our English correspondents. On January 14, an English journal announced that the Bishops were unable to speak Latin; and that Cardinal Altieri (who laid down his life for his flock in the cholera three years ago), in whose rooms the Bishops met, " was beside himself." " What is there," the correspondent of another paper asked, "in seven hundred old men dressed in white, and wearing tall paper caps?" " The Oriental Bishops," he says, " refused to wear white mitres:" reasonably, because they never wear them. " The Bishop of Thun attacked the Bishop of Sura with a violence which threatened personal collision." There is no Bishop of Thun. The same paper, July 7, says, "I was positively shocked, yesterday, at finding that the Roman Catholic Hierarchy of my own country is a sham; at least, so far as regards its territorial and independent pretensions. Every one of them, including the Archbishop, is in charge of a Vicar Apostolic, Cardinal Maddalena, titular Archbishop of Corfu, within whose diocese, it would appear, our island is situated." This has more foundation in fact than the other statements, for until the Archbishop of Corfu could find a carriage, we used daily to go together to the Council.

A leading journal, in May last, announced: "At a recent sitting of the Council, Cardinal Schwarzenberg made a speech which created even a greater uproar than the former one of Bishop Strossmayer." In this speech he defended Protestants with such vigor that "the presiding Legate, Cardinal De Angelis, interrupted the speaker, and a warm dispute between the two Cardinals ensued. The President strove repeatedly, but in vain, to silence the Cardinal with his bell; and at length the Bishops drowned his protest in a storm of hisses, in the midst of which the Cardinal was carried from the tribune, half fainting with excitement, to his seat." The Cardinal was indeed called to order, but no such tragedy was ever acted. "The Papal authorities," says another journal, "have housed the Bishops with discriminating hospitality. Those who could not be absolutely trusted have been lodged with safe companions, in the proportion of one weak brother to half-a-dozen strong." "The Jesuits have had the manipulation of the flock and have done it well." The distribution of the Bishops was made by the Government, and months before the Council opened, with as much theological manipulation as the filling of a train from Paddington. Again, we hear on May

17, that "Cardinal Bilio, the Prefect of the Deputation for Dogma, and author of the Syllabus, has
passed over to the opposition." When the Holy
Father heard of this defection " he was seized with
faintness," and told the Cardinal "to go on a tour
for the benefit of his health." The " Times" at last
confessed: "To find out the truth of what is going
on . . . . . . is difficult beyond conception." . . . . . .
" Every day, even every hour, brings up its story,
. . . . . which, in nine cases out of ten, will prove an
ingenious hoax." Therefore nine-tenths of these
histories are labelled " hoaxes." The " Times"
adds: "To pick one's way amidst these snares,
without becoming the victims of delusions, is what
no man can feel quite sure of." A warning of
which I hope the readers of newspapers will fully
avail themselves.

The " Standard," wiser than its fellows, said in
February: " It is a thousand pities that English
correspondents should childishly swallow cock-
and-bull stories of what never did and never could
have occurred in the Council, and thus damage
their own reputation for accuracy, as well as infer-
entially that of their colleagues."

Another journal damaged something more than
its reputation for accuracy, when, after having announced that the Roman Clergy, that is, the Parish
Priests of Rome, had, all but eight, declined to
petition in favor of the definition, it was again and
again called upon to. publish the fact that the Roman Clergy unanimously petitioned for the definition, in a form so explicit that the Clergy of
England and Scotland afterwards adopted it as
their own, and presented it to the Holy Father.

The newspaper in question was never pleased to
nsert the correction.

But these are flowers plucked at random.

I will now endeavor to give shortly a more connected outline of the Vatican Council, as drawn by
the newspapers of the last eight or nine months;
and as their representations will be one day read
up as contemporaneous records for a future history, I wish to leave in the Archives of the Diocese
a contemporaneous record of their utter worth-
lessness, and, for the most part, of their utter falsehood.

As the highest point attracts the storm, so the
chief violence fell upon the head of the Vicar of
Jesus Christ. On this I shall say nothing. Pos-
terity will know Pius the Ninth; and the world
already knows him now too well to remember,
except with sorrow and disgust, the language of
his enemies. " If they have called the master of
the house Beelzebub, how much more them of his
household?" No one has this privilege above the
Vicar of the Master; and it is a great joy and distinct source of strength and confidence to all of
the household to share this sign, which never fails
to mark those who are on His side against the
world.

The Council was composed, at first, of 767 Fathers. We were told that their very faces were
such as to compel an enlightened correspondent,
at the first sight of them, to lament " that the spiritual welfare of the world should be committed to
such men."

Then, by a wonderful disposition of things, for
the good, no doubt, of the human race, and, above

all, of the Church itself, the Council was divided
into a majority and a minority ; and, by an even
more beneficent and admirable provision, it was so
ordered that the theology, philosophy, science,
culture, intellectual power, logical acumen, eloquence, candor, nobleness of mind, independence
of spirit, courage, and elevation of character in
the Council, were all to be found in the minority.
The majority was naturally a Dead Sea of superstition, narrowness, shallowness, ignorance, prejudice ;
without theology, philosophy, science, or eloquence ; gathered from " old Catholic countries ; "
bigoted, tyrannical, deaf to reason ; with a herd
of " Curial and Italian Prelates," and mere " Vicars
Apostolic."

The Cardinal Presidents were men of imperious
and overbearing character, who by violent ringing
of bells and intemperate interruptions cut short
the calm and inexorable logic of the minority.

But the conduct of the majority was still more
overbearing. By violent outcries, menacing ges-
tures, and clamorous manifestations round the
tribune, they drowned the thrilling eloquence of
the minority, and compelled unanswerable orators
to descend.

Not satisfied with this, the majority, under the
pretext that the method of conducting the discus-
· sions was imperfect, obtained from the supreme
authority a new regulation, by which all liberty of
discussion was finally taken from the noble few
who were struggling to redeem the Council and
the Church from bondage.

From that date the non-œcumenicity of the
Council was no longer doubtful. Indeed, " Janus "

had told the world in many tongues, long before it met, that the Council would not be free. Nevertheless, the minority persevered with heroic courage, logic which nothing could resist, and eloquence which electrified the most insensible, until a tyrannous majority, deaf to reason and incapable of argument, cut discussion short by an arbitrary exercise of power; and so silenced the only voices nobly lifted up for science, candor and common sense.

This done, the definition of new dogmas became inevitable, and the antagonism between the ultra-romanism of a party and the progress of modern society, between independence and servility, became complete,

Such is the history of the Council written *ab extra* in the last nine months. I believe that every epithet I have given may be verified in the mass of extracts now before me.

A leading English journal, ten days after the Definition of the Infallibility of the Roman Pontiff, with great simplicity observed, " It is curious to compare the very general and deep interest taken by all intelligent observers in the early deliberations of the Council with the equally marked indifference to the culmination of its labors. Every rumor that came from Rome six or seven months ago was canvassed with great eagerness, even by men who cared little for ordinary theological disputations; while the proclamation of the astonishing dogma of papal infallibility has produced in any but ecclesiastical circles little beyond a certain amount of prefunctory criticism."

The main cause of this contrast is, of course,

not far to seek. The writer proceeds to assign the
cause, and in so doing passes at once, with a gravity
befitting the occasion, to a disquisition on Sir
William Hamilton's theory of perception, and on
" the gigantic gooseberry."

Such is the earnestness and the sincerity with
which English journals, even of high repute, have
treated the subject of the Œcumenical Council.

Let me, also, assign the cause why the un-Cath-
olic and anti-Catholic world took so clamorous an
interest in the opening of the Council, and in the
end affected so ill-sustained a tone of indifference.
I know of no public event in our day the explanation of which is more transparent and self-evident.
It is this :

When the Council assembled, it was both hoped
and believed that the " Roman Curia " and the
" Ultramontane party " would be checked and
brought under by the decisions of the Bishops.
A controversy had been waged against what was
termed " Ultramontanism," or " Ultra - Catholic-
ism," or " Ultra-Romanism," in Germany, France,
and England. When I last addressed you I used
the following words, which I now repeat, because
I can find none more exact. They have been ful-
filled to the very letter :

" Facts like these give a certain warrant to the
assertions and prophecies of politicians and Protestants. They prove that in the Catholic Church
there is a school at variance with the doctrinal
teaching of the Holy See in matters which are not
of faith. But they do not reveal how small that
school is. Its centre would seem to be at Munich ;
it has, both in France and in England, a small

number of adherents. They are active, they correspond, and, for the most part, write anonymously. It would be difficult to describe its tenets, for none of its followers seem to be agreed in all points. Some hold the infallibility of the Pope, and some defend the Temporal Power. Nothing appears to be common to all, except an animus of opposition to the acts of the Holy See in matters outside the faith.

" In this country, about a year ago, an attempt was made to render impossible, as it was confidently but vainly thought, the definition of the infallibility of the Pontiff, by reviving the monotonous controversy about Pope Honorius. Later we were told •of I know not what combination of exalted personages in France for the same end. It is certain that these symptoms are not sporadic and disconnected, but in mutual understanding, and with a common purpose. The anti-Catholic press has eagerly encouraged this school of thought. If a Catholic can be found out of tune with authority by half a note, he is at once extolled for unequalled authority and irrefragable logic. The anti-Catholic journals are at his service, and he vents his opposition to the common opinions of the Church by writing against them anonymously. Sad as this is, it is not formidable. It has effect almost alone upon those who are not Catholic. Upon Catholics its effect is hardly appreciable ; on the theological Schools of the Church, it will have little influence ; upon the Œcumenical Council it can have none,* "

Many publications had appeared in French, Eng-

---

* Pastoral on " The Œcumenical Council, 1869," &c. pp. 132, 133.

lish, and German, from which it became evident
that a common purpose and plan of co-operation
had been formed. Certain notorious letters published in France, and the infamous book " Janus,"
translated into English, French, and Italian, proclaimed open war upon the Council within the
unity of the Catholic Church. This alone was
enough to set the whole anti-Catholic world on
fire with curiosity, hope, and delight. The learning, the science of the intellectual freemen of the
Roman Church were already under arms to reduce
the pretensions of Rome.

A belief had also spread itself that the Council
would explain away the doctrines of Trent, or give
them some new or laxer meaning, or throw open
some questions supposed to be closed, or come to
a compromise or transaction with other religious
systems ; or at least that it would accommodate
the dogmatic stiffness of its traditions to modern
thought and modern theology. It is strange
that any one should have forgotten that every
General Council, from Nicæa to Trent, which has
touched on the faith, has made new definitions, and
that every new definition is a new dogma, and
closes what was before open, and ties up more
strictly the doctrines of faith. This belief, however, excited an expectation, mixed with hopes,
that Rome by becoming comprehensive might become approachable, or by becoming inconsistent
might become powerless over the reason and the
will of men.

But the interest excited by this preliminary skir-
mishing external to the Council, was nothing compared to the exultation with which the anti-Catho-

lic opinion and anti-Catholic press of Protestant
countries, and the anti-Roman opinion and press
even of Catholic countries, beheld, as they believed,
the formation of an organized " international opposition " of more than a hundred Bishops within the
Council itself. The day was come at last. What
the world could not do against Rome from without, its own Bishops were going to do against
Rome, and in the world's service, from within. I
shall hereafter show how little the world knew the
Bishops whom it wronged by its adulation, and
damaged by its praise. They were the favorites
of the world, because they were believed to be
fighting the Pope. In a moment, all the world
rose up to meet them. Governments, politicians,
newspapers, schismatical, heretical, infidel, Jewish,
revolutionary, as with one unerring instinct, united
in extolling and setting forth the virtue, learning,
science, eloquence, nobleness, heroism of this " international opposition." With an iteration truly
Homeric, certain epithets were perpetually linked
to certain names. All who were against Rome were
written up ; all who were for Rome were written
down. The public eye and ear of all countries
were filled, and taught to associate all that is noble
and great with the " international opposition ; " all
that is neither noble nor great, not to say more,
with others. The interest was thus wrought up to
the highest pitch ; and a confident expectation was
raised, and spread abroad, that the Council would
be unable to make a definition, and that Rome
would be defeated. I can hardly conceive a keen-
er or more vivid motive of interest to the anti-
Catholic world than this. For this cause Rome

was full of correspondents, " our own," " our special," and " our occasional." Private persons for-
sook great interests and duties, to reside in Rome
for the support of the "international opposition."
A league of newspapers, fed from a common centre, diffused hope and confidence in all countries,
that the science and enlightenment of the minority
would save the Catholic Church from the immod-
erate pretensions of Rome, and the superstitious
ignorance of the universal Episcopate. Day after
day, the newspapers teemed with the achievements
and orations of the opposition. The World believed that it had found its own in the heart of the
Episcopate, and loved it as its own. There was
nothing it might not hope for, expect, and predict.
In truth, it is no wonder that a very intense interest should be excited in minds hostile to Rome by
such a spectacle as the outer world then believed
itself to see. And such, we may safely affirm, were
the chief motives of its feverish excitement, at the
opening and during the early period of the Council.

But how shall we account for the indifference
with which the World affects to treat its close ?

By two very obvious reasons. First, because it
became gradually certain that the World had not
found its own in the Council; and that the " opposition " on which it counted were not the servants
of the World, but Bishops of the Catholic Church,
who, while using all freedom which the Church
abundantly gave them, would, in heart, mind, and
will, remain faithful to its divine authority and
voice. And secondly, because it became equally
certain, indeed was self-evident, that no opposition,

from without or from within, could move the Council a hair's breadth out of the course in which it was calmly and irresistibly moving to its appointed work.

The hopes and confidence of the miscellaneous alliance of nominal Catholics, Protestants, rationalists, and unbelievers, received its first sharp check when some five hundred Fathers of the Council desired of the Holy See that the doctrine of the Infallibility of the Roman Pontiff should be defined.* This event manifested a mind and a will so united and so decisive, as to reduce the proportions of the opposition, both numerically and morally, to very little. Still it was confidently hoped that some event, in the chapter of accidents, might yet hinder the definition ; that either the minority might become more powerful by increase, or the majority less solid by division.

This expectation again was rudely shaken by the unanimous vote of the third public Session. The first Constitution *De Fide* had been so vehemently assailed, and, as it was imagined, so utterly defeated, that if ever voted at all it would be voted only by a small majority, or at least it would be resisted by an imposing minority. It was therefore no small surprise that the whole Council, consisting then of 664 Fathers, should have affirmed it with an unanimous vote. I well remember that when the " *Placets* " of the " opposition leaders " sounded through the Council Hall, certain high diplomatic personages looked significantly at each other. This majestic unanimity, after the alleged internal

---

* See Appendix, p. 9.

contentions of the Council, was as perplexing as it was undeniable. The World began to fear that, after all, the international opposition would neither serve its purpose nor do its work. A sensible change of tone was then perceived. The correspondents wrote of everything but of this unanimity. The newspapers became almost silent. The leading articles almost ceased. From that time they exchanged the tone of confidence and triumph for a tone of iritation and of no little bitterness.

Nevertheless, a new hope arose. Governments were acted upon to make representations, and all but to menace the Holy Father.* For a time, confidence revived. It was thought impossible that the joint note of so many Powers, and the joint influence of so many diplomatists, could fail of their effect. It did not seem to occur to those who invoked the interference of the Civil Powers that they were thereby endeavoring to deprive the Council of its liberty; which, in those who were complaining, in all languages, that the Council was not free, involved a self-contradiction on which I need not comment. Neither did they seem to remember that those who invoke the secular power against the spiritual authority of the Church, whether to defeat a sentence already given, or to prevent the delivery of such a sentence, are *ipso facto* excommunicate, and that their case is reserved to the Pope.† This, which applies to any ordi-

---

* See Appendix, p. 181.

† *Appellantes seu recurrentes ad curiam sæcularem ab ordinationibus alicujus judicis ecclesiastici* excommunicationem incurrunt Papæ reservatum ex cap. 16 Bullæ *In Cœna Domini*, sive illi judices ecclesiastici sint ordinarii sive delegati, ut patet in eadem Bulla : et

nary ecclesiastical judge in matters of law, surely applies in an eminent degree to an Œcumenical Council in matters of faith. Be this as it may, for a time the interest of the World was re-awakened by the hope that Rome would be in some way baffled after all.

But this hope also was doomed to disappointment. The distribution by the Cardinal Presidents of the *Additamentum*, or additional chapter on the doctrine of Infallibility ; the introduction of the *Schema de Romano Pontifice* before the *Schema de Ecclesia ;* the closing of the general discussion by a vote of the Council; all alike showed that the Council knew its own mind, and was resolved to do its duty. It became unmistakably clear how few were in opposition; and equally certain that, when the definition should be completed, all opposition would cease. The interest in the Council, manifested by the anti-Catholic World, at once collapsed. The correspondents became silent, or only found reasons why nobody cared any longer for the Council. A period of supercilious disdain followed ; and then the correspondents of the English journals, one by one, left Rome. The game was played out; and the last hope of an intestine conflict in the Church was over. A more disappointing end to the high hopes and excited anti-

---

multi dicunt hoc procedere, etiamsi sic appellantes et recurrentes nulla decreta pœnalia aut inhibitiones contra eosdem judices ecclesiasticos obtineant ; alii tamen contrarium tenent. Vide interpretes super dicta Bulla cap. 19, et Bonacina *de Censur.* in partic. disp. 1, q. 17, punct. 1, num. 28, qui auctores pro utraque parte allegat. Et continet etiam judices seculares, qui ea occasione decernunt contra dictos judices ecclesiasticos, et eos qui illa decreta exequuntur ; et,

cipations with which the adversaries of the Catholic Church cheered on the opposition at the opening of the year, cannot be conceived. They little knew the men whom they were mortifying and dishonoring by their applause. They forgot that Bishops are not deputies, and that an Œcumenical Council is not a Parliament. And when, of the eighty-eight who on the thirteenth of July voted *Non placet*, two only repeated their *Non placet* on the eighteenth, proving thereby that what two could do eighty might have done, the World was silent, and has steadfastly excluded the Constitution *De Romano Pontifice* from the columns of its newspapers.

Here is the simple and self-evident reason of this pretended loss of interest in the Council. It is the affected indifference of those who, having staked their reputation on the issue of a contest, have been thoroughly and hopelessly disappointed.

Before I conclude this part of the subject, I will give one passage as a supreme example of what I have been describing. I take it from the chief newspaper in England. It is from an article evidently written by a cultivated and practiced hand. It appeared when the definition was seen to be certain and near. It was intended to ruin its effects beforehand. The writer could not narrate what

---

continet dantes consilium, patrocinium, et favorem in eisdem, ut patet ex eadem Bulla.

In hac materia vide plures pœnas infra verb. *Curia*, c. 8, et verb. *Jurisdictio*, et procedit etiam in tacita, seu anticipata appellatione ad procurandum impediri futuras ordinationes judicii ecclesiastici, ut Bonac. num. 23, juxta probabiliorem.—Giraldus *de Pœnis Eccl.* pars ii. c. iii. vol. v. p. 96.

had taken place, because it was before the event;
nor what would really take place, because nothing
was known; but what he thought would excite
contempt, *that* he pleased to say would take place.
Nevertheless, he spoke as if the events were certain, and already so ordered; which truth forbade:
and he taxed his ingenuity to make the whole account in the highest degree odious or ridiculous;
which revealed his motive. The reader will bear
in mind that not one particle of the following elaborate description is true, or had even a shadow of
truth. But nobody would perceive the fine verbal
distinctions on which the writer would defend himself from a charge of deliberate falsehood.

On June 8, we read as follows:—

" The British public have some reason to regret
that the pressure of subjects nearer home, and
more directly concerning this country, has put
their interest in the Œcumenical Council some-
what in abeyance. A great event is at hand.
There can no longer be any doubt that at the approaching Feast of St. Peter and St. Paul, the 29th
instant, the priceless blessing of Papal Infallibility
will be vouchsafed to the world. The day is the
Feast of St. Peter in our Calendar, and it is usually
called St. Peter's Day at Rome, the Apostle to the
Gentiles having been associated only to disappear.
The day is on this occasion to be observed as a day
of days, and the era of a new revelation. Fireworks,
illuminations, transparencies, triumphal arches, and
all that taste and money can do to demonstrate and
delight, are already in hand, and, whoever the
guests, the marriage feast is in preparation. . . . An
extraordinary effort is to be made. Rome is to

excel herself in her mimic meteors, her artistic transfigurations, her new heavens and new earths, her angelic radiance, her divine glories, and infernal horrors. If the Council has been chary of its utterances and coy in its appearances, that will be made up by explosions and spectacles of a more intelligible character. We can promise that it will be worth many miles of excursion trains to go and see. The Campagna will be deserted, that all the Pope's temporal lieges may be there in their picturesque costumes. They and the astonished strangers will there see with their own eyes the Pope of Rome, the actual successor of St. Peter, invested with absolute authority over all souls, hearts and minds. They will see him welcoming the faithful .' *Placets*,' and consigning the ' *Non-Placets* ' to the flames of a Tartarean abyss. They will see hideous forms, snakes, dragons, hydras, centipedes, toads, and nondescript monsters under the feet, or the lance, or the thunderbolt of conquering Rome; and they will not fail to recognize in them the Church of England, the Protestant communities, and the German philosophers. It will be a grand day, and great things will be done on that 29th of June. We will not believe it possible that a single mishap will disturb the sacred programme—that the lightnings may miss their aim, or the Powers of Darkness prevail. We cannot doubt all will go off well, for the simple reason that all is ready and forecasted, down to the very Dogma. Artists of surpassing skill and taste are working hard on the Upholstery of the Divine manifestation, not knowing whether to think it a blasphemy or a good joke. It is their poverty and not their will that consents to the task. As we see the illuminations expiring, the Roman candles lost in smoke, and the exhibitors taking the old properties back to the vast magazines of Rome, we cannot help thinking of the poor fathers put off with glare and noise in place of conviction and peace of mind. Think of poor MacHale exhausting in vain his logic, his learning, and his powerful style, and taking back to his poor flock on the Atlantic shore a strange story of Chinese lanterns, fiery bouquets, showers of gold, and transparencies more striking even than the illustrations of our prophetic almanacks."   .

When it is borne in mind that the definition of the Infallibility of the Head of the Christian Church is a subject of deep religious faith to the most cultivated nations of the world, and that a fifth part of the population of our three kingdoms was profoundly interested in the subject, I shall refrain from saying that this article from the leading newspaper of England has as little decency as truth.

I will now endeavor briefly to sketch the outline of the Council as viewed from within. As I was enabled to attend, with the exception of about three or four days, every Session of the Council, eighty-nine in number, from the opening to the close, I can give testimony, not upon hearsay, but as a personal witness of what I narrate.

Cardinal Pallavicini, after relating the contests and jealousies of the Orators of Catholic States assembled in the Council of Trent, goes on to say that to convoke a General Council, except when absolutely demanded by necessity, is to tempt

God.* I well remember, at the time of the centenary of St. Peter's Martyrdom, when the Holy Father first announced his intention to convene the General Council, one of the oldest and most experienced of foreign diplomatists expressed to me his great alarm. He predicted exactly what came to pass in the beginning of the Council. His diplomatic foresight fully appreciated the political dangers. They were certainly obvious and grave; for no one perhaps, at that time, could anticipate the majestic unity and firmness of the Council, which exceeded all hopes, and has effectually dispelled all fears.

For three hundred years, the Church dispersed throughout the world has been in contact with the corrupt civilization of old Catholic countries, and with the anti-Catholic civilization of countries in open schism. The intellectual traditions of nearly all nations have been departing steadily from the unity of the Faith and of the Church. In most countries, public opinion has become formally hostile to the Catholic religion. The minds of Catholics have been much affected by the atmosphere in which they live. It was to be feared and to be expected that the Bishops of all the world, differing so widely in race, political institutions, and intellectual habits, might have imported into the Council elements of divergence, if not of irreconcilable division. Some had indeed met before, at the Canonizations of 1862 or 1867; but for the most part the Bishops met for the first time. The Pas-

---

* Hist. Conc. Trid. lib. xvi. c. 10, tom. ii. p. 800. Antwerp, 1670.

tors of some thirty nations were there, bringing together every variety of mental and social culture and experience: but in the midst of this variety there reigned a perfect identity of faith. On this, three centuries of separation and divergence in all things of the natural order, had produced no effect. Nothing but the Church of God alone could have lived on immutable through three hundred years of perpetual changes, and under the most potent influences of the world. Nothing has ever more luminously exhibited the supernatural endowments of the Church than the Council of the Vatican. In these three centuries it had passed through revolutions which have dissolved empires, laws, opinions. But the Episcopate of the Catholic Church met again last December in Rome, as it met in Trent, Lyons, or Nicæa. At once it proceeded to its work; and began as if by instinct, or by the prompt facility of an imperishable experience, to define doctrines of faith and to decree laws of discipline. Such unity of mind and will is above the conditions of human infirmity; it can be traced to one power and guidance alone, the supernatural assistance of the Spirit of Truth, by Whom the Church of God is perpetually sustained in the light and unity of faith.

To those who were within the Council, this became, day by day, almost evident to sense. It was no diminution from this, that a certain number were found who were of opinion that it was inopportune to define the Infallibility of the Roman Pontiff. This was a question of prudence, policy, expedience; not of doctrine or of truth. It was thus that the Church was united twenty years ago

in the belief of the Immaculate Conception, while
some were still to be found who doubted the prudence of defining it. Setting aside this one question of opportuneness, there was not in the Council of the Vatican a difference of any gravity, and
certainly no difference whatsoever on any doctrine
of faith. I have never been able to hear of five
Bishops who denied the doctrine of Papal Infallibility. Almost all previous Councils were distract-
ed by divisions, if not by heresy. Here no heresy
existed. The question of opportunity was altogether subordinate and free. It may truly be affirmed that never was there a greater unanimity
than in the Vatican Council. Of this the world
had a first evidence in the unanimous vote by
which the first Constitution on Faith was affirmed
on the 24th of April.

I should hardly have spoken of the outward conduct of the Council, if I had not seen, with surprise
and indignation, statements purporting to be descriptions of scenes of violence and disorder in the
course of its discussions. Having from my earliest
remembrance been a witness of public assemblies
of all kinds, and especially of those among ourselves, which for gravity and dignity are supposed
to exceed all others, I am able and bound to say
that I have never seen such calmness, self-respect
mutual-forbearance, courtesy and self-control, as in
the eighty-nine sessions of the Vatican Council.
In a period of nine months, the Cardinal President
was compelled to recall the speakers to order perhaps twelve or fourteen times. In any other assembly they would have been inexorably recalled
to the question sevenfold oftener and sooner.

2*

Nothing could exceed the consideration and respect with which this duty was discharged. Occa-
sionally murmurs of dissent were audible; now
and then a comment may have been made aloud.
In a very few instances, and those happily of an
exceptional kind, expressions of strong disapproval
and of exhausted patience at length escaped. But
the descriptions of violence, outcries, menace, de-
nunciation, and even of personal collisions, with
which certain newspapers deceived the world, I
can affirm to be calumnious falsehoods, fabricated
to bring the Council into odium and contempt.
That such has been the aim and intent of certain
journals and their correspondents is undeniable.
They at first attempted to write it down; but an
Œcumenical Council cannot be written down.
Next, they endeavored to treat it with ridicule;
but an Œcumenical Council cannot be made ridiculous. The good sense of the world forbids it.
But it may be made odious and hateful; and
thereby the minds of men may be not only turned
from it, but even turned against it. For this in
every way the anti-Catholic world has labored;
and no better plan could be found than to describe
its sessions as scenes of indecent clamor and personal violence, unworthy even in laymen, criminal
in Bishops of the Church. I have read descriptions of scenes of which I was a personal witness, so
absolutely contrary to fact and truth, that I cannot
acquit the anonymous writer on the plea of error.
The animus was manifest, and its effect has been
and will be to poison a multitude of minds which
the truth will never reach.

It has been loudly declared, that a tyrannical

majority deprived the minority of liberty of discussion.

Now it is hard to believe this allegation to be sincere, for many reasons.

First, there was only one rule for both majority and minority. If either were deprived of liberty, both were; if both were, it might be unwise, it could not be unjust; but if both were not, then neither. The majority spontaneously and freely imposed upon itself the same conditions it accepted for all.

. But secondly, the mode of conducting the discussions afforded the amplest liberty of debate.

The subject matter was distributed in print to every Bishop, and a period of eight or ten days was given for any observations they might desire to make in writing.

These observations were carefully examined by the deputation of twenty-four; and when found to be pertinent were admitted, either to modify or to reform the original Schema.

The text so amended was then proposed for the general discussion, on which every Bishop in the Council had a free right to speak, and the discussions lasted so long as any Bishop was pleased to inscribe his name.

The only limit upon this freedom of discussion consisted in the power of the Presidents, on the petition of ten Bishops to interrogate the Council whether it desired the discussion to be prolonged. The Presidents had no power to close the discussion. The Council alone could put an end to it. This right is essential to every deliberative assembly; which has a two-fold liberty, the one, to listen as long as it shall see fit; the other, to refuse to listen when it shall judge that a subject has been sufficiently discussed. To deny this liberty to the Council is to claim for individuals the liberty to force the Council to listen as long as they are pleased either to waste its time or to obstruct its judgment. In political assemblies, the house puts an end to debates by a peremptory and inexorable cry of "question" or "divide." The assemblies of the Church are of another temper. But they are not deprived of the same essential rights; and by a free vote they may decide either to listen, or not to listen, as the judgment of the Council shall see fit. To deny this is to deny the liberty of the Council; and under the pretext of liberty to claim a tyranny for the few over the will of the many.*

Obvious as is this liberty and right of the Council to close its discussions when it shall see fit, there exists only one example on record in which it did so. With exemplary patience it listened to what the House of Commons would have pro-

---

* I cannot help here marking a historical parallel. Those who had been invoking the anti-Catholic public opinion, and even the civil governments of all countries, to control the Holy See and the Council, complained of oppression and the violation of their liberty.

When Napoleon held Pius VII. prisoner at Fontainebleau, and by every form of threat and influence had deprived him of liberty, the following warning was given by Colonel Lagorse to Cardinal Pacca, then in attendance upon the Pope: "That the Emperor was displeased with the Cardinals, for having, ever since their arrival at Fontainebleau, continually restricted the Pope from a condition of free agency; that provided they were desirous of remaining at Fontainebleau, they must abstain from all matters of interference in matters of business. . . . Failing in the above conditions, they would expose themselves to the hazard of losing their liberty."— *Memoirs of Cardinal Pacca,* vol. ii. p. 192.

nounced to be interminable discussions and interminable speeches.   On the general discussion of
the Schema *De Romano Pontifice* some eighty Bishops had spoken.   Of these, nearly half were of
what the newspapers called the Opposition; but
the proportion of the Opposition to the Council
was not more than one sixth.   They had therefore
been heard as three to six.   But further, there still
remained the special discussion on the Prœmium
and the four chapters; that is to say, five distinct
discussions still remained, in which every Bishop.
of the six or seven hundred in the Council would,
therefore, have a right to speak five times.   Most
reasonably, then, the Council closed the general
discussion, leaving to the Bishops still their un-
diminished right, if they saw fit, still to speak five
times.   No one but those who desired the discussion never to end, that is, who desired to render
the definition impossible by speaking against time,
could complain of this most just exercise of its liberty on the part of the Council.   I can conscientiously declare, that long before the general discussion was closed, all general arguments were
exhausted.   The special discussion of details also
had been to such an extent anticipated, that nothing
new was heard for days. The repetition became hard
to bear.   Then, and not till then, the President, at
the petition not of ten, but of a hundred and fifty
Bishops, at least, interrogated the Council whether
it desired to prolong or close the general discussion.   By an overwhelming majority it was closed.
When this was closed, still, as I have said, five distinct discussions commenced; and were continued
so long as any one was to be found desirous to

speak. Finally, for the fifth or last discussion, a hundred and twenty inscribed their names to speak. Fifty at least were heard, until on both sides the burden became too heavy to bear; and, by mutual consent, an useless and endless discussion, from sheer exhaustion, ceased.

So much for the material liberty of the Council. Of the moral liberty it will be enough to say, that the short-hand writers have laid up in its Archives a record of discourses which will show that the liberty of thought and speech was perfectly unchecked. If they were published to the world, the accusation would not be of undue suppression. The wonder would be, not that the Opposition failed of its object, but that the Council so long held its peace. Certain Bishops of the freest country in the world said truly: "The liberty of our Congress is not greater than the liberty of the Council." When it is borne in mind that out of more than six hundred Bishops, one hundred, at the utmost, were in opposition to their brethren, it seems hardly sincere to talk of the want of liberty. There was but one liberty of which this sixth part of the Council was deprived, a liberty they certainly would be the last to desire, namely, that of destroying the liberty of the other five. The Council bore long with this truthless accusation of politicians, newspapers, and anonymous writers; and never till the last day, when the work was finally complete, except only the voting of the public session, took cognizance of this mendacious pretence. On the 16th of July, after the last votes had been given, and the first Constitution *De Ecclesia Christi*, had been finally approved, then for the first time it turned its attention to this attempt upon its authority. Two calumnious libels on the Council had appeared ; the one entitled, *Ce qui se passe au Concile*, the other, *La dernière heure du Concile* : in both, the liberty of the Vatican Council was denied, with a view to denying its authority. The General Congregation by an immense majority adopted the following protest, and condemned these two slanderous pamphlets, thereby placing on record a spontaneous declaration of the absolute freedom of the Council.

"Most Reverend Fathers,

"From the time that the Holy Vatican Synod opened, by the help of God, a most bitter warfare instantly broke out against it; and in order to diminish its venerable authority with the faithful, and, if it could be, to destroy it altogether, many writers vied with each other in attacking it by contumelious detraction, and by the foulest calumnies; and that, not only among the heterodox and open enemies of the Cross of Christ, but also among those who give themselves out as sons of the Catholic Church; and what is most to be deplored, among even its sacred ministers.

"The infamous falsehoods which have been heaped together in this matter in public newspapers of every tongue, and in pamphlets without the author's name, published in all places and stealthily distributed, all men well know ; so that we have no need to recount them one by one. But among anonymous pamplets of this kind there are two especially, written in French, and entitled, *Ce qui se passe au Concile*, and *La dernière heure du Concile*, which for the arts of calumny and the license of detraction bear away the palm from all others. For in these not only is the dignity and full liberty of the Council assailed with the basest falsehoods, and the rights of the Holy See overthrown, but even the august person of our Holy Father is attacked with the gravest insults. Wherefore we, being mindful of our office, lest our silence, if longer maintained, should be perversely interpreted by men of evil will, are compelled to lift up our voice, and before you all, Most Reverend Fathers, to protest and to declare all such things as have been uttered in the aforesaid newspapers and pamphlets to be altogether false and calumnious, whether in contempt of our Holy Father and of the Apostolic See, or the dishonor of this Holy Synod, and on the score of its asserted want of legitimate liberty.

" From the Hall of the Council, the 16th day of July, 1870.

" PHILIP, CARDINAL DE ANGELIS, *President.*

" ANTONIUS, CARDINAL DE LUCA.

" ANDREAS, CARDINAL BIZZARI.

" ALOYSIUS, CARDINAL BILIO.

" HANNIBAL, CARDINAL CAPALTI."*

We have thus carried down our narrative to the eve of the Definition, and with one or two general remarks I will conclude this part of the subject.

A strange accusation has been brought against the Council of the Vatican, or, to speak more truly, against the Head of the Church, who summoned it ; namely, that its one object was to define the   ·

---

* See Appendix, p. 192.

Infallibility of the Pope. With the knowledge I have, in common with a large part of the Episcopate, I am able to give to this a direct denial. But this denial is not given as if the admission of the charge would be in any way inconsistent with the wisdom, dignity, or duty of the Council. It is simply untrue in fact. Even though it were true, I should have no hesitation in undertaking to show that the Council, if it had been assembled chiefly to define the Infallibility of the Roman Pontiff, would have been acting in strict analogy with the practice of the Church in the eighteen Œcumenical Councils already held.

Each several Council was convened to extinguish the chief heresy, or to correct the chief evil, of the time. And I do not hesitate to affirm that the denial of the Infallibility of the Roman Pontiff was the chief intellectual or doctrinal error as to faith, not to call it more than proximate to heresy, of our times.

It was so, because it struck at the certainty of the pontifical acts of the last three hundred years; and weakened the effect of pontifical acts at this day over the intellect and conscience of the faithful. It kept alive a dangerous controversy on the subject of Infallibility altogether, and exposed even the Infallibility of the Church itself to difficulties not easy to solve. As an apparently open or disputable point, close to the very root of faith, it exposed even the faith itself to the reach of doubts.

Next, practically, it was mischievous beyond measure. The divisions and contentions of " Gallicanism" and " Ultramontanism" have been a scandal and a shame to us. Protestants and unbelievers have been kept from the truth by our intestine controversies, especially upon a point so high and so intimately connected with the whole doctrinal authority of the Church.

Again, morally, the division and contention on this point, supposed to be open, has generated more alienation, bitterness, and animosity between Pastors and people, and what is worse, between Pastor and Pastor, than any other in our day. Our internal contests proclaimed by Protestant newspapers, and, worse than all, by Catholic also, have been a reproach to us before the whole world.

It was high time to put an end to this; and if the Council had been convened for no other purpose, this cause would have been abundantly sufficient; if it had defined the Infallibility at its outset, it would not have been an hour too soon; and perhaps it would have averted many a scandal we now deplore. But this last I say with submission, for the times and seasons of a Council are put in a power above our reach.

In the midst of all these graver events and cares, there were, now and then, some things which gave rise to hearty, and I hope harmless, amusement. Of these, one was what may be called the panic fear lest the definition of the Infallibility of the Pope should suddenly be carried by acclamation; and the amusing self-gratulation of those who imagined that with great dexterity and address they had defeated this intention. The acclamation, like the rising of a conspiracy, was to have taken place first on one day, and then, being frustrated, on another. The Feast of the Epiphany was named, then the Feast of St. Joseph, then the Feast of the Annun-

ciation. But by the masterly tactics of certain leaders, this conspiracy could never accomplish itself.
Janus first announced the discovery of the plot.
The minds of men from that time, it seems, were
haunted with it. They lived in perpetual alarm.
They were never safe, they tell us, from a surprise
which would create an article of faith before they
could protest. I refrain, out of respect, from nam-
ing the distinguished prelates of whom our anonymous teachers speak so freely, when they affirm
that at the first general congregation Papal Infallibility was to be carried by acclamation, but that
"the scheme was foiled by the tact and firmness
of" such an one; and that "a similar attempt was
projected for a later day (March 19), when the
prompt action of four American prelates again
frustrated the design." *

Now the truth is, that nobody, so far as my
knowledge reaches, and I believe I may speak with
certainty, ever for a moment dreamed of this defi-
· nition, by acclamation. All whom I have ever
heard speak of these rumors were unfeignedly
amused at them. The last men in the Council who
would have desired or consented to an acclamation
were those to whom it was imputed; and that for
a reason as clear as day. They had no desire for
acclamations, because acclamations define nothing.
They had already had enough of acclamations in
the Council of Chalcedon, which cried unanimously,
"Peter hath spoken by Leo;" and in the Council
of Constantinople which acclaimed, "Peter hath
spoken by Agatho;" and in the address of the five

---

* "Saturday Review," Aug. 2, 1870.

hundred Bishops at the centenary of St. Peter, in 1867, in which they unanimously declared that "Peter had spoken by Pius:" for they well knew that many, even of those who joined most loudly in that acclamation, deny that these words ascribe infallibility to the Successor of Peter. Experience therefore proved, even if theology long ago had not, that an acclamation is not a definition; and that an acclamation leaves the matter as it found it, as disputable after as it was before. Nothing short of a definition would satisfy either reason or conscience; and nothing but this was ever for a moment thought of.

Such, then, is a slight outline of the internal history of this protracted contest. It passed through nine distinct phases; and it must be confessed that they who desired to avert the definition held their successive positions with no little tenacity.

The first attack came from the World without, in support of a handful of professors and writers, who denied the truth of the doctrine: the second position was to admit its truth but to deny that it was capable of being defined: the third, to admit that it was definable, but to deny the opportuneness of defining it: the fourth, to resist the introduction of the doctrine for discussion: the fifth, to render discussion impossible by delay: the sixth, to protract the discussion till a conclusion should become physically impossible before the summer heats drove the Council to disperse: the seventh, when the discussion closed, to defer the definition to the future: the eighth, after the definition was made, to hinder its promulgation: the ninth—I will not say the last, for who can tell what may still come?—to affirm that the definition, though solemnly made, confirmed, and published by the Head of the Church in the Œcumenical Council, and promulgated *urbi et orbi* according to the traditional usage of the Church, does not bind the conscience of the faithful till the Council is concluded, and subscribed by the Bishops.

This last is the only remnant of the controversy now surviving. I can hardly believe that any one, after the letter of Cardinal Antonelli to the Nunzio at Brussels, can persist in this error. Nevertheless, it may be well to add one or two words, which you will anticipate, and well know how to use.

1. A definition of faith declares that a doctrine was revealed by God.

Are the faithful, then, dispensed from believing Divine revelation till the Council is concluded, and the Bishops have subscribed it?

I hope, for the sake of the Catholic religion in the face of the English people, that we shall hear no more of an assertion so uncatholic and so dangerous.

2. But perhaps it may mean that the Council is not yet confirmed, because not yet concluded.

The Council may not yet be confirmed because not yet concluded; but the Definition is both concluded and confirmed.

The Council is as completely confirmed, in its acts hitherto taken, as it ever will or can be. The future confirmation will not add anything to that which is confirmed already. It will confirm future acts, not those which are already perfect.

3. But perhaps some may have an idea that the

question is not yet closed, and that the Council may hereafter undo what it has done. We have been told that " Its decrees may have to be corrected," and that two years elapsed before the Œcumenical pretensions of the *Latrocinium* of Ephesus were formally superseded. Some have called it " Ludibrium Vaticanum."

Let those who so speak, or think, for many so speak without thinking, look to their faith. The past acts of the Council are infallible. No future acts will retouch them. This is the meaning of " irreformable." Infallibility does not return upon its own steps. And they who suspend their assent to its acts on the plea that the Council is not concluded, are in danger of falling from the faith. They who reject the Definitions of the Vatican Council are already in heresy.

CHAPTER II.

THE TWO CONSTITUTIONS.

HAVING so far spoken on the less pleasing and less vital part of this subject, I gladly turn to the authoritative acts of the Council.

The subject matter of its deliberations was divided into four parts, and for each part a Deputation of twenty-four Fathers was elected by the Council. The four divisions were, on Faith, Discipline, Religious Orders, and on Rites, including the Missions of the Church.

Hitherto, the subjects of Faith and Discipline alone have come before the Council; and of these two chiefly the first has been treated, as being the basis of all, and in its nature the most important.

In what I have to add, I shall confine myself to the two Dogmatic Constitutions, *De Fide* and *De Ecclesia Christi.**

The history of the Faith cannot be adequately written without writing both the history of heresy and the history of definitions; for heresies are partial aberrations from the truth, and definitions are rectifications of those partial errors. But the Faith is co-extensive with the whole Revelation of

---

* See Appendix, p. 192, etc.

Truth; and though every revealed truth is definite and precise, nevertheless, all are not defined. The need of definition arises when any revealed truth has been obscured or denied. The general history of the Church will therefore give the general history of the Faith; but the history of Councils will give chiefly, if not only, the history of those parts of revelation which have been assailed by heresy and protected by definition.

The Divine Tradition of the Church contains truths of the supernatural order which without revelation could not have been known to man, such as the Incarnation of God and the mystery of the Holy Trinity, and truths of the natural order, which are known also by reason, such as the existence of God. The circumference of this Divine Tradition is far wider than the range of definitions. The Church guards, teaches, and transmits the whole divine tradition of natural and supernatural truth, but defines only those parts of the deposit which have been obscured or denied.

The eighteen Œcumenical Councils of the Church have therefore defined such specific doctrines of the Faith as were contested. The Council of the Vatican has, for this reason, treated of two primary truths greatly contested but never hitherto defined, namely: the Supernatural order and the Church. It is this which will fix the character of the Vatican Council, and will mark in history the progress of error in the Christian world at this day.

The series of heresy has followed the order of the Baptismal Creed. It began by assailing the nature and Unity of God, the Creator; then of the Redeemer; then the doctrine of the Incarnation of the Godhead and the Manhood of the Son of God; then of the Holy Trinity, and of the personality and Godhead of the Holy Ghost. To these succeeded controversies on sin, grace, and the Holy Sacraments; finally the heresies of the so called Reformation, which spread over what remained unassailed in the Catholic Theology, especially the Divine authority and the institution of the Church itself. The Councils before Trent have completely guarded all doctrines of faith hitherto contested, by precise definition, excepting only the two primary and preliminary truths anterior to all doctrine, namely, the revelation of the supernatural order and the Divine authority and institution of the Church. To affirm and to define these seems to be, as I said, the mission and character of the Vatican Council, and indicates the state of the Christian world; because in the last three hundred years the rapid development of the rationalistic principle of Protestantism has swept away all intermediate systems and fragmentary Christianities. The question is reduced to a simple choice of faith and unbelief, or, of the natural or the supernatural order.

This, then, is the starting-point of the first dogmatic Constitution, *De Fide Catholica*.

In the Procemium, the Council declares that none can fail to know how the heresies condemned at Trent have been subdivided into a multitude of contending sects, whereby Faith in Christ has been overthrown in many; and the Sacred Scriptures, which at first were avowedly held to be the source and rule of faith, are now reputed as fables. The cause of this it declares to be, the rejection of the Divine authority of the Church, and the license of private judgment.

"Then sprang up," it goes on to say, "and was widely spread throughout the world, the doctrine of rationalism or naturalism, which opposing itself altogether to Christianity as a supernatural institution, studiously labors to exclude Christ, our only Lord and Saviour, from the minds of men and from the life and morality of nations, and to set up the dominion of what they call pure reason and nature. After forsaking and rejecting the Christian religion, and denying the true God and His Christ, the minds of many have lapsed at length into the depth of pantheism, materialism, and atheism, so that, denying the rational nature of man, and all law of justice and of right, they are striving together to destroy the very foundations of human society.

"While this impiety spreads on every side, it miserably comes to pass, that many even of the sons of the Catholic Church have wandered from the way of piety, and while truth in them has wasted away, the Catholic instinct has become feeble. For, led astray by many and strange doctrines, they have recklessly confused together nature and grace, human science, and divine faith, so as to deprave the genuine sense of dogmas which the Holy Church our Mother holds and teaches; and have brought into danger the integrity and purity of the Faith."

Such is the estimate of the condition of the Christian world in the judgment of the Vatican

Council; and from this point of sight we may
appreciate its decrees.

Its first chapter is of God the Creator of all
things.* In this is decreed the personality, spiritu-
ality and liberty of God, the creation of corporeal
and of spiritual beings, and the existence of body
and soul in man. These truths may be thought so
primary and undeniable as to need no definition.
To some it may be hardly credible, that, at this
day, there should exist men who deny the existence
of God, or His personality, or His nature distinct
from the world, or the existence of spiritual beings,
or the creation of the world, or the liberty of the
Divine will in creation. But such errors have existed and do exist, not only in obscure and inco-
herent minds, but in intellects of power and cultivation, and in philosophies of elaborate subtilty,
by which the faith of many has been undermined.

The second Chapter is on Revelation. It affirms
the existence of two orders of truth : the order of
nature, in which the existence of God as the beginning and end of creatures may be certainly known
by the things which He has made; and the order
which is above created nature, that is, God and His
action by truth and grace upon mankind. The
communication of supernatural truth to man is revelation; and that revelation is contained in the
Word of God written and unwritten, or in the divine tradition committed to the Church. These
truths, elementary and certain as they seem, have
been and are denied by errors of a contradictory

---

* The text of the Constitutions will be found in the Appendix,
No. IV.

kind. By some it is denied that God can be known
by the light of reason; by others it is affirmed not
only that God may be known by the light of reason,
but that no revelation is necessary for man; once
more, others deny that man can be elevated to a
supernatural knowledge and perfection; again,
others affirm that he can attain to all truth and
goodness of and from himself. These errors also
are widespread; and in the multifarious literature
which Catholics incautiously admit into their
homes and minds, have made havoc of the faith of
many.

The third Chapter is on Faith. It may be truly
said, that in this chapter every word is directed
against some intellectual aberration of this century.

It affirms the dependence of the created intelligence upon the uncreated, and that this dependence is by the free obedience of faith; or, in other
other words, that inasmuch as God reveals to man
truths of the supernatural order, man is bound to
believe that revelation by reason of the authority
or veracity of God, who can neither deceive nor
be deceived. The infallibility of God is the motive
of faith. And this faith, though it be not formed
in us by perceiving the intrinsic credibility of what
we believe, but by the veracity of God, nevertheless is a rational or intellectual act, the highest and
most normal in its nature. For no act of the reason
can be more in harmony with its nature than to
believe the Word of God. To assure mankind that
it is God who speaks, God has given to man signs
and evidences of His revelation, which exclude
reasonable doubt. The act of faith therefore is not

a blind act, but an exercise of the highest reason.
It is also an act not of necessity but of perfect freedom, and therefore in itself an act of normal obedience to God, and meritorious in its nature. And
this act of faith, in which both the intellect and the
·will have their full and normal exercise, is nevertheless an act not of the natural order, but of the
supernatural, and springs from the preventing
grace of the Holy Spirit, Who illuminates the intelligence and moves the will. Faith is therefore
a gift of God, and a moral duty which may be required of us by the commandment of God.

But inasmuch as the grace of faith is given to
man that he may believe the revelation of God, it
is co-extensive with that whole revelation. Whatsoever God has revealed, man, when he knows it, is
bound to believe. But God has made provision
that man should know His revelation, because
He has committed it to His Church as the guardian and teacher of truth. Whatsoever, therefore,
the Church proposes to our belief as the Word of
God, written or unwritten, whether by its ordinary
and universal teaching, or by its solemn judgment
and definition, we are bound to believe by divine
and Catholic faith.

To this end, God has instituted in the world His
visible Church, one, universal, indefectible, immutable, ever multiplying ; the living witness of the
Incarnation, and the sufficient evidence of its own
mission to the world. The maximum of extrinsic
evidence for the revelation of Christianity is the
witness of the Church, considered even as an historical proof; and that evidence is not only sufficient to convince a rational nature that Christianity

is a Divine revelation, but to convict of unreason-
able unbelief any intelligence which shall reject its
testimony. But the visible Church is not merely
a human witness. It was instituted and is guided
perpetually by God Himself, and is therefore a divine witness, ordained by God as the infallible motive of credibility, and the channel of His revelation to mankind.

I need hardly point out what errors are excluded
by these definitions. The whole world outside the
Catholic Church is full of doctrines diametrically
contrary to these truths. It is affirmed that the
reason of man is so independent of God, that He
cannot justly lay upon it the obligation of faith;
again, that faith and science are so identified that
they have the same motives, and that there is neither need nor place in our convictions for the authority of God; again, that extrinsic evidence is
of no weight, because men ought to believe only
on their own internal experience or private inspiration; again, that all miracles are myths, and all
supernatural evidences useless, because intrinsically incredible; once more, that we can only believe
that of which we have scientific proof, and that it
is lawful for us to call into doubt the articles of our
faith when and as often as we will, and to submit
them to a scientific analysis, in the meanwhile suspending our faith until we shall have completed the
scientific demonstration.

The fourth and last Chapter is on the relation of
faith to reason. In this three things are declared:
first, that there are two orders of knowledge; secondly, that they differ as to their object; thirdly,
that they differ as to their methods of procedure.

The order of nature contains the subject-matter of natural religion and of natural science. The order of faith contains truths which without revelation we might have known, though not certainly nor easily; and also truths which, without revelation, we could not have known. Such then are the two objects of reason and of faith. The two methods of procedure likewise differ, inasmuch as in the order of nature the instrument of knowledge is discovery; in the supernatural order, it is faith, and the intellectual processes which spring from faith.

From these principles it is clear that science and faith can never be in real contradiction. All seeming opposition can only be either from error as to the doctrine of the Church, or error in the assumptions of science. Every assertion, therefore, contrary to the truth of an illuminated faith, is false. "For the Church, which, together with the Apostolic office of teaching, received also the command to guard the deposit of faith, is divinely invested with the right and duty of proscribing science falsely so-called, lest any man be deceived by philosophy and vain deceit." "For the doctrine of Faith which God has revealed, was not proposed to the minds of men to be brought to perfection like an invention of philosophy, but was delivered to the Spouse of Christ as a divine deposit to be faithfully guarded, and to be *infallibly* declared."

The importance of this first Constitution on Catholic Faith cannot be over-estimated, and, from its great breadth, may not as yet be fully perceived.

It is the broadest and boldest affirmation of the

supernatural and spiritual order ever yet made in
the face of the world; which is now, more than
ever, sunk in sense and heavy with materialism. It
declares that a whole order of being and power, of
truth and agency, exists, and is in full play upon
the world of sense. More than this, that this supernatural and spiritual order is present in the world,
and is incorporated in a visible and palpable form,
over which the world has no authority. That God
and His operations are sensible; visible to the eye,
and audible to the ear. That they appeal to the
reason of man; and that men are irrational, and
therefore act both imprudently and immorally, if
they do not listen to, and believe in the Word of
God. It affirms also, as a doctrine of revelation,
that the visible Church is the great motive of credibility to faith, and that it is "the irrefragable testimony of its own divine legation." It moreover
asserts that the Church has a divine commission
to guard the deposit of revelation, and "a divine
right to proscribe errors of philosophy and vain
deceit," that is, all intellectual aberrations at variance with the deposit of revelation. Finally, it
affirms that the Church has a divine office to declare *infallibly* the deposit of truth.

I am not aware that in any previous Œcumenical
Council the doctrine of the Church, and of its divine and infallible authority, has been so explicitly
defined. And yet the Council of the Vatican was
not at that time engaged upon the *Schema de Ecclesia,* which still remains to be treated hereafter.
It was not however without a providential guidance that the first Constitution on Catholic Faith
was so shaped, especially in its closing chapter.

Neither is it without a great significance that at its conclusion was appended a Monitum, in which the Roman Pontiff by his supreme authority, enjoins all the faithful, Pastors and people, to drive away all errors contrary to the purity of the faith ; and moreover warns Christians that it is not enough to reject positive heresies, but that all errors which more or less approach to heresy must be avoided; and all erroneous opinions which are proscribed and prohibited by the Constitutions and decrees of the Holy See.

When these words were written, it was not foreseen that they were a preparation, unconsciously made, for the definition of the Infallibility of the Roman Pontiff. If the first Constitution had been designedly framed as an introduction, it could hardly have been more opportunely worded. It begins with God and His revelation ; it closes with the witness and office of the Visible Church, and with the supreme authority of its Head. The next truth demanded by the intrinsic relations of doctrine was the divine endowment of infallibility. And when treated, this doctrine was, contrary to all expectation, and to all likelihood, presented first to the Council, and by the Council to the world, in the person and office of the Head of the Church.

In all theological treatises, excepting indeed one or two of great authority, it had been usual to treat of the Body of the Church before treating of its Head. The reason of this would appear to be, that in the exposition of doctrine the logical order was the more obvious; and to the faithful, in the first formation of the Church, the body of the Church was known before its Head. We might have expected that the Council would have followed the same method. It is, therefore, all the more remarkable that the Council inverted that order, and defined the prerogative of the Head before it treated of the Constitution and endowments of the Body. And this, which was brought about by the pressure of special events, is not without significance. The Schools of the Church have followed the logical order: but the Church in Council, when for the first time it began to treat of its own constitution and authority, changed the method, and, like the Divine Architect of the Church, began in the historical order, with the foundation and Head of the Church. Our Divine Lord first chose Cephas, and invested him with the primacy over the Apostles. Upon this Rock all were built, and from him the whole unity and authority of the Church took its rise. To Peter alone first was given the plenitude of jurisdiction and of infallible authority. Afterwards, the gift of the Holy Ghost was shared with him by all the Apostles. From him and through him, therefore, all began. For which cause a clear and precise conception of his primacy and privilege is necessary to a clear and precise conception of the Church. Unless it be first distinctly apprehended, the doctrine of the Church will be always proportionally obscure. The doctrine of the Church does not determine the doctrine of the Primacy, but the doctrine of the Primacy does precisely determine the doctrine of the Church. In beginning therefore with the Head, the Council has followed our Lord's example, both in teaching and in fact; and in this will be found one of the causes of the singular and lu-

minous precision with which the Council of the
Vatican has, in one brief Constitution, excluded
the traditional errors on the Primacy and Infallibility of the Roman Pontiff.

The reasons which prevailed to bring about this
change of method were not only those which demonstrated generally the opportuneness of defining
the doctrine, but those also which showed specially
the necessity of bringing on the question while as
yet the Council was in the fulness of its numbers.
It was obvious that the length of time consumed
in the discussion, reformation, and voting of the
schemata was such, that unless the Constitution *De
Romano Pontifice* were brought on immediately after
Easter, it could not be finished before the setting
in of summer should compel the Bishops to disperse. Once dispersed, it was obvious they could
never again re-assemble in so large a number.
Many who, with great earnestness, desired to share
the blessing and the grace of extinguishing the
most dangerous error which for two centuries has
disturbed and divided the faithful, would have been
compelled to go back to their distant sees and missions, never to return. It was obviously of the first
moment that such a question should be discussed
and decided, not, as we should have been told, in
holes and corners, or by a handful of Bishops, or
by a faction, or by a clique, but by the largest possible assembly of the Catholic Episcopate. All
other questions, on which little divergence of opinion existed, might well be left to a smaller number
of Bishops. But a doctrine which for centuries
had divided both Pastors and people, the defining
of which was contested by a numerous and organ-

ized opposition, needed to be treated and affirmed by the most extensive deliberation of the Bishops of the Catholic Church. Add to this, the many perils which hung over the continuance of the Council; of which I need but give one example. The outbreak of a war might have rendered the definition impossible. And in fact, the Infallibility of the Roman Pontiff was defined on the eighteenth of July, and war was officially declared on the following day.

With these and many other contingencies fully before them, those who believed that the definition was not only opportune but necessary for the unity of the Church and the Faith, urged its immediate discussion. Events justified their foresight. The debate was prolonged into the heats of July, when, by mutual consent, the opposing sides withdrew from a further prolonging of the contest, and closed the discussion. If it had not been already protracted beyond all limits of reasonable debate, for not less than a hundred fathers in the general and special discussions had spoken, chiefly if not alone, of infalliblity, it could not so have ended.* Both sides were convinced that the matter was exhausted.

We will now examine, at least in outline, the first Dogmatic Constitution on the Church of Christ; and I will then confine what I have to add to the definition of Infallibility; thereby completing a part of the subject which in the two previous Pastorals it would have been premature to treat.

---

* During the session of the council four hundred and twenty speeches were delivered, of which nearly one-fourth were on the Infallibility alone.

The Proœmium of the Constitution declares that the institution of the visible Church was ordained to preserve the twofold unity of faith and of communion, and that for this end one principle and foundation was laid in Peter.

The first Chapter declares the Primacy of Peter over the Apostles; and that his primacy was conferred on him immediately and directly by our Lord, and consists not only in honor but also in jurisdiction.

The second Chapter affirms this primacy of honor and jurisdiction to be perpetual in the Church; and that the Roman Pontiffs, as successors of Peter, inherit this primacy; whereby Peter always presides in his see, teaching and governing the Universal Church.

The third Chapter defines the nature of his jurisdiction, namely, 'totam plenitudinem hujus supremæ potestatis," the plenitude of power to feed, rule, and govern the Universal Church. It is therefore jurisdiction episcopal, ordinary, and immediate over the whole Church, over both pastors and people, that is, over the whole Episcopate, collectively and singly, and over every particular church and diocese. The ordinary and immediate jurisdiction which every several Bishop in the Church exercises in the flock over which the Holy Ghost has placed him, is thereby sustained and strengthened.

From this Divine primacy three consequences follow : the one, that the Roman Pontiff is the supreme judge over all the Church, from whom lies no appeal; the second, that no power under God may come between the chief pastor of the Church and any, from the highest to the humblest, member of the flock of Christ on earth ; the third, that this supreme power or primacy is not made up of parts, as the sovereignty of constitutional states, but exists in its plenitude in the successor of Peter.[*]

The fourth and last Chapter defines the infallible doctrinal authority of the Roman Pontiff as the supreme teacher of all Christians.

The Chapter opens by affirming that to this supreme jurisdiction is attached a proportionate grace, whereby its exercise is directed and sustained.

This truth has been traditionally held and taught by the Holy See, by the *praxis* of the Church, and by the Œcumenical Councils, especially those in which the East and the West met in union together, as for instance the fourth of Constantinople, the second of Lyons, and the Council of Florence.

It is then declared, that in virtue of the promise of our Lord, " I have prayed for thee, that thy faith fail not,"[†] a perpetual grace of stability in faith was divinely attached to Peter and to his successors in his See.

The definition then affirms "that the Roman Pontiff, when he speaks *ex cathedra*, that is, when in

---

[*] In order to fix this doctrine more exactly, and to exclude all possible equivocation, after full and ample and repeated discussion, the words " aut eum habere tantum potiores partes, non vero totam plenitudinem hujus supremæ potestatis," were inserted in the Canon appended to this Chapter. I notice this, because it has been most untruly and most invidiously said, that these words were interpolated after the discussion. They were fully and amply discussed, and the proof of the fact exists in the short-hand report of the speeches, laid up in the Archives of the Council.

[†] St. Luke xxii. 31, 32.

discharge of the office of Pastor and Doctor of all Christians, by virtue of his supreme Apostolic authority, he defines a doctrine regarding faith or morals to be held by the Universal Church, by the Divine assistance promised to him in Blessed Peter, is possessed of that infallibility with which the Divine Redeemer willed that His Church should be endowed for defining doctrine, regarding faith and morals. And that therefore such definitions of the Roman Pontiff are irreformable of themselves, and not from the consent of the Church."

In this definition there are six points to be noted.

1. First, it defines the meaning of the well-known phrase, *loquens ex cathedra ;* that is, speaking from the Seat, or place, or with the authority of the supreme teacher of all Christians, and binding the assent of the Universal Church.

2. Secondly, the subject-matter of his infallible teaching, namely, the doctrine of faith and morals.

3. Thirdly, the efficient cause of infallibility, that is, the divine assistance promised to Peter, and in Peter to his successors.

4. Fourthly, the act to which this divine assistance is attached, namely, the defining of doctrines of faith and morals.

5. Fifthly, the extension of this infallible authority to the limits of the doctrinal office of the Church.

6. Lastly, the dogmatic value of the definitions *ex cathedra*, namely, that they are in themselves irreformable, because in themselves infallible, and not because the Church, or any part or member of the Church, should assent to them.

These six points contain the whole definition of

Infallibility. I will therefore take them in order, and then answer certain objections.

I. First, the definition limits the infallibility of the Pontiff to the acts which emanate from him *ex cathedra*. This phrase, which has been long and commonly used by theologians, has now, for the first time, been adopted into the terminology of the Church ; and in adopting it the Vatican Council fixes its meaning. The Pontiff speaks *ex cathedra* when, and only when, he speaks as the Pastor and Doctor of all Christians. By this, all acts of the Pontiff as a private person, or a private doctor, or as a local Bishop, or as sovereign of a state, are excluded. In all these acts the Pontiff may be subject to error. In one, and one only, capacity he is exempt from error ; that is, when, as teacher of the whole Church in things of faith and morals.

Our Lord declared, " Super cathedram Moysi sederunt scribæ et Pharisæi : " the scribes and Pharisees sit in the chair of Moses. The seat or " cathedra " of Moses signifies the authority and the doctrine of Moses ; the *cathedra Petri* is in like manner the authority and doctrine of Peter. The former was binding by Divine command and under pain of sin, upon the people of God under the old law ; the latter is binding by Divine command and under pain of sin, upon the people of God under the new.

I need not here draw out the traditional use of the term *cathedra Petri*, which in St. Cyprian, St. Optatus, and St. Augustine is employed as synonymous with the successor of Peter, and is used to express the centre and test of Catholic unity. *Ex cathedra* is therefore equivalent to *ex cathedra Petri* and distinguishes those acts of the successor of Peter which are done as supreme teacher of the whole Church.

The value of this phrase is great, inasmuch as it excludes all cavil and equivocation as to the acts of the Pontiff in any other capacity than that of Supreme Doctor of all Christians, and in any other subject matter than the matters of faith and morals.

II. Secondly, the definition limits the range, or, to speak exactly, the object of infallibility, to the doctrine of faith and morals. It excludes, therefore, all other matter whatsoever.

The great commission or charter of the Church is, in the words of our Lord, " Go ye, therefore, and teach all nations ... teaching them to observe all things whatsoever I have commanded you ; and behold, I am with you all days, even to the consummation of the world."*

In these words are contained five points.

1. First, the perpetuity and universality of the mission of the Church as the teacher of mankind.

2. Secondly, the deposit of the Truth and of the commandments, that is, of the Divine Faith and law entrusted to the Church.

3. Thirdly, the office of the Church, as the sole interpreter of the Faith and of the Law.

4. Fourthly, that it has the sole Divine jurisdiction existing upon earth, in matters of salvation, over the reason and will of man.

5. Fifthly, that in the discharge of this office our Lord is with His Church always, and to the consummation of the world.

---

* St. Matthew xxviii. 19, 20.

The doctrine of faith and the doctrine of morals are here explicitly described. The Church is infallible in this deposit of revelation.

And in this deposit are truths and morals both of the natural and of the supernatural order; for the religious truths and morals of the natural order are taken up into the revelation of the order of grace, and form a part of the object of infallibility.

1. The phrase, then, "faith and morals," signifies the whole revelation of faith; the whole way of salvation through faith; or the whole supernatural order, with all that is essential to the sanctification and salvation of man through Jesus Christ.

Now, this formula is variously expressed by the Church and by theologians; but it always means one and the same thing.

The Second Council of Lyons says, "If any questions arise concerning faith," they are to be decided by the Roman Pontiff.*

The Council of Trent uses the formula "in things of faith and morals, pertaining to the edification of Christian doctrine."†

Bellarmine says, "in things which pertain to faith," and again, "The Roman Pontiff cannot err in faith;" and further he says, "Not only in decrees of faith the Supreme Pontiff cannot err, but neither (can he err) in moral precepts which are

---

* "Si quæ subortæ fuerint quæstiones de fide, suo (i. e. Rom. Pont.) debent judicio definiri."—Labbe, *Concil.* tom. xiv. p. 512. Venice, 1731.

† "In rebus fidei et morum ad ædificationem doctrinæ Christianæ pertinentium."—Labbe, *Concil.* tom. xx. p. 23.

enjoined on the whole Church, and which are conversant with things that are necessary to salvation, or with those which are in themselves good or evil."*

Gregory of Valentia says, " Without any restriction it is to be said, that whatsoever the Pontiff determines in controverted matters which have respect to piety, he determines infallibly ; when, as it has been stated, he obliges the whole Church ; " and again, " Whatsoever the Pontiff asserts in any controverted matter of religion, it is to be believed that he asserts infallibly by his Pontifical authority, that is, by Divine assistance," †

Bannez proposes the thesis in these words; "Can (the Roman Pontiff) err in defining matters of faith ? " ‡

S. Antoninus says, " It is necessary to admit one head in the Church, to whom it belongs to clear up

---

* " In his quæ *ad fidem pertinent.*" " Pontifex Romanus non potest errare *in fide.*" " Non solum in decretis fidei errare non potest Summus Pontifex, sed neque in præceptis morum, quæ toti Ecclesiæ præscribuntur, et quæ *in rebus necessariis ad salutem*, vel in iis quæ per se bona vel mala sunt, versantur."—Bellarmine, *De Romano Pontifice*, lib. iv. capp. iii. v. pp. 795, 804. Venice, 1599.

† " Absque ulla restrictione dicendum est, quicquid Pontifex in rebus controversis *ad pietatem* spectantibus determinat, infallibiliter illum determinare, quando, ut expositum est, universam Ecclesiam obligat." Greg. de Valentia, *Opp.* tom. iii. disp. 1. qu. i. " De Objecto Fidei," punct. vii. s. 40, p. 312. Ingolstadt, 1595.

" Quæcumque Pontifex in aliqua re de religione controversa sic asserit, certa fide credendum est illum infallibiliter, utpote ex auctoritate Pontificia, i.e. ex Divina assistentia, asserere."—Ibid. s. 39, p. 303.

‡ " An possit in rebus fidei definiendis errare ?"—*In Sum. S. Th.* Q. 2. q. 1. art. 10.

the traditionary expression of the object of the infallibility of the Church.

It is clear that these phrases are all equivalent. They are more or less explicit, but they contain the same ultimate meaning, namely, that the Church has an infallible guidance in treating of all matters of faith, morals, piety, and the general good of the Church.

The object of infallibility, then, is the whole revealed Word of God, and all that is so in-contact with revealed truth, that without treating of it, the Word of God could not be guarded, expounded, and defended. As, for instance, in declaring the Canon and authenticity and true interpretation of Holy Scripture, and the like.

Further, it is clear that the Church has an infallible guidance, not only in all matters that are revealed, but also in all matters which are opposed to revelation. For the Church could not discharge its office as the Teacher of all nations, unless it were able with infallible certainty to proscribe doctrines at variance with the word of God.

From this, again, it follows that the *direct* object

---

tifex ad doctrinæ controversias finiendas erroresque exterminandos fidelium proposuit, tanquam a Deo revelata et credende ex fide. Cæterum, quoniam Pastorem suum semper audire tenetur Ecclesia, et Ecclesiam divina Scriptura absolute prædicat esse columnam et firmamentum veritatis (1 Tim. iii.), ideoque nunquam errare tota potest ; dubium esse non debet quin in aliis quoque rebus omnibus asserendis, *quæ ad pietatem spectent*, et Ecclesiam totam concernent,infallibilis sit Pontificis auctoritas. Neque sane arbitror, hoc absque errore negari posse. . . Quæ sane certitudo iisdem illis Dei promissionibus nititur ex quibus compertum habemus nunquam esse futurum ut universa Ecclesia in rebus religionis fallatur."—Ibid s. 40, p. 300.

of infallibility is the Revelation, or Word, of God; the *indirect* object is whatsoever is necessary for its exposition or defence, and whatsoever is contrariant to the Word of God, that is, to faith and morals. The Church having a divine office to condemn errors in faith and morals, has therefore an infallible assistance in discerning and in proscribing false philosophies and false science.* Under this head comes the condemnation of heretical texts, such as the Three Chapters proscribed in the Fifth Council, the " Augustinus " of Jansenius, and the like; and also censures, both greater and less, those, for instance, of heresy and of error, because of their contrariety to faith; those also of temerity, scandal, and the like, because of their contrariety to morals at least.

2. It is therefore evident that the doctrinal authority of the Church is not confined to matters of revelation, but extends also to positive truths which are not revealed, whensoever the doctrinal authority of the Church cannot be duly exercised in the promulgation, explanation, and defence of revelation without judging and pronouncing on such matters and truths. This will be clear from the following propositions :

(1.) First, the doctrinal authority of the Church is infallible in all matters and truths which are necessary to the custody of the Depositum.

---

* Porro Ecclesia, quæ una cum apostolico munere docendi, mandatum accepit fidei depositum custodiendi, jus etium et officium divinitus habet falsi nominis scientiam proscribendi, ne quis decipiatur per philosophiam, et inanem fallaciam (Coloss. ii. 8.)—*Constitutio Prima de Fide Catholica*, cap. iv. De Fide et Ratione. Appendix, No. IV.

This extends to certain truths of natural science, as, for example, the existence of substance; and to truths of the natural reason, such as that the soul is immaterial; that it is "the form of the body;"* and the like. It extends also to certain truths of the supernatural order, which are not revealed; as, the authenticity of certain texts or versions of the Holy Scripture.

The Council of Trent by a dogmatic decree declared, under anathema, that the Vulgate edition is authentic. Now this is a definition or dogmatic judgment, to be believed on the infallible authority of the Church. But this truth or fact is not revealed.

(2.) Secondly, there are truths of mere human history, which therefore are not revealed, without which the deposit of the Faith cannot be taught or guarded in its integrity. For instance, that St. Peter was Bishop of Rome; that the Council of Trent and the Council of the Vatican are Œcumenical, that is, legitimately celebrated and confirmed; that Pius IX. is the successor of Peter by legitimate election. These truths are not revealed. They have no place in Scripture; and except the first, they have no place in tradition; yet they are so necessary to the order of faith, that the whole would be undermined if they were not infallibly certain. But such infallible certainty is impossible by means of human history and human evidence alone. It is created only by the infallible authority of the Church.

(3.) Thirdly, there are truths of interpretation,

---

* Concil. Later. V. Bulla *Apostolici Regiminis.*

not revealed, without which the deposit of the faith cannot be preserved.

The Council of Trent* declares that to the Church it belongs to judge of the true sense and interpretation of Holy Scripture. Now the sense of the Holy Scripture is two-fold; namely, the literal and grammatical, or, as it is called, the *sensus quis*; and the theological and doctrinal, or the *sensus qualis*. The Church judges infallibly of both. It judges of the question that such and such words or texts have such and such literal and grammatical meaning. It judges also of the conformity of such meaning with the rule of faith, or of its contradiction to the same. The former is a question of fact, the latter of dogma. That the latter falls within the infallible judgment of the Church has been denied by none but heretics. The former has been denied, for a time, by some who continued to be Catholics : for this is, in truth, the question of dogmatic facts. But the Jansenists never ventured to extend their denial to the text of Scripture, though the argument is one and the same. The Church has the same assistance in judging of the grammatical and theological sense of texts, whether sacred or simply human : and has exercised it in all ages.

For instance: Pope Hormisdas † says, "The venerable wisdom of the Fathers providently defined by faithful ordinance what doctrines are Catholic : fixing also certain parts of the ancient books to be received as of authority, the Holy Ghost so instructing them ; lest the reader, indulging in his

---

* Sess. iv.

† Hormisdæ Ep. LXX. Labbe, *Concil.* tom. v. p. 664.

own opinion ... should assert not that which tends to the edification of the Church, but what his own pleasure had conceived."

Pope Nicholas I.[*] writes, "by their decree (i. e. that of the Roman Pontiffs) the writings of other authors are approved or condemned, so that what the Apostolic See approves, is to be held at this day, and what it has rejected, is to be esteemed of no effect," &c.

Pope Gelasius, in a Council held at Rome, decreed as follows: "Also the writings of Cæcilius Cyprianus, Martyr, Bishop of Carthage, are in all things to be received; also the writings of Blessed Gregory, Bishop of Nazianzum .... also the writings and treatises of all orthodox Fathers, who in nothing have deviated from the fellowship of the Holy Roman Church, nor have been separated from its faith and preaching; but have been partakers by the Grace of God of its communion unto the last day of their life, we decree to be read."[†]

Turrecremata says, "It is to be believed that the Roman Pontiff is directed by the Holy Ghost in things of faith, and consequently in these cannot err; otherwise any one might as easily say that there was error in the choice (or discernment) of the four Gospels, and of the canonical epistles, and of the books of other doctors, approving some, and disapproving others; which, however, we read, and as is evident, was determined by the Roman Pontiffs Gregory and Gelasius."[‡]   Again, he says,

---

[*] Nic. Ep. ad Univ. Episc. Galliæ, Labbe, *Concil.* tom. x. p. 262.

[†] Labbe, *Concil.* tom. v p. 887.

[‡] Turrecremata, *De potestate Papali,* lib. ii. cap. 112, in Bibl. M. Rocaberti, tom. xiii. p. 453.

" The sixth kind of Catholic truths are those which are asserted by doctors, approved by the Universal Church for the defence of the faith and the confutation of heretics. . . . This is evident: for since the Church, which is directed by the Holy Ghost, approves certain doctors, receiving their doctrine as true, it necessarily follows that the doctrine of such (writers), delivered by way of assertion, and never otherwise retracted, is true and ought to be held by all the faithful with firm belief, in so far as it is received by the Universal Church; otherwise, the Universal Church would appear to have erred in approving and accepting their doctrine as true, which however was not true." *

And Stapleton lays down, "Bishops . . . when they treat of the Scripture as doctors, have not this certain and infallible authority of which we are speaking: until their treatises, approved by sacred authority, are commended by the Church as Catholic and certainly orthodox interpretation, which Gelasius first did," † &c.

I will give one more example, as it is eminently in point.

The Church has approved in a special manner the works of St. Augustine as containing the true doctrines of grace against the Pelagian and semi-Pelagian heresies.

In this particular, his works have been declared to be orthodox by St. Innocent I., St. Zosimus, St. Boniface I., St. Celestine, St. Hormisdas, St. Felix IV., and Boniface II. For that reason Clement XI. justly condemned the book of Launoy called

---

* Ibid. lib. iv. p. ii. c. ii. 382.
† *Controv. Fidei*, lib. x. c. ii. p. 355, ed. Paris, 1620.

" Véritable tradition de l'Église sur la Prédestina-
tion et la Grâce," &c., as "at least impious and
blasphemous, and injurious to St. Augustine, the
shining light and chief doctor of the Catholic
Church; as also to the Church itself and to the
Apostolic See." *

Now, in this approbation the Church approved
the doctrine of St. Augustine, not only in the *sensus
qualis* but also in the *sensus quis;* that is, it approved
not only a possible theological sense which was orthodox, but the very and grammatical sense of the
text. It was therefore a true doctrinal judgment
as to a dogmatic fact.

For, as Cardinal Gerdil argues, the doctrine of
St. Augustine was proposed by the Church as a
rule of faith against the Pelagian and semi-Pelagian
errors. " When it is said that the doctrine of St.
Augustine in the matter of grace was adopted by
the Church, it must not be understood in the sense
as if St. Augustine had worked out a peculiar system for himself, which the Church then adopted as
its own. . . . . " The great merit of St. Augustine is,
that with marvellous learning he expounded and
defended the antient belief of the faithful." † The
Church infallibly discerned the orthodoxy of his
writings, and approving them, commended them
as a rule of faith.

If the Church have this infallible discernment of
the meaning, grammatical and theological, of orthodox texts, it has *eodem intuitu* the same discern-

---

* Brev. "*Cum. sicut,*" 28 Jan. 1704. D'Argentré, *Collec. Jud.* tom.
vi. p. 444.

  † *Saggio d' Istruz. teol.* "De gratia," ed. Rom. p. 189.

ment of heterodox texts. For the universal practice of the Church in commending the writings of
orthodox, and of condemning those of heterodox
authors, is a part of the doctrinal authority of the
Church in the custody and defence of the faith.
It falls therefore within the limits of its infallibility.

The commendation of the works of St. Augustine, and the commendation of the Thalia of Arius
at Nicæa, of the Anathematisms of Nestorius at
Ephesus, and of the Three Chapters of Ibas, Theo-
dore, and Theodoret, in the Second Council of
Constantinople, all alike involved a judgment of
dogmatic facts.

The subterfuge of the Jansenists as to the literal
meaning of " Augustinus " came too late. The
practice of the Church and the decrees of Councils
had already pronounced its condemnation.

(4.) What has here been said of the condemnation of heretical texts, is equally applicable to the
censures of the Church..

The condemnation of propositions is only the
condemnation of a text by fragments.

The same discernment which ascertains the orthodoxy of certain propositions, detects the heterodoxy of those which are contradictory. And in
both processes that discernment is infallible. To
define doctrines of faith, and to condemn the con-
tradictions of heresy, is almost one and the same
act. The infallibility of the Church in condemning heretical propositions is denied by no Catholic.

In like manner, the detection and condemnation
of propositions at variance with theological cer-

tainty is a function of the same discernment by
which theological certainty is known.   But the
Church has an infallible discernment of truths
which are theologically certain; that is, of conclusions resulting from two premises of which one is
revealed and the other evident by the light of
nature.

In these two kinds of censures, at least, it is
therefore of faith that the Church is infallible.

As to the other censures, such as temerity, scandal, offence to pious ears, and the like, it is evident
that they all relate to the moral character of propositions.   It is not credible that a proposition
condemned by the Church as rash should not be
rash, and as scandalous should not be scandalous,
or as offensive to pious ears should not be such,
and the like.   If the Church be infallible in faith
and morals, it is not to be believed that it can err
in passing these moral judgments on the ethical
character of propositions.   In truth, all Catholic
theologians, without exception, so far as I know,
teach that the Church is infallible in all such censures.*   They differ only in this: that some declare
this truth to be of faith, and therefore the denial of
it to be heresy; others declare it to be of faith as to
the condemnation of heretical propositions, but in
all others to be only of theological certainty; so
that the denial of it to be not heresy, but error.

To deny the infallibility of the Church in the
censures less than for heresy, is held to be heretical
by De Panormo, Malderus, Coninck, Diana, Ovie-

---

* Of course, I am not speaking of writers whose works are under
censure.

do, Amici, Matteucci, Pozzobonelli, Viva, Nannetti. Murray calls it objective heresy. Griffini, Herincx, Ripalda, Ferraris, and Reinerding do not decide whether it be heretical, erroneous, or proximate to error. Cardenas and Turrianus hold it to be erroneous; Anfossi, erroneous, or proximate to error. De Lugo in one place maintains that it is erroneous; in another, that to deny the infallibility of the Church in the condemnation of erroneous propositions, is heresy.* All, therefore, affirm the Church in passing such censures to be infallible.

The infallibility of the Church in all censures less than heresy may be proved from the Acts of the Council of Constance. In the eleventh article of the Interrogatory proposed to the followers of Huss are included condemnations of all kinds.

---

* De Panormo, *Scrutinium Doctrinarum*, cap. iii. art. xiii. num. 7 sqq. p. 196, Rome, 1709; Diana, *Opp.* tom. ix. De infall. Rom. Pont. resol. x. num. 8 sqq. p. 262, Venice, 1698; Amici, *Cursus Theologicus*, tom. iv. De Fide, disp. vii. num. 55, p. 146, Douay, 1641; Matteucci, *Opus Dogmatic.* De Controv. Fidei, vii. cap. iii. num. 33, p. 359, Venice, 1755; Viva, *Theses Damnatæ*, quæst. prodrom. num. xviii. p. 10, Padua, 1737; Murray, *De Ecclesia*, tom. iii. fasc. i. p. 226, Dublin, 1865; Herincx, *Summ. Theol. Schol. et Moral.* dub. ix. num. 98, p. 186, Antwerp, 1663; Ripalda, tom. iii. disp. i. sect. 7, num. 59, p. 16, Cologne, 1648; Ferraris, *Bibliothec. Canonic.* tom. vi. sub. v. Prop. Damn. num. 37, p. 565, Rome, 1789; Reinerding, *Theol. Fundamental.* tract. i. num. 408, p. 237, Münster, 1864; Cardenas, *Crisis Theologica*, dis. procem. num. 140, p. 35, Cologne, 1690; Turrianus, *Select. Disput. Theol.* pars i. disp. xxx. dub. 3, p. 149, Lyons, 1634; Anfossi, *Difesa dell' "Auctorem Fidei,"* lett. x. tom. ii. p. 141, Rome, 1816; De Lugo, *De Virtute Fidei*, tom. iii. disp. xx. sect. 3, num. 109, p. 324, and num. 113–117, p. 325, Venice, 1751. For the summary and for the references to Pozzobonelli, Malderus, Coninck, Oviedo, Nannetti and Griffini, I am indebted to an unpublished work of Fr. Granniello of the congregation of Barnabites in Rome.

They were asked whether they believed the articles of Wickliffe and Huss to be "not Catholic,
but some of them notoriously .heretical, some erroneous, others temarious and seditious, others
offensive to pious ears."*   Martin V., therefore, in
the Bull "Inter cunctos" requires belief, that is,
interior assent, to all such condemnations made by
the Council of Constance, which therein extended
its infallible jurisdiction to all the minor censures,
less than that of heresy.

In like manner, again, in the Bull "Auctorem
Fidei," the propositions condemned as heretical are
very few, but the propositions condemned as erroneous, scandalous, offensive, schismatical, injurious, are very numerous.

During the last three hundred years, the Pontiffs have condemned a multitude of propositions
of which perhaps not twenty were censured with
the note of heresy.

Now in every censure the Church proposes to
us some truth relating to faith or morals; and
whether the matter of such truths be revealed or
not revealed, it nevertheless so pertains to faith and
morals that the deposit could not be guarded if
the Church in such judgments were liable to error.

The Apostle declares that "the Church is the
pillar and ground of the Truth."† On what authority these words can be restricted to revealed

* "Utrum credat sententiam sacri Constantiensis concilii, . . .
scilicet quod supradicti 45 articuli Joannis Wicliff, et Joannis Huss
triginta, non sunt Catholici; sed quidam ex eis sunt notorie hæretici, quidam erronei, alii temerarii et seditiosi, alii piarum aurium
offensivi."—Labbe, *Concil.* tom. xvi. p. 194.

† 1 Tim. iii. 15.

truth alone, I do not know. I know of no com-
mentator, ancient or modern, who so restricts
them. On the other hand St. Peter Damian, Six
tus V., Ferré, Cardinal de Lugo, Gregory de Valentia, expressly extend these words to all truths
necessary to the custody of the deposit.

This doctrine is abundantly confirmed by the
following declarations of Pius IX. "For the
Church by its Divine institution is bound with all
diligence to guard whole and inviolate the deposit
of Divine faith, and constantly to watch with supreme zeal over the salvation of souls, driving
away therefore, and eliminating with all exactness,
all things which are either contrary to faith or can
in any way bring into peril the salvation of souls.
Wherefore the Church, by the power committed
to it by its Divine Author, has not only the right
but above all the duty, of not tolerating but of
proscribing and of condemning all errors, if the
integrity of the faith and the salvation of souls
should so require. On all philosophers who desire
to remain sons of the Church, and on all philosophy, this duty lies, to assert nothing contrary to
the teachings of the Church, and to retract all such
things when the Church shall so admonish. The
opinion which teaches contrary to this we pronounce and declare altogether erroneous, and in
the highest degree injurious to the faith of the
Church, and to its authority."[*]

From all that has been said, it is evident that the
Church claims no jurisdiction over the processes

---

[*] Litteræ Pii IX., "Gravissimas inter," ad Archiep. Monac. et
Frising. Dec. 1862.

of philosophy or science, except as they bear upon revealed truths ; nor does it claim to intervene in philosophy or science as a judge or censor of the principles proper to such philosophy or science. The only judgment it pronounces regards the conformity or variance of such processes of the human intelligence with the deposit of faith, and the principles of revealed morality ; that is, in order to the end of the infallible office, namely, the guardianship of Divine revelation.

I will not here attempt to enumerate the subject-matters which fall within the limits of the infallibility of the Church. It belongs to the Church alone to determine the limits of its own infallibility. Hitherto it has not done so except by its acts, and from the practice of the Church we may infer to what matter its infallible.discernment extends. It is enough for the present to show two things :

1. First, that the infallibility of the Church extends, as we have seen, directly to the whole matter of revealed truth, and indirectly to all truths which though not revealed are in such contact with revelation that the deposit of faith and morals cannot be guarded, expounded, and defended without an infallible discernment of such unrevealed truths.

2. Secondly, that this extension of the infallibility of the Church is, by the unanimous teaching of all theologians, at least theologically certain ; and, in the judgment of the majority of theologians, certain by the certainty of faith.

Such is the traditional doctrine respecting the infallibility of the Church in faith and morals. By the definition of the Vatican Council, what is traditionally believed by all the faithful in respect to the Church is expressly declared of the Roman Pontiff. But the definition of the extent of that infallibility, and of the certainty on which it rests, in matters not revealed, has not been treated as yet, but is left for the second part of the " Schema De Ecclesia."

III. Thirdly, the definition declares the efficient cause of infallibility to be a Divine assistance promised to Peter, and in Peter to his successors.

The explicit promise is that of our Divine Lord to Peter. " I have prayed for thee that thy faith fail not, and thou being once converted, confirm thy brethren."*

The implicit promise is in the words " On this rock I will build my Church, and the Gates of Hell shall not prevail against it."†

The traditional interpretation of these promises is precise.

The words, " Ego rogavi pro te, ut non deficiat fides tua, et tu aliquando conversus confirma fratres tuos," are interpreted, by both Fathers and Councils, of the perpetual stability of Peter's faith in his see and his successors; and of this assertion I give the following proofs.

St. Ambrose, A.D. 397, in his treatise on Faith, says, Christ " said to Peter, I have prayed for thee, that thy faith fail not. Was He not therefore able to confirm the faith of him to whom by His own authority He gave the kingdom? whom he pointed

---

* St. Luke xxii. 32.   † St. Matth. xvi. 18.

out as the foundation of the Church, when He called him the Rock?"[*]

St. John Chrysostom, A.D. 407, in his commentary on the Acts of the Apostles, writes, " He (i. e. Peter) takes the lead in the matter, as he was himself entrusted with the care of all. For Christ said to him, Thou, being converted, confirm thy brethren."[†]

St. Augustine, A.D. 430, in his commentary on the words of Psalm cxviii. 43, " And take not Thou the word of truth utterly out of my mouth," says, " Therefore the whole body of Christ speaks ; that is the universality of the Holy Church. And the Lord Himself said to Peter, I have prayed for thee, that thy faith fail not, that is, that the word of truth be not utterly taken out of thy mouth."[‡]

St. Cyril of Alexandria, A.D. 444, in his commentary on St. Luke, says, " The Lord, when He hinted at the denial of His disciple and said, I have prayed for thee, that thy faith fail not, immediately utters a word of consolation, thou being converted, confirm thy brethren ; that is, be the con-

---

[*] Habes in evangelio quia Petro dixit, Rogavi pro to ut non deficiat fides tua.—Ergo cui propria auctoritate regnum dabat, hujus fidem firmare non poterat ; quem cum petram dixit firmamentum Ecclesiæ indicavit ?—St. Ambrose De Fide, lib. iv. cap. v. tom. iii. p. 672, ed. Ben. Venice, 1751.

[†] Πρῶτος τοῦ πράγματος αὐθεντεῖ, ἅτε αὐτὸς πάντας ἐγχειρισθείς, πρὸς γὰρ τοῦτον εἶπεν ὁ Χριστός· Καὶ σύ ποτε ἐπιστρέψας στήριξον τοὺς ἀδελ.- φούς σου.—St. Joann. Chrys. Opp. tom. ix. p. 26, ed. Ben. Paris, 1731.

[‡] Totum itaque corpus Christi loquitur, id est Ecclesiæ sanctæ universitas —Et ipse Dominus ad Petrum, Rogavi, inquit, pro te, ne deficiat fides tua ; hoc est ne auferatur ex ore tuo verbum veritatis usque valde.—St. Augustin. Enarratio in Psalmos, tom. iv. p. 1310. ed. Ben. Paris, 1681.

firmer and teacher of those who came to Me by faith.*

St. Leo the Great, A. D. 460, in a discourse on the anniversary of his election to the Pontificate, says, " If anything in our time and by us is well administered and rightly ordained, it is to be ascribed to his operation and to his government, to whom it was said, 'Thou being converted, confirm thy brethren,' and to whom after His resurrection, in answer to his threefold declaration of everlasting love, the Lord with mystical meaning thrice said, 'Feed my sheep.'"†

St. Gelasius, A. D. 496, writes to Honorius, Bishop of Dalmatia, "Though we are hardly able to draw breath in the manifold difficulties of the times; yet in the government of the Apostolic See we unceasingly have in hand the care of the whole fold of the Lord, which was committed to blessed Peter by the voice of our Saviour Himself, ' And thou being converted, confirm thy brethren,' and again, ' Peter, lovest thou Me ? Feed My sheep.'"‡

---

* Ὁ μέντοι Κύριος τὴν τοῦ μαθητοῦ ἄρνησιν αἰνιξάμενος ἐν οἷς ἔφη, ἐδεήθην περὶ σοῦ ἵνα μὴ ἐκλίπῃ ἡ πίστις σου, εἰσφέρει παραχρῆμα τὸν τῆς παρακλήσεως λόγον, καί φησι, Καὶ σύ ποτε ἐπιστρέψας στήριξον τοὺς ἀδελφούς σου · τούτεστι γενοῦ στήριγμα καὶ διδάσκαλος τῶν διὰ πίστεως προσιόντων ἐμοί.—St. Cyrill. Alex. *Comment. in Luc.* xxii. tom. v. p. 916, ed. Migne, Paris, 1848.

† Tantam potentiam dedit ei quem totius Ecclesiæ principem fecit, ut si quid etiam nostris temporibus recte per nos agitur recteque disponitur illius operibus illius sit gubernaculis deputandum, cui dictum est, Et tu conversus confirma fratres tuos ; et cui post ressurectionem suam Dominus ad trinam æterni amoris professionem mystica insinuatione ter dixit, Pasce oves meas.—St. Leo, serm. iv. cap. iv. tom. i. p. 19, ed. Ballerini, Venice, 1753.

‡ Licet inter varias temporum difficultates vix respirare valeamus, pro sedis tamen apostolicæ moderamine totius ovilis dominici

Pelagius II., A. D. 590, in like manner writes to the Bishops of Istria, " For you know how the Lord in the gospel declares: Simon, Simon, behold Satan has desired you that he might sift you as wheat, but I have prayed the Father for thee, that thy faith fail not, and thou being converted, confirm thy brethren. See, beloved, the truth cannot be falsified, nor can the faith of Peter ever be shaken or changed."*

St. Gregory the Great, A. D. 604, in his celebrated letter to Maurice, Emperor of the East, says, " For it is clear to all who know the Gospel, that the care of the whole Church was committed to the Apostle St. Peter, prince of all the Apostles. For to him it is said, 'Peter, lovest thou me? Feed My sheep.' To him it is said, 'Behold, Satan has desired to sift you as wheat: but I have prayed for thee, Peter, that thy faith fail not, and thou being once converted, confirm thy brethren.' To him it is said, 'Thou art Peter, and upon this rock I will build My church.' "†

---

curam sine cessatione tractantes, quæ beato Petro salvatoris ipsius nostri voce delegata est, Et tu conversus confirma fratres tuos; et item, Petre, amas me? pasce oves meas.—St. Gelasius, epist. v.; in Labbe, *Concil.* tom. v. p. 298, Venice, 1728.

* Nostis enim in evangelio dominum proclamantem, Simon, Simon, ecce Satanas expetivit vos, ut cribraret sicut triticum, ego autem rogavi pro te Patrem, ut non deficiat fides tua, et tu conversus confirma fratres tuos. Considerate, carissimi, quia veritas mentiri non potuit, nec fides Petri in æternum quassari poterit vel mutari.—Pelagius. II. epist. v. in Labbe, *Concil.* tom. vi. p. 626.

† Cunctis enim Evangelium scientibus liquet, quod voce dominica sancto et omnium apostolorum Petro Principi Apostolo totius Ecclesiæ cura commissa est. Ipsi quippe dicitur, Petre, amas me? pasce oves meas. Ipsi dicitur, Ecce Satanas expetiit cribrare vos sicut triticut; et ego pro te rogavi, Petre, ut non deficiat fides tua ;

Stephen, Bishop of Dori, A. D. 649, at a Lateran Council under Martin I. says, in a *libellas supplex* or memorial read and recorded in the acts, "Peter the Prince of the Apostles was first commanded to feed the sheep of the Catholic Church, when the Lord said, ' Peter, lovest thou Me? Feed My sheep." And again, he chiefly and especially, having a faith firm above all, and unchangeable in our Lord God, was found worthy to convert and to confirm his fellows and his spiritual brethren who were shaken."*

Pope St. Vitalian, A. D. 669, says, in a letter to Paul, Archbishop of Crete, "What things we command thee and thy Synod according to God and for the Lord, study at once to fulfil, lest we be compelled to bear ourselves not in mercy but according to the power of the sacred canons, for it is written; The Lord said, ' Peter, I have prayed for thee, that thy faith fail not, and thou being once converted, confirm thy brethren.'· And again, ' Whatsoever thou, Peter, shall bind on earth, shall be bound in heaven, and whatever thou shalt loose on earth shall be loosed in heaven.' "†

---

et tu aliquando conversus confirma fratres tuos. Ipsi dicitur, Tu es Petrus et super hanc Petram, etc.—St. Gregor. *Epist.* lib. v. ep. xx. tom. ii. 748, ed. Ben. Paris, 1705.

* Princeps apostolorum ₁Petrus pascere primus jussus est oves Catholicæ Ecclesiæ, cum Dominus dicit, Petre, amas me? Pasce oves meas; et iterum ipse præcipue ac specialiter firmam præ omnibus habens in Dominum Deum nostrum et immutabilem fidem, convertere aliquando et confirmare exagitatos consortes suos et spiritales meruit fratres.—Labbe, *Concil.* tom. vii. p. 107.

† Quæ præcipimus tibi secundum Deum et propter Dominum tuæque synodo, stude illico peragere, ne cogamur non misericorditer sed secundem virtutem sacratissimorum canonum conversari.

The quotations given in the Pastoral Letter of last year, united with these, afford the following result. The application of the promise *Ego rogavi pro te*, &c., to the infallible faith of Peter and his successors, is made by St. Ambrose, St. Augustine, St. Leo, St. Gelasius, Pelagius II., St. Gregory the Great, Stephen Bishop of Dori in a Lateran Council, St. Vitalian, the Bishops of the IV. Œcumenical Council A. D. 451, St. Agatho in the VI. A. D. 680, St. Bernard A. D. 1153, St. Thomas Aquinas A. D. 1274, St. Bonaventure A. D. 1274 : that is, this interpretation is given by three out of the four doctors of the Church, by six Pontiffs down to the seventh century. It was recognized in two Œcumenical Councils. It is explicitly declared by the Angelic Doctor, who may be taken as the exponent of the Dominican school, and by the Seraphic Doctor, who is likewise the witness of the Franciscan; and by a multitude of Saints. This catena, if continued to later times, might, as all know, be indefinitely prolonged.

The interpretation by the Fathers of the words " On this rock," &c., is fourfold, but all four interpretations are no more than four aspects of one and the same truth, and all are necessary to complete its full meaning. They all implicitly or explicitly contain the perpetual stability of Peter's faith. It would be out of place to enter upon this here. It is enough to refer to Ballerini *De vi et ratione Primatus*, where the subject is exhausted.

Scriptum namque est, Dominus inquit, Petre, rogavi pro te ut n deficeret fides tua ; et tu aliquando conversus confirma fratres tuos. Et rursum, Quodcunque ligaveris, etc.—St. Vitalian, epist. i. in Labbe, *Concil.* tom. vii. p. 460.

In these two promises a divine assistance is pledged to Peter and to his successors, and that divine assistance is promised to secure the stability and indefectibility of the Faith in the supreme Doctor and Head of the Church, for the general good of the Church itself.

It is therefore a *charisma*, a grace of the supernatural order, attached to the Primacy of Peter which is perpetual in his successors.

I need hardly point out that between the charisma, or *gratia gratis data* of infallibility and the idea of impeccability there is no connection. I should not so much as notice it, if some had not strangely obscured the subject by introducing this confusion. I should have thought that the gift of prophecy in Balaam and Caiaphas, to say nothing of the powers of the priesthood, which are the same in good and bad alike, would have been enough to make such confusion impossible.

The preface to the Definition carefully lays down that infallibility is not inspiration. The Divine assistance by which the Pontiffs are guarded from error, when as Pontiffs they teach in matters of faith and morals, contains no new revelation. Inspiration contained not only assistance in writing but sometimes the suggestions of truth not otherwise known. The Pontiffs are witnesses, teachers, and judges of the revelation already given to the Church; and in guarding, expounding, and defending that revelation, their witness, teaching and judgment, is by Divine assistance preserved from error. This assistance, like the revelation which it guards, is of the supernatural order. They, therefore, who argue against the infallibility of the Pontiff because he is an individual person, and still profess to believe the infallibility of Bishops in General Councils, and also of the Bishops dispersed throughout the world, because they are many witnesses, betray the fact that they have not as yet mastered the idea that infallibility is not of the order of nature, but is of the order of grace. In the order of nature, indeed, truth may be found rather with the many than with the individual, though in this the history of mankind would give a host of contrary examples. But in the supernatural order, no such argument can have place. It depends simply upon the ordination of God; and certainly neither in the Old Testament nor in the New have we examples of infallibility depending upon number. But in both we have the example of infallibility attaching to persons as individuals; as for instance the Prophets of the old and the Apostles of the new law. It is no answer to say that the Apostles were united in one body. They were each one possessed of that which all possessed together. To this may be also added the inspired writers, who were preserved from error individually and personally, and not as a collective body. The whole evidence of Scripture, therefore, is in favor of the communication of Divine gifts to individuals. The objection is not scriptural nor Catholic, nor of the supernatural order, but natural, and, in the last analysis, rationalistic.

IV. Fourthly, the Definition precisely determines the acts of the Pontiff to which this Divine assistance is attached; namely, " *in doctrina de fide vel moribus definienda*," to the defining of doctrine of faith and morals.

The definition, therefore, carefully excludes all ordinary and common acts of the Pontiff as a private person, and also all acts of the Pontiff as a private theologian, and again all his acts which are not in matters of faith and morals; and further, all acts in which he does not define a doctrine, that is, in which he does not act as the supreme Doctor of the Church in defining doctrines to be held by the whole Church.

The definition therefore includes, and includes only, the solemn acts of the Pontiff as the supreme Doctor of all Christians, defining doctrines of faith and morals, to be held by the whole Church.

Now the word *doctrine* here signifies a revealed truth, traditionally handed down by the teaching authority, or *magisterium infallibile*, of the Church; including any truth which, though not revealed, is yet so united with a revealed truth as to be inseparable from its full explanation and defence.

And the word definition here signifies the precise judgment or sentence in which any such traditional truth of faith or morals may be authoritatively formulated; as, for instance, the consubstantiality of the Son, the procession of the Holy Ghost by one only Spiration from the Father and the Son, the Immaculate Conception, and the like.

The word " definition " has two senses, the one forensic and narrow, the other wide and common; and this in the present instance is more correct. The forensic or narrow sense confines its meaning to the logical act of defining by *genus* and *differentia*. But this sense is proper to dialectics and disputations, not to the acts of Councils and Pontiffs. The wide and common sense is that of an authoritative

termination of questions which have been in doubt
and debate, and therefore of the judgment or sentence thence resulting.   When the second Council
of Lyons says, " Si quæ subortæ fuerint fidei quæstiones suo judicio debere definiri," it means that the
questions of faith ought to be *ended* by this judgment of the Pontiff. *Definire* is *finem imponere*, or
finaliter judicare.   It is therefore equivalent to *determinare*, or *finaliter determinare*, which words are
those of St. Thomas when speaking of the supreme
authority of the Roman Pontiff.   It is in this sense
that the Vatican Council uses the word *definienda*.
It signifies the final decision by which any matter
of faith and morals is put into a doctrinal form.

Now it is to be observed that the definition does
not speak of either controversies, or questions of
faith and morals.   It speaks of the doctrinal authority of the Pontiff in general ; and therefore both of
what may be called pacific definitions like that of
the Immaculate Conception, and of controversial
definitions like those of St. Innocent against the Pe-
lagians,   or   St.   Leo   against   the   Monophysites.
Moreover, under the term definitions, as we have
seen, are included all dogmatic judgments.   In the
Bull *Auctorem Fidei* these terms are used as synonymous.   The tenth proposition of the Synod of
Pistoia is condemned as " Detrahens firmitati defin-
itionum, judiciorumve dogmaticorum Ecclesiæ."
In the Italian version made by order of the Pope
these words are translated, "detraente alla fermezza
delle definizioni o giudizj dommatici della Chiesa."
Now, dogmatic judgments included all judgments
in matters of dogma ; as for instance, the inspiration and authenticity of sacred books, the ortho-

doxy or heterodoxy of human and uninspired books. But intimately connected with dogma in these judgments, as we have already seen, is the grammatical and literal sense of such texts. The theological sense of such texts cannot be judged of without a discernment of their grammatical and literal sense; and both are included in the same dogmatic judgment, that is, both the dogmatic truth and the dogmatic fact.

The example above given, in which the Pontiffs approved and commended to the Church, as a rule of faith against Pelagianism, the writings of St. Augustine, was a true definition of doctrine in faith and morals. The condemnation of the " Augustinus" of Jansenius, and of the five propositions extracted from it, was also a doctrinal definition, or a dogmatic judgment.

In like manner all censures, whether for heresy or with a note less than heresy, are doctrinal definitions in faith and morals, and are included in the words *in doctrina de fide vel moribus definienda.*

In a word, the whole *magisterium* or doctrinal authority of the Pontiff as the supreme Doctor of all Christians, is included in this definition of his infallibility. And also all legislative or judicial acts, so far as they are inseparably connected with his doctrinal authority; as, for instance, all judgments, sentences, and decisions, which contain the motives of such acts as derived from faith and morals. Under this will come laws of discipline, canonization of Saints, approbation of religious Orders, of devotions, and the like; all of which intrinsically contain the truths and principles of faith, morals, and piety.

The Definition, then, limits the infallibility of the Pontiff to his supreme acts *ex cathedra* in faith and morals, but extends his infallibility to all acts in the fullest exercise of his supreme *magisterium* or doctrinal authority.

V. Fifthly, the definition declares that in these acts the Pontiff *"ea infallibilitate pollere*, qua Divinus Redemptor Ecclesiam suam in definienda doctrina de fide et moribus instructam esse voluit;" that is, that he is possessed of the infallibility with which our Divine Saviour willed that His Church should be endowed.

It is to be carefully noted that this definition declares that the Roman Pontiff possesses by himself the infallibility with which the. Church in unison with him is endowed.

The definition does not decide the question whether the infallibility of the Church is derived from him or through him. But it does decide that his infallibility is not derived from the Church, nor through the Church. The former question is left untouched. Two truths are affirmed; the one, that the supreme and infallible doctrinal authority was given to Peter, the other, that the promise of the Holy Spirit was afterwards extended to the Apostles. The promises " Ego rogavi pro te," and " Non prævalebunt," were spoken to Peter alone. The promises " He shall lead you into all truth," and " Behold, I am with you all days," were spoken to Peter with all the Apostles. The infallibility of Peter was, therefore, not dependent on his union with them in exercising it; but, their infallibility was evidently dependent on their union with him. In like manner, the whole Episcopate gathered in

Council is not infallible without its head. But the
head is always infallible by himself. Thus far the
definition is express, and the infallibility of the
Vicar of Christ is declared to be the *privilegium
Petri*, a charisma attached to the primacy, a Divine
assistance given as a prerogative of the Head.
There is, therefore, a special fitness in the word
pollere in respect to the Head of the Church. This
Divine assistance is his special prerogative depending on God alone; independent of the Church,
which in dependence on him is endowed with the
same infallibility. If the definition does not decide
that the Church derives its infallibility from the
Head, it does decide that the Head does not derive
his infallibility from the Church; for it affirms this
Divine assistance to be derived from the promise
to Peter and in Peter to his successors.

VI. Lastly, the definition fixes the dogmatic
value of these Pontifical acts *ex cathedra*, by declaring that they are " *ex sese, non autem ex consensu Ecclesiæ irreformabilia*," that is, irreformable in and
of themselves, and not because the Church or any
part or any members of the Church should assent
to them. These words, with extreme precision, do
two things. First, they ascribe to the Pontifical
acts *ex cathedra*, in faith or morals an intrinsic infallibility; and secondly, they exclude from them
all influx of any other cause of such intrinsic infallibility. It is ascribed alone to the Divine assistance given to the Head of the Church for that end
and effect.

I need not add, that by these words many forms
of error are excluded: as, first, the theory that the
joint action of the Episcopate congregated in

Council is necessary to the infallibility of the Pontiff; secondly, that the consent of the Episcopate dispersed is required; thirdly, that if not the express at least the tacit assent of the Episcopate is needed. All these alike deny the infallibility of the Pontiff till his acts are confirmed by the Episcopate. I know, indeed, it has been said by some, that in so speaking they do not deny the infallibility of the Pontiff, but affirm him to be infallible when he is united with the Episcopate, from which they further affirm that he can never be divided. But this, after all, resolves the efficient cause of his infallibility into union with the Episcopate, and makes its exercise dependent upon that union; which is to deny his infallibility as a privilege of the primacy, independent of the Church which he is to teach and to confirm. The words "*Ex sese, non autem ex consensu Ecclesiæ*," preclude all ambiguity by which for two hundred years the promise of our Lord to Peter and his successors has in some minds been obscured.

CHAPTER III.

THE TERMINOLOGY OF THE DOCTRINE OF
INFALLIBILITY.

I WILL now add a few words respecting the terms which have been used, not only in the course of the last months, but in the traditional theology of the Schools, on the doctrine of Infallibility.

Certain well-known writers have rendered memorable the formula of "personal, separate, independent and absolute infallibility." It has not only been used in pastoral letters, and pamphlets, but introduced into high diplomatic correspondence.

The frequency and confidence with which this formula was repeated, as if taken from the writings of the promoters of the Definition, made it not unnatural to examine into the origin, history, and meaning of the formula itself. I therefore set myself to search it out; and I employed others to do the same. As it had been ascribed to myself, our first examination was turned to anything I might have written. After repeated search, not only was the formula as a whole nowhere to be discovered, but the words of which it is composed were, with the exception of the word "independent," equally nowhere to be found. I mention this, that I may clear away the supposition that in what I add I have any motive of defending myself or anything I may have written. I speak of it now simply for the truth's sake, and for charity, which is always promoted by a clear statement of truth, and never by the confused noise of controversy; and also to justify some of the most eminent defenders of Catholic doctrine, by showing that this terminology is to be found in the writings of many of our greatest theologians.

I may remind you, in passing, that in the Definition not a trace of this formula nor of its component words is to be found.

First, as to the word *personal*, Cardinal Toletus, speaking of the doctrine of infallibility, says, " The first opinion is, that the privilege of the Pope, that of not erring in faith, is *personal;* and cannot be communicated to another." After quoting our Lord's words, "I have prayed for thee," etc., he adds, "I concede that this privilege is personal."*

Ballerini says, that the jurisdiction of St. Peter, by reason of the primacy, was "singular and personal" to himself. The same right he affirms to belong also to the Roman Pontiffs, St. Peter's successors." †

This doctrine he explains diffusely.

---

* "Prima est quod privilegium Papæ ut in fide errare non possit est personale, nec ipse potest alteri communicare, Luc. xxii. : ' Ego rogavi pro te, Petre, et tu aliquando conversus confirma fratres tuos.' Ad primum concedo esse illud privilegium personale: ob id communicari non potest."—Toletus. *In Summ. Enarr.* tom. ii. pp. 62, 64. Rome, 1869.

† "Jurisdictio et prærogativæ quæ eidem sedi ab antiquis asseruntur ratione primatus ejusdem Petri ac successorum singulares et personales judicandæ sunt."—Ballerini, *de Vi et Ratione Primatus,* cap. iii. sect. 5, p. 14. Rome, 1849.

"This primacy of chief jurisdiction, not of mere order, in St. Peter and the Roman Pontiffs his successors, is *personal*, that is, attached to their person; and therefore a supreme personal right, which is communicated to no other, is contained in the primacy.

"Hence, when there is question of the rights and the jurisdiction proper to the primacy, and when these are ascribed to the Roman See, or Cathedra, or Church of St. Peter; by the name of the Roman See, or Cathedra, or Church, to which this primacy of jurisdiction is ascribed, the single person of the Roman Pontiff is to be understood, to whom alone the same primacy is attached.

"Hence again it follows, that whatsoever belongs to the Roman See or Cathedra or Church, by reason of the primacy, is so to be ascribed to the person of the Roman Pontiffs that they need help or association of none for the exercise of that right." *

From this passage three conclusions flow:

1. First, that the Primacy is a personal privilege in Peter and his successors.

---

* "Hic præcipuæ jurisdictionis et non meri ordinis primatus S. Petri et Romanorum Pontificum ejus successorum personalis est, seu ipsorum personæ alligatus; ac proinde jus quoddam præcipuum ipsorum personale, id est, nulli alii commune, in eo primatu contineri debet. Hinc cum de jure, seu jurisdictione propria primatus agitur, hæcque Romanæ S. Petri sedi, cathedræ, vel Ecclesiæ tribuitur; sedis cathedræ vel Ecclesiæ Romanæ nomine, cui ea jurisdictio primatus propria asseratur, una Romani Pontificis persona intelligenda est, cui uni idem primatus est alligatus. Hinc quoque sequitur, quidquid juris ratione primatus Romanæ sedi cathedræ, vel Ecclesiæ competit, Romanorum Pontificum personæ ita esse tribuendum ut nullius adjutorio vel societate ad idem jus exercendum indigeant."—Ballerini, *de Vi et Ratione Primatus*, cap. iii. propositio 3, p. 10.

2. Secondly, that this personal privilege attaches to Peter and to the Roman Pontiffs alone.

3. Thirdly, that in exercising this same primacy the Roman Pontiff needs the help and society of no other.

Ballerini then adds:

"That what was personal in Peter by reason of the primacy, is to be declared personal in his successors the Roman Pontiffs, on whom the same primacy of Peter with the same jurisdiction has devolved, no one can deny.

"Therefore to Peter alone, and to the person alone of his successors, the dignity and jurisdiction of the Primacy is so attached, that it can be ascribed to no other Bishop, even though of the Chief Sees; and much less can it be ascribed to any number whatsoever of Bishops congregated together; nor in that essential jurisdiction of· the primacy ought the Roman Pontiff to depend on any one whomsoever; nor can he; especially as the jurisdiction received from Christ was instituted by Christ un-circumscribed by any condition, and personal in Peter alone and his successors: like as He instituted the primacy of jurisdiction to be personal, which without personal jurisdiction is unintelligible." *

---

* "Quod autem personale in Petro fuit ratione primatus, idem in successoribus ejus Romanis Pontificibus, in quos idem primatus Petri cum eadem jurisdictione transivit, personale esse dicendum, inficiari potest nemo. Soli igitur Petro et soli successorum ejus personæ ita alligata est propria primatus dignitas et jurisdictio ut nulli alii Episcopo præstantiorum licet sedium, et minus multo pluribus aliis Episcopis quantumvis in unum collectis, possit adscribi: neque in ea jurisdictione primatus essentiali Romanus Pontifex dependere ab alio quopiam debet aut potest, cum præsertim ipsam a Christo acceptam idem Christus nulla conditione circum-

From these statements it follows:

1. First, that what depends on no other is altogether independent.

2. Secondly, that what is circumscribed by no condition is absolute.

3. Thirdly, that what is by God committed to one alone, depends on God alone.

But perhaps it will be said that all this relates not to infallibility, but to the power of jurisdiction only.

To this I answer:

1. That if the primacy be personal, all its prerogatives are personal.

2. That the doctrinal authority of the Pontiff is a part of his jurisdiction, and is therefore personal.

3. That infallibility is, as the Definition expressly declares, a supernatural grace, or *charisma*, attached to the primacy, in order to its proper exercise. Infallibility is a quality of the doctrinal jurisdiction of the Pontiff in faith and morals.

And such also is the doctrine of Ballerini, who lays down the following propositions:

"Unity with the Roman faith is absolutely necessary, and therefore the prerogative of absolute infallibility is to be ascribed to it, and a coercive power to constrain to unity of faith, in like manner, absolute; as also the infallibility and coercive power of the Catholic Church itself, which is bound to adhere to the faith of Rome, is absolute." *

---

scriptam, personalem solius Petri ac successorum esse instituerit, uti primatum jurisdictionis instituit personalem, qui sine personali jurisdictione intelligi nequit."—Ballerini, *de Vi et Ratione Primatus*, cap. iii. sect. 4, p. 13.

* Ballerini *de Vi et Rat. Primatus:* Unitas cum Romana fide

But Ballerini has declared that whatsoever is ascribed to the Roman See, Cathedra, or Church is to be ascribed to the Person of the Roman Pontiff only. Therefore this infallibility and coercive power are to be ascribed to him, and are personal.

Here we have the infallibility personal, independent, and absolute, fully and explicitly taught by two chief theologians of great repute.

But hitherto we have not met the word *separate*, though in truth the word *sole*, or *alone*, is equivalent.

I will therefore add certain quotations from the great Dominican School.

Bzovius, the continuator of the Annals of Baronius, says, " To Peter alone, and after him to all the Roman Pontiffs legitimately succeeding, the privilege of infallibility, as it is called, was conceded by the Prince of Pastors, Christ, who is God."*

Dominicus Marchese writes : " This privilege was conceded to the successors of Peter alone without the assistance of the College of Cardinals; " and again, " To the Roman Pontiff alone,

---

absolute necessaria est, ac proinde infallibilatis prærogativa absoluta illi est tribuenda, et vis coactiva ad fidei unitatem pariter absoluta: sicuti absoluta est item infallibilitas et vis coactiva ipsius Ecclesiæ Catholicæ, quæ Romanæ fidei adhærere oportet. Appendix De infall. Pont. Prop. vii.

* " Soli Petro et post eum omnibus Romanis Pontificibus legitime sedentibus, infallibilitatis quod vocant privilegium, a Principe pastorum Christo Deo concessum, ut in rebus fidei, morum doctrina, et universalis Ecclesiæ administratione certissima nullaque fallaciæ nota inumbrata decreta veritatis ipsius radio scribant edicant et sanciant."—Bzovius, *de Pontifice Romano*, cap. xiv. p. 106; apud Rocaberti, Biblioth. Pontif. tom. i. Rome, 1698.

in the person of Peter, was committed the care of the Universal Church, and firmness, and certainty in defining matters of faith." *

Gravina teaches as follows: "To the Pontiff, as one (person) and alone, it was given to be the head;" and again, "The Roman Pontiff for the time being is one, therefore he alone has infallibility." †

Vincentius Ferré says, "The exposition of certain Paris (doctors) is of no avail, who affirm that Christ only promised that the faith should not fail of the Church founded upon Peter; and not that it should not fail in the successors of Peter taken apart from (seorsum) the Church." He adds that our Lord said, "I have prayed for thee, Peter; sufficiently showing that the infallibility was not promised to the Church as apart from (seorsum) the head, but promised to the head, that from him it should be derived to the Church." ‡

---

* "Soli Petro secluso ab Apostolis ac proinde soli ejus successori Summo Pontifici secluso Cardinalium Collegio hoc privilegium concessit."—Marchese, *de Capite visibili Ecclesiæ*, disput. iii. dub. 2, p. 719 ; apud Rocaberti, tom. ix.

"Soli Romano Pontifici in persona Petri commissa est cura totius Ecclesiæ et firmitas et certitudo in definiendo res fidei."—Marchese, disput. v. dub. 1, sect. 2, p. 785 ; apud Rocaberti, tom. ix.

† "Uni et soli Pontifici datum est esse caput."—Gravina, *de supremo Judice controv. Fidei*, quæst. i. apud Rocaberti, tom. viii. p. 892.

"Nullus in terra reperitur alter, qui cæteris sit in fide firmior et constantior sciatur esse quam unus Pontifex Romanus pro tempore ; ergo et ipse *solus* habet infallibilitatem."—Gravina, quæst. ii. apud Rocaberti, tom. viii. p. 422.

‡ "Nec valet expositio aliquorum Parisiensium affirmantium hic Christum tantum promisisse fidem non defecturam Ecclesiæ fundatæ super Petrum, non vero promisisse non defecturam in successoribus

Marchese, before quoted, repeats the same words, "The infallibility in faith which (our Lord) promised, not to the Church apart from (seorsum) the head, but to the head, that from him it should be derived to the Church."[*]   Billuart also says, "(Christ) makes a clear distinction of Peter from the rest of the Apostles, and from the whole Church, when He says, And thou, &c."[†]

Peter Soto writes: "When this (Pasce oves meas, &c.) was said to Peter in the presence of the rest of the Apostles, it was said to Peter as one, and as apart from (seorsum) the rest."[‡]

And Marchese again, "Therefore to Peter alone set apart from the Apostles (secluso ab Apostolis), and therefore to his successor alone, the Supreme Pontiff, set apart from the College of Cardinals, He (our Lord) conceded this privilege."[§]

Petri seorsum ab Ecclesia sumptis. Christus dicens, ego autem rogavi pro te Petre, satis designat hanc infallibilitatem non promissam Ecclesiæ ut seorsum a capite, sed promissam capiti, ut ex illo derivetur ad Ecclesiam."—Ferre, *De Fide*, quæst. xii. apud Rocaberti, tom. xx. p. 388.

[*] "Satis designat infallibilitatem in fide quam promisit, non Ecclesiæ seorsum a Capite sed Capiti ut ex illo derivetur ad Ecclesiam."—Marchese, *de capite Visib. Eccles.* disput. iii. dub. 2 ; apud Rocaberti, tom. ix. p. 719.

[†] "Facit enim apertam distinctionem Petri ab aliis apostolis et a tota Ecclesia cum dicit, et tu aliquando conversus confirma fratres tuos."—Billuart, *de Regulis Fidei*, dissert. iv. art. 5, sect. 2, tom. iv p. 78.   Venice, 1787.

[‡] "Dum vero hoc Petro coram cæteris apostolis dicitur, uni inquam, Petro et a cæteris seorsum."—Petrus Soto, *Defensio Catholicæ Confessionis*, cap. 82, apud Rocaberti, tom. xviii. p. 73.

[§] "Ergo soli Petro secluso ab Apostolis ac proinde soli ejus successori summo Pontifici, secluso Cardinalium collegio, hoc privilegium concessit."—Marchese, *de Capite visib. Eccles.* disp. iii. dub. 2 ; apud Rocaberti, tom. ix. p. 715.

Lastly, F. Gatti, the learned professor of theology of the Dominican Order at this day, writing of the words, "I have prayed for thee," &c., says, "indefectibility is promised to Peter apart from (seorsum) the Church, or from the Apostles; but it is not promised to the Apostles, or to the Church, apart from (seorsum) the head, or with the head," and afterwards he adds, "Therefore Peter, even apart from (seorsum) the Church, is infallible." *

Muzzarelli, in his treatise on the primacy and infallibility of the Pontiff, uses the same terms again and again; of which the following is an example: Speaking as in the person of the Pontiff, he says, "If I *separately* from a Council propose any truth to be believed by the Universal Church, it is most certain that I cannot err." †

In like manner Mauro Cappellari, afterwards Gregory XVI., affirms that the supreme judge of controversies is the Pontiff, "distinct and *separate* from all other Bishops; and that his decree in things of faith ought by them to be held without doubt." ‡

---

* "Indefectibilitas promittitur Petro seorsum ab Ecclesia seu ab Apostolis; non vero promittitur Apostolis seu Ecclesiæ sive seorsum a capite, sive una cum capite.—Ergo Petrus etiam seorsum ab Ecclesia spectatus est infallibilis."—Gatti, *Institutiones Apologetico-Polemicæ*. apud Bianchi *de Constitutione Monarchica Ecclesiæ*, p. 124. Rome, 1870.

† "Ne viene che se anch' io separatamente dal concilio vorrò proporre alla chiesa universale la verità da credersi su questo articolo, non potrò certamente errare."—Muzzarelli, *Primato ed Infallibilità del Papa*, in *Il Buon Uso della Logica*, tom. i. p. 183. Florence, 1821.

‡ Il Trionfo della Santa Sede, Cap. v. Sect. 10, p. 124. Venezia, 1832.

Lastly, Clement VI., in the fourteenth century, proposed to the Armenians certain interrogations, of which the fourth is as follows :

" Hast thou believed, and dost thou still believe, that the Roman Pontiff *alone* can, by an authentic determination to which we must inviolably adhere, put an end to doubts which arise concerning the Catholic faith ; and that whatsoever he, by the authority of the keys delivered to him by Christ, determines to be true, is true and Catholic ; and what he determines to be false and heretical is to be so esteemed ? " *

In the above passages we have infallibility personal, absolute, independent, without the Apostles, without the college of Cardinals, alone, apart from the Church, separate from Councils and from Bishops.

I am not aware of any modern writer who has used language so explicit and fearless.

We will now ascertain the scholastic meaning of these terms ; and we shall see that they are in precise accordance with the definition of the Council.

You need not be reminded, Reverend and dear Brethren, of the terminology of Canonists in treating the subject of privileges.

A privilege is a right, or faculty, bestowed upon persons, places, or things.

---

* " Si credidisti et adhuc credis solum Romanum Pontificem, dubiis emergentibus circa fidem catholicam posse per determinationem authenticam cui sit inviolabiliter adhærendum, finem imponere et esse verum et Catholicum quidquid ipse auctoritate clavium sibi traditarum a Christo determinat esse verum ; et quod determinat esse falsum et hæreticum sit censendum."—Baronius, tom. xxv. ad ann. 1351, p. 529. Lucca, 1750.

Privileges, therefore, are of three kinds, personal, real, and mixed.*

A personal privilege is that which attaches to the person as such.

A real privilege attaches either to a place, or to a thing, or to an office.

A mixed privilege may be both personal and real; it may also attach to a community or body of persons, as to an University, or a College, or a Chapter.

The primacy, including jurisdiction and infallibility, is a privilege attaching to the person of Peter and of his successors. It is therefore a personal privilege in the Pontiffs.

It is personal, as Toletus says, because it cannot be communicated to others. It is not a real privilege attached to the See, or Cathedra, or Church of Rome, and therefore to the person; but to the person of the Roman Pontiff, and, therefore, to the See.

It is not a mixed privilege, attaching to the Pontiff, only in union with a community or body, such as the Episcopate, congregated or dispersed; but attaching to his person, because inherent in the primacy, which he alone personally bears.

The use of the word *personal* is therefore precise and correct, according to the scholastic terminology; not, indeed, according to the sense of newspaper theologians. Theology, like chancery law, has its technical language; and the common sense of Englishmen would keep them from using it in any other meaning.

---

* Reiffenstuel. Tit. de Privileg. lib. v. 34, 12.

In this sense it is that the Dominican theologian De Fiume says, " There are two things . . . in Peter: one personal, and another public; as Pastor and Head of the Church. Some things, therefore, belong to the person of Peter alone, and do not pass to his successors; as the saying, Get thee behind me, Satan . . . and the like. Some, again, are spoken of him as a *public person*, and by reason of his office as supreme Head and Pastor of the Universal Church, as, Feed My Sheep, &c." *

Therefore, infallibility is the privilege of Peter, not as a private person, but as a public person, holding the primacy over the Universal Church.

In the Pastoral addressed to you so long ago as the year 1867, this was pointed out in the unmistakable words of Cardinal Sfondratus. " The Pontiff," he says, " does some things as a man, some things as a prince, some as doctor, some as Pope, that is, as head and foundation of the Church; and it is only to these (last-named) actions that we attribute the gift of infallibility. The others we leave to his human condition. As then not every action of the pope is papal, so not every action of the Pope enjoys the papal privilege." †

---

* " Duo namque sunt in Petro. Unum personale et aliud publicum, ut Pastor et caput Ecclesiæ. Quædam ergo tantummodo personæ Petri conveniunt, ad successores non transeunt; ut quod dicatur: Vade post me, Satana, et similia. Quædam vero dicuntur de eo quatenus est persona publica, et ratione officii Supremi Capitis et Pastoris Ecclesiæ universalis; ut Pasce oves meas, &c."— Ignatius de Fiume, *Schola veritatis orthodoxæ*, apud Bianchi, *de Constitutione Monarchica Ecclesiæ*, p. 88. Rome, 1870.

† " Pontifex aliqua facit ut homo, aliqua ut Princeps, aliqua ut Doctor, aliqua ut Papa, hoc est ut caput et fundamentum Ecclesiæ; et his solis actionibus privilegium infallibilitatis adscribimus: alias

The value, therefore, of this traditional language of the schools is evident.

When the infallibility of the Pontiff is said to be personal, it is to exclude all doubt as to the source from which infallibility is derived; and to declare that it is not a *privilegium mixtum* inherent in the Episcopate, or communicated by it to the head of the Church; but a special assistance of the Spirit of Truth attaching to the primacy, and therefore to the person who bears the primacy, Peter and his successors; conferred on them by Christ Himself for the confirmation of the Church in faith.

2. Next, as to the term *separate*. The sense in which theologians have used this term is obvious. They universally and precisely apply it to express the same idea as the word *personal*; namely, that in the possession and exercise of this privilege of infallibility the successor of Peter depends on no one but God. The meaning of decapitation, decollation, and cutting off, of a headless body, and a bodiless head, I have hardly been able to persuade myself, has ever, by serious men, at least in serious moods, been imputed to such words as *separatim, seorsum,* or *seclusis Episcopis*.

My reason for this doubt is, that such a monstrous sense includes at least six heresies; and I could hardly think that any Catholic would fail to know this, or, knowing it, would impute it to Catholics, still less to Bishops of the Church.

The words *seorsum*, &c., may have two meanings, one obviously false, the other as obviously true.

---

humanæ conditioni relinquimus: sicut ergo non omnis actio Papæ est papalis, ita non omnis actio Papæ papali privilegio gaudet."— Sfondrati, *Regale Sacerdotium*, lib. iii. sec. 1.

The former sense would be disunion of the head from the body of the episcopate and the faithful, or separation from Catholic communion; the latter, an independent action in the exercise of his supreme office.

And first of the former:

1. It is *de fide*, or matter of faith, that the head of the Church, as such, can never be separated, either from the *Ecclesia docens*, or the *Ecclesia discens;* that is, either from the Episcopate or from the faithful.

To suppose this, would be to deny the perpetual indwelling office of the Holy Ghost in the Church, by which the mystical body is knit together; the head to the Body, the Body to the head, the members to each other; and to "dissolve Jesus," * that is, to destroy the perfect symmetry and organization which the Apostle describes as the body of Christ; and St. Augustine speaks of as "one man, head and body, Christ and the Church a perfect man." † On this unity all the properties and endowments of the Church depend; indefectibility, unity, infallibility. As the Church can never be separated from its invisible Head, so never from its visible head.

2. Secondly, it is matter of faith that the *Ecclesia docens* or the Episcopate, to which, together with Peter, and as it were, in one person with him, the assistance of the Holy Ghost was promised, can never be dissolved; but it would be dissolved if it

---

* St. John iv. 3, "Omnis spiritus qui solvit Jesum," &c.

† "Unus homo caput et corpus, unus homo Christus et Ecclesia vir perfectus."—S. Augustin. *In Psalm xviii.* tom. iv. p. 85, 86, ed. Ben. Paris, 1681.

were separated from its head. Such separation
would destroy the infallibility of the Church itself.
The Ecclesia docens would cease to exist; but this
is impossible, and without heresy cannot be supposed.

3. Thirdly, it is also matter of faith that not only
no separation of communion, but even no disunion
of doctrine and faith between the Head and the
Body, that is, between the *Ecclesia docens* and *discens*, can ever exist. Both are infallible ; the one
actively, in teaching, the other passively, in believing ; and both are therefore inseparably, because
necessarily, united in one faith. Even though a
number of bishops should fall away, as in the Arian
and Nestorian heresies, yet the Episcopate could
never fall away. It would always remain united,
by the indwelling of the Holy Ghost, to its head ;
and the reason of this inseparable union is precisely the infallibility of its head. Because its head
can never err, it, as a body, can never err. How
many soever, as individuals, should err and fall
away from the truth, the Episcopate would remain,
and therefore never be disunited from its head in
teaching or believing. Even a minority of the
Bishops united to the head, would be the Episcopate of the Universal Church. They, therefore,
and they only, teach the possibility of such a separation, who assert that the Pontiff may fall into
error. But they who deny his infallibility do expressly assert the possibility of such a separation.
And yet, it is they who have imputed to the defenders of the Pontifical infallibility, that separation
which on "Ultramontane" principles is impossible ;
but, on the principles of those who lay the charge,

such a separation is not only possible, but even of probable occurrence.

So far, we have spoken of the idea of separation from communion, or disunion in faith and doctrine. But further, the separate or independent exercise of the supreme Pontifical authority in no way imports separation or disunion of any kind.

1. It is *de fide* that the plenitude of jurisdiction was given to Peter and his successors; and that its exercise over the whole body, pastors and people, imports no separation or disunion from the Body. How then should the exercise of infallibility, which is attached to that jurisdiction, import separation?

2. Again, it is *de fide* that this supreme jurisdiction and infallibility was given to maintain and perpetuate the unity of the Church. How then can its exercise produce separation, which it is divinely ordained to prevent?

It is therefore *de fide* that its exercise excludes separation, and binds the whole Church, both Body and Head, in closer bonds of communion, doctrine and faith.

3. Lastly, it is *de fide* that in the assistance promised to Peter and his successors, all the means necessary for its due exercise are contained. An infallible office fallibly exercised is a contradiction in terms. The infallibility of the head consists in this, that he is guided both as to the means and as to the end. It is therefore contrary to faith to say, that the independent exercise of this office, divinely assisted, can import separation or disunion of any kind. It is a part of the promise, that in the selection of the means of its exercise, the successor

of Peter will not err.   If he erred as to the means,
either he would err as to the end, or he would be
preserved only by a series of miracles.   In escap-
ing from the supernatural, the objectors fall into
the miraculous.   The Catholic doctrine of infallibility invokes no such interventions.   It affirms
that a Divine assistance, proportionate to the burden of the primacy, is attached to it as a condition
of its ordinary exercise *in bonum Ecclesiæ*.   The
freedom as well as the prudence of the Pontiffs, in
selecting the means of exercising their office of
universal Doctor, is carefully expressed in the
fourth Chapter of this Constitution.   " The Roman
Pontiffs, as the state of times and events induced
them, sometimes by convoking Œcumenical Councils, or by ascertaining the mind of the Church dispersed throughout the world, sometimes by local
Synods, sometimes by employing other helps
which Divine providence supplied, have defined
as truths to be held, such things as they by God's
assistance knew to be in harmony with the Scriptures and Apostolical traditions."*

It may be well here to add two passages which
complete this subject.

Melchior Canus says: " Inasmuch as God promised firmness of faith to the Church, He cannot
be wanting to it, so as not to bestow upon the
Church prayers and other helps whereby that
firmness is preserved.   Nor can it be doubted that
what happens in natural things, the same occurs
in supernatural; namely, that he who gives the
end gives the means to the end."

---

* Constit. Dogmat. Prima, de Eccl. Christi, cap. iv.

"If God should promise an abundant harvest next year, what could be more foolish than to doubt whether men would sow seeds in the earth? So will I never admit that either Pontiff or Council have omitted any necessary diligence in deciding questions of faith. It might happen to any private man, that he should not use diligent attention in seeking truth, and yet to do so should entirely give himself to the work, and, though his error be inculpable, nevertheless fall into error. But even inculpable error is far from the Church of God, as we have proved in a former book. Which fact is an abundant argument that neither Pontiff nor Council has omitted, in deliberation, any necessary thing." "Let us therefore grant that to the Judges constituted by God in the Church, none of those things can be wanting which are necessary for a right and true judgment."*

---

* "Cum Ecclesiæ fidei firmitatem fuerit pollicitus, deesse non potest quominus tribuat Ecclesiæ preces, cæteraque præsidia, quibus hæc firmitas conservatur. Nec vero dubitari potest, quod in rebus naturalibus contingit, idem in supernaturalibus usu venire ; ut qui dat finem, det consequentia ad finem.—Quod si Deus in sequentem annum frugum abundantiam polliceretur, ecquid stultius esse posset quam dubitare, anne homines semina terræ mandaturi sint ?—Ita nunquam ego admittam aut Pontificem aut concilium diligentiam aliquam necessariam quæstionibus fidei decernendis omisisse. Id quod privato cuicunque alteri homini accidere potest, ut nec diligentem navet operam ad disquirendam veretatem, et ut navaverit integrumque sese in ea re præsterit, errat ad huc tamen, quamvis error sine culpa sit. Error autem vel inculpatus ab Ecclesia Dei longissime abest, quemadmodum libro superiore constituimus. Quæ res abunde magno argumento est ut nec Pontifex nec concilia necessarium quicquam in deliberando prætermiserint.—Concedamus ergo judicibus a Deo in Ecclesia constitutis nihil eorum deesse

Cerboni, a theologian of the Dominican order, says:

"When once anything of faith has been defined by the Supreme Pontiff, it is not permitted to doubt whether he has used all diligence before such definition."

" It absolutely cannot be said, that the means necessary for the Supreme Pontiff in the investigation of truth have been neglected by him, even though he should be supposed to have defined anything *ex cathedra*, without first seeking the judgment of others."

" The privilege of infallibility, when the Supreme Pontiff defines anything *ex cathedra*, is to be ascribed not to those whom he has previously consulted, but to the Roman Pontiff himself.

"Inasmuch as the truth and certainty of those things which are defined ' ex cathedra ' depend on the authority and infallibility of the Supreme Pontiff, it is not necessarily requisite, that he should first consult these (counsellors) rather than others, this rather than that body, concerning the matter which he is about to define ex cathedra."*

---

posse, quæ ad rectum verumque judicium sunt necessaria."—Melchior Canus, *De Locis Theol.*, lib. v. cap. 5, pp. 120, 121, Venice, 1776.

* " Semel ac a Summo Pontifice quidpiam ad fidem spectans definitum habeatur, dubitare non licet, utrum omnem diligentiam anti hujusmodi definitionem ille præmiserit.

Quæ ad investigandam veritatem media in summo Pontifice requiruntur, ab eo neglecta fuisse, absolute dici non potest, etiamsi aliorum non exquisita sententia quidpiam ex cathedra definiisse præsupponatur.

Privilegium infallibilitatis, dum a Summo Pontifice aliquid ex cathedra definitur, non iis qui antea consulti fuerint, sed ipsi Romano Pontifici tribui debet.

Ex eo quod veritas et certitudo eorum quæ ex cathedra definiun-

From all that has been said, three things are beyond question; first, that the privilege of infallibility in the head of the Church, neither by its possession nor by its exercise, can in any way import separation or disunion between the head and the body. Such a supposition involves, as we have seen, heretical notions at every turn. The very reverse is true: that the supreme privilege of infallibility in the head is the divinely ordained means to sustain for ever the unity of the Universal Church in communion, faith, and doctrine.

And further, that the independent exercise of this privilege by the head of the Episcopate, and as distinct from the Bishops, is the divinely ordained means of the perpetual unity of the Episcopate in communion and faith with its head and with its own members.

And lastly, that though the consent of the Episcopate or the Church be not required, as a condition, to the intrinsic value of the infallible definitions of the Roman Pontiff, nevertheless, it cannot without heresy be said or conceived that the consent of the Episcopate and of the Church can ever be absent. For if the Pontiff be divinely assisted, both the active and passive infallibility of the Church exclude such a supposition as heretical. To deny such infallible assistance now after the definition, is heresy. And even before the defin-

---

tur, a Summi Pontificis auctoritate et infallibilitate pendeant non necessario requiritur, ut Summus Pontifex de eo quod est ex cathedra definiturus, hos vel illos potius quam alios hunc vel illum cœtum præ alio antea consulat."—Cerboni, *De Jure et Legum Disciplina*, lib. 23, cap. 6, apud Bianchi de constitutione mon. Eccles. p. 158. Rome, 1870.

ition, to deny it was proximate to heresy, because it was a revealed truth, and a Divine fact, on which the unity of the Church has depended from the beginning.

From what has been said, the precise meaning of the terms before us may be easily fixed.

1. The privilege of infallibility is *personal*, inasmuch as it attaches to the Roman Pontiff, the successor of Peter, as a *public person*, distinct from, but inseparably united to, the Church ; but it is not personal, in that it is attached, not to the private person, but to the primacy, which he alone possesses.

2. It is also *independent*, inasmuch as it does not depend upon either the *Ecclesia docens* or the *Ecclesia discens ;* but it is not independent, in that it depends in all things upon the Divine Head of the Church, upon the institution of the primacy by Him, and upon the assistance of the Holy Ghost.

3. It is *absolute*, inasmuch as it can be circumscribed by no human or ecclesiastical law ; it is not absolute, in that it is circumscribed by the office of guarding, expounding, and defending the deposit of revelation.

4. It is *separate* in no sense, nor can be, nor can so be called, without manifold heresy, unless the word be taken to mean *distinct*. In this sense, the Roman Pontiff is distinct from the Episcopate, and is a distinct subject of infallibility ; and in the exercise of his supreme doctrinal authority, or magisterium, he does not depend for the infallibility of his definitions upon the consent or consultation of the Episcopate, but only on the Divine assistance of the Holy Ghost.

CHAPTER IV.

SCIENTIFIC HISTORY AND THE CATHOLIC RULE OF FAITH.

IT may here be well to answer an objection which is commonly supposed to lie against the doctrine of the Pontifical Infallibility; namely, that the evidence of history is opposed to it.

The answer is twofold.

1. First, that the evidence of history distinctly proves the infallibility of the Roman Pontiff.

I shall be told that this is to beg the question.

To which I answer, they also who affirm the contrary beg the question.

Both sides appeal to history, and with equal confidence; sometimes with equal clamor, and often equally in vain.

By some people " The Pope and the Council," by Janus, is regarded as the most unanswerable work of scientific history hitherto published.

By others it is regarded as the shallowest and most pretentious book of the day.

Between such contradictory judgments who is to decide? Is there any tribunal of appeal in matters of history? or is there no ultimate judge? Is history a road where no one can err; or is it a wilderness in which we must wander without guide or

path ?   Are we all left to private judgment alone?
If any one say, that there is no judge but right
reason or common sense, he is only reproducing in
history what Luther applied to the Bible.

This theory may be intellectually and morally
possible to those who are not Catholics.   In Catholics such a theory is simple heresy.   That there is
an ultimate judge in such matters of history as
affect the truths of revelation, is a dogma of faith.
But into this we will enter hereafter.

For the present, I will make only one other ob-
servation.

Let us suppose that the divinity of our Lord
were in controversy.   Let us suppose that two
hundred and fifty-six passages from the Fathers
were adduced to prove that Jesus Christ is God.
These two hundred and fifty-six passages, we will
say, may be distributed into three classes ; the first
consisting of a great number, in which the divinity
of our Lord is explicitly and unmistakably declared ;
the second, a greater number which so assume or
imply it as to be inexplicable upon any other hypothesis ; the third, also numerous, capable of the
same interpretation, and incapable of the contrary
interpretation, though in themselves inexplicit.

We will suppose, next, one passage to exist in
some one of the Fathers, the aspect of which is adverse.   Its language is apparently contradictory to
the hypothesis that Jesus Christ is God.   Its terms
are explicit; and, if taken at the letter, cannot be
reconciled with the doctrine of His divinity.

I need only remind you of St. Justin Martyr's
argument that the Angel who appeared to Moses
in the bush could not be the Father, but the Son,

because the Father could not be manifested "in a narrow space on earth ;"* or even of the words of our Divine Lord Himself, " The Father is greater than I."†

Now, I would ask, what course would any man of just and considerate intelligence pursue in such a case?

Would he say, one broken link destroys a chain? One such passage adverse to the divinity of Christ outweighs two hundred and fifty-six passages to the contrary?

Would this be scientific history? or would it be scientific to assume that the one passage, however apparently explicit and adverse, can bear only one sense, and cannot in any other way be explained? If so, scientific historians are bound to the literal *prima facie* sense of the words of St. Justin Martyr, and of our Lord above quoted.

Still, supposing the one passage to remain explicit and adverse, and therefore an insoluble difficulty, I would ask whether any but a Socinian, ὑποθέσει δουλεύων, servilely bound, and pledged by the perverseness of controversy, would reject the whole cumulus of explicit and constructive evidence contained in two hundred and fifty-six passages, because of one adverse passage of insoluble difficulty? People must be happily unconscious of the elements which underlie the whole basis of their most confident beliefs if they would so proceed. But into this I will not enter now. Enough to say, that such a procedure would be so far from

---

* Dialog. cum Tryph. sect. 60, p. 157.   Ed. Ben. Paris, 1742.

† St. John xiv. 28.

scientific that it would be superficial, unintellectual, and absurd. I would ask, then, is it science, or is it passion, to reject the cumulus of evidence which surrounds the infallibility of two hundred and fifty-six pontiffs, because of the case of Honorius, even if supposed to be an insoluble difficulty? Real science would teach us that in the most certain systems there are residual phenomena which long remain as insoluble difficulties, without in the least diminishing the certainty of the system itself.

But, further, the case of Honorius is not an insoluble difficulty.

In the judgment of a cloud of the greatest theologians of all countries, schools, and languages, since the controversy was opened two hundred years ago, the case of Honorius has been completely solved. Nay more, it has been used with abundant evidence, drawn from the very same acts and documents, to prove the direct contrary hypothesis, namely, the infallibility of the Roman pontiffs. But into this again I shall not enter. It is enough for my present argument to affirm that inasmuch as the case of Honorius has been for centuries disputed, it is disputable. Again, inasmuch as it has been interpreted with equal confidence for and against the infallibility of the Roman pontiff— and I may add that they who have cleared Honorius of personal heresy, are an overwhelming majority compared with their opponents, and let it be said for argument's sake, and with more than moderation, that the probability of their interpretations at least equals that of the opponents—for all these reasons I may, with safety, affirm that, if the case of Honorius be not solved, it is certainly not insoluble; and that the long, profuse, and confident controversy of men whom I will assume to be sincere, reasonable, and learned on both sides, proves beyond question that the case of Honorius is doubtful.

I would ask, then, is it scientific, or passionate to reject the cumulus of evidence surrounding the line of two hundred and fifty-six pontiffs, because one case may be found which is doubtful? doubtful, too, be it remembered, only on the theory that history is a wilderness without guide or path; in no way doubtful to those who, as a dogma of faith, believe that the revelation of faith was anterior to its history and is independent of it, being divinely secured by the presence and assistance of Him who gave it.

And this is a sufficient answer to the case of Honorius, which of all controversies is the most useless, barren, and irrelevant.

I should hardly have thought, at this time of day, that any theologian or scholar would have brought up again the cases of Vigilius, Liberius, John XXII., etc. But as these often-refuted and senseless contentions have been renewed, I give in the note references to the works and places in which they are abundantly answered.*

Such is the first part of the answer to the alleged opposition of history.

2. We will now proceed to the second and more complete reply.

The true and conclusive answer to this objection consists, not in detailed refutation of alleged diffi-

---

* Appendix, p. 244.

culties, but in a principle of faith; namely, that whensoever any doctrine is contained in the Divine tradition of the Church, all difficulties from human history are excluded, as Tertullian lays down, by prescription. The only source of revealed truth is God, the only channel of His revelation is the Church. No human history can declare what is contained in that revelation. The Church alone can determine its limits, and therefore its contents.

When then the Church, out of the proper fountains of truth, the Word of God, written and unwritten, declares any doctrine to be revealed, no difficulties of human history can prevail against it. I have before said: "The pretentious historical criticism of these days has prevailed, and will prevail, to undermine the peace and the confidence, and even the faith of some. But the city seated on a hill is still there, high and out of reach, It cannot be hid, and *is its own evidence, anterior* to its *history*, and *independent* of it. Its history is to be learned of itself." "It is not therefore by criticism on past history, but by acts of faith in the living voice of the Church at this hour, that we can know the faith."*

On these words of mine, Quirinus makes the following not very profound remark: "The faith which removes mountains will be equally ready— such is clearly his meaning—to make away with the facts of history. Whether any German Bishop will be found to offer his countrymen these stones to digest, time will show." † Time has shown, faster than Quirinus looked for. The German Bishops at Fulda, in their pastoral letter on the Council,

---

* Pastoral, etc., 1869, p. 125.

† Letters from Rome, etc., by Quirinus, second series, p. 848-9.

speak as follows: "To maintain that either the one or the other of the doctrines decided by the General Council is not contained in the Holy Scripture, and in the tradition of the Church—those two sources of the Catholic faith—or that they are even in opposition to the same, is a first step, irreconcilable with the very first principles of the Catholic Church, which leads to separation from her communion. Wherefore, we hereby declare that the present Vatican Council is a legitimate General Council; and, moreover, that this Council, as little as any other General Council, has propounded or formed a new doctrine at variance with the ancient teaching, but has simply developed and thrown light upon the old and faithfully-preserved truth contained in the deposit of faith, and in opposition to the errors of the day has proposed it expressly to the belief of all faithful people; and, lastly, that these decrees have received a binding power on all the faithful by the fact of their final publication by the Supreme Head of the Church in solemn form at the Public Session." *

Let us, then, go on to examine the relation of history to faith.

The objection from history has been stated in these words: "There are grave difficulties, from the words and acts of the Fathers of the Church, from the genuine documents of history, and from the doctrine of the Church itself, which must be altogether solved, before the doctrine of the infallibility of the Roman Pontiff can be proposed to the faithful as a doctrine revealed by God."

---

* "Times," Sept. 22, 1870

Are we to understand from this that the words
and acts of the Fathers, and the documents of human history, constitute the Rule of Faith, or that
the Rule of Faith depends upon them, and is either
more or less certain as it agrees or disagrees with
them? or, in other words, that the rule of faith is
to be tested by history, not history by the rule of
faith? If this be so, then they who so argue lay
down as a theological principle that the doctrinal
authority of the Church, and therefore the certainty
of dogma, depends, if not altogether, at least in
part, on human history. From this it would follow
that when critical or scientific historians find, or
suppose themselves to find, a difficulty in the writings of the Father or other human histories, the
doctrines proposed by the Church as of Divine
revelation are to be called into doubt, unless such
difficulties can be solved. The gravity of this objection is such, that the principle on which it rests
is undoubtedly either a doctrine of faith or a heresy.

In order to determine whether it be the one or
the other, let us examine first what is the authority
and place of human history.

To do so surely and shortly, I will transcribe the
rules of Melchior Canus, which may be taken as
the doctrine of all theological Schools.

The eleventh chapter of his work "De Locis
Theologicis," is entitled "de Humanæ Historiæ
Auctoritate." In it he lays down the following
principles:

1. "Excepting the sacred authors, no historian
can be *certain*, that is, sufficient to constitute a certain faith in theological matter. As this is obvious

and manifest to every one, it has no need to be proved by our arguments.

2. "Historians of weight, and worthy of confidence, as some without doubt have been, both in Ecclesiastical and in secular matters, furnish to a theologian, *a probable argument.*

3. "If all approved historians of weight concur in the same narrative of an event, then from their authority a *certain* argument can be educed, so that the dogmas of theology may be confirmed also by reason."

Let us apply these rules to the case of Honorius, and to the alleged historical difficulties. Is this one in which "all approved historians of weight concur in the same narration of events?" In the case of Honorius, it is well known that great discrepancy prevails among historical critics. The histories themselves are of doubtful interpretation. But the Rule of Faith is the Divine tradition of revelation proposed to us by the *magisterium*, or doctrinal authority, of the Church. Against this, no such historical difficulties can prevail. Into this they cannot enter. They are excluded, as I have said, by a prescription which has its origin in the Divine institution of the Church. The revelation of the faith, and the institution of the Church, were both perfect and complete, not only before human histories existed, but even before the inspired Scriptures were written. The Church itself is the Divine witness, teacher, and judge, of the revelation entrusted to it. There exists no other. There is no tribunal to which appeal from the Church can

---

* Melchior Canus, *Loci theol.* lib. xi. c. 4.

lie. There is no co-ordinate witness, teacher, or judge, who can revise, or criticise, or test, the teaching of the Church. It is sole and alone in the world. And to it may be applied the words of St. Paul, as St. John Chrysostom has applied them: " The spiritual man judgeth all things and he himself is judged by no one." The *Ecclesia docens*, or the pastors of the Church, with their head, are a witness divinely sustained and guided to guard and to declare the faith. They were antecedent to history, and are independent of it. The sources from which they draw their testimony of the faith are not in human histories, but in Apostolical tradition, in Scripture, in Creeds, in the Liturgy, in the public worship and law of the Church, in Councils; and in the interpretation of all these things by the supreme authority of the Church itself.

The Church has indeed a history. Its course and its acts have been recorded by human hands. It has its annals, like the empire of Rome or of Britain. But its history is no more than its footprints in time, which record indeed, but cause nothing and create nothing.

The tradition of the Church may be historically treated; but between history and the tradition of the Church there is a clear distinction. The school of scientific historians, if I understand it, lays down as a principle that history is tradition, and tradition history: that they are one and the same thing under two names. This seems so be the πρῶτον ψεῦδος of their system; it is a tacit elimination of the supernatural, and of the Divine authority of the Church.

The tradition of the Church is not human in its origin, in its perpetuity, in its immutability. The matter of that tradition is Divine. But history, excepting so far as it is contained in the tradition of the Church, is not Divine but human, and human in its mutability, uncertainty, and corruption. The matter of it is human. Under the name "tradition" come two elements altogether Divine; namely, that which is handed down as the Word of God written and unwritten, and the mode of handing it down, which is the "magisterium" or teaching authority of the Church. But against neither the one nor the other of these things can human histories, written by men not inspired by the Spirit of God, not seldom inspired by any other than the Spirit of God, prevail; because against the Church the gates of hell cannot prevail. The visible Church itself is Divine tradition. It is also the Divine depository, and the Divine guardian of Faith. But this Divine tradition contains both the "Ecclesia docens" and the "Ecclesia discens;" both infallible, the latter passively, the former passively and actively, by the perpetual assistance of the Spirit of Truth. It contains also the Creed of the Universal Church, the decrees of Pontiffs, the definitions of Councils, the common and constant doctrine of the Church delivered by its living voice in all the world, of which our Divine Lord said, "He that heareth you, heareth Me."*

Now if this be so, of what weight or authority is human history in matters of faith?

For instance, the Vatican Council affirms that the

* See Appendix, p. 199.

doctrine of the immutable stability of Peter and of his successors in the faith, and therefore the infallibility of the Roman Pontiff in matters of faith and morals, in virtue of a Divine assistance promised to St. Peter, and in Peter to his successors, is a revealed truth.

What has human history to say to this declaration? Human history is neither the source nor the channel of revelation.

Scientific history may, however, mean a scientific handling of the Divine tradition and the authoritative documents of the Church. But before these things can be thus scientifically handled, they must be first taken out of the hands of the Church by the hands of the scientific critics. And this simply amounts to saying: "You are the Catholic Church indeed, and possess these documents and histories of your own past. But either you do not know the meaning of them, because you are not scientific, or you will not declare the real meaning of them, because you are not honest. We are the men; honesty and science is with us, if it will not die with us. Hand over your documents, the forged and the true; the forgeries we will find out; the true we will interpret; and by science we will prove that you have erred and led the world into error; and therefore that your claim to be a Divine tradition, and to have a Divine authority, is an imposture. The case of Honorius alone is enough. You say that Pope Leo and Pope Agatho interpreted the Councils of Constantinople so as to show, that whatever faults of infirmity were in Honorius, a doctrinal heretic he was not. We, by scientific treatment of history, have proved that your contemporaneous

Popes were wrong; and we are scientifically right in declaring that Honorius was a heretic, not in a large, but in a strict sense, not only as a private person, but as a pope, 'ex cathedra:' and therefore that the infallibility of the Pope is a fable."

But why should the school of scientific history prevail over the immemorial tradition of the Church, even in a matter of fact?

And how can it prevail over the definition of the Vatican Council, except by claiming to be infallible, or denying the infallibility of the Catholic Church?

And here lies the true issue. My purpose has been to bring out this one point, namely, that under this pretext of scientific history lurks an assumption which is purely heretical. It has already destroyed the faith of some; and will that of more. Our duty is to expose it, and to put the faithful on their guard against what I believe to be the last and most subtle form of Protestantism. This school of error has partly sprung up in Germany by contact with Protestantism, and partly in England by the agency of those who, being born in Protestantism, have entered the Catholic Church, but have never been liberated from certain erroneous habits of thought.

The first form of Protestantism was to appeal from the Divine authority of the Church to the text of Scripture: that is, from the interpretation of the Holy Scriptures traditionally declared by the Church, to the interpretation of private judgment. This is the pure Lutheran or Calvinistic Protestantism.

. The next was, to appeal from the Divine authority of the Church to the faith of the undivided

Church before the separation of the East and West. Such was the Anglican Protestantism of Jewell and others.

The third was, to appeal from the Divine authority of the Church to the consent of the Fathers, to the canons of Councils, and the like. Such is the more modern form of Anglicanism; of which I wish to speak with all charity, for the sake of so many whom I respect and love.

Thus far, we have to deal with those who are not in communion with the Holy See.

But there has been growing up, both in Germany and in England, a school, if I may so call it, not numerous nor likely to have succession, which places itself in constant antagonism to the authority of the Church, and, to justify its attitude of antagonism, appeals to "scientific history." "The Pope and the Council," by Janus, and the attacks on Honorius are its fruits. These were all avowedly written to prevent the definition of the infallibility of the Roman Pontiff. It was an attempt to bar the advance of the "magisterium Ecclesiæ" by scientific history.

Now, before the definition of the Vatican Council, the infallibility of the Roman Pontiff was a doctrine revealed by God, delivered by the universal and constant tradition of the Church, recognized in Œcumenical Councils, pre-supposed in the acts of the Pontiffs in all ages, taught by all the Saints, defended by every religious Order, and by every theological school except one, and in that one disputed only by a minority in number, and during one period of its history; believed, at least implicitly, by all the faithful, and therefore attested by the passive infallibility of the Church in all ages and lands, with the partial and transient limitations already expressed.

The doctrine was therefore already *objectively* de fide, and also *subjectively* binding in conscience upon all who knew it to be revealed.

The definition has added nothing to its intrinsic certainty, for this is derived from Divine revelation.

It has added only the extrinsic certainty of universal promulgation by the Ecclesia docens, imposing obligation upon all the faithful.

Hitherto, therefore, the authors of Janus, and the like, who appealed to scientific history, appealed indeed from the doctrinal authority of the Church in a matter of revelation; but they may be, so far as God knows their good faith, protected by the plea that the doctrine had not yet been promulgated by a definition.

Nevertheless, the process of their opposition was essentially heretical. It was an appeal from the traditional doctrine of the Catholic Church, delivered by its common and constant teaching, to history interpreted by themselves.

It does not at all diminish the gravity of this act to say that the appeal was not to mere human history, nor to history written by enemies, but to the acts of Councils, and to the documents of Ecclesiastical tradition.

This makes the opposition more formal; for it amounts to an assumption that scientific history knows the mind of the Church, and is better able to interpret its acts, decrees, condemnations, and documents, either by superiority of scientific criticism, or by superiority of moral honesty, than the Church itself.

But surely the Church best knows its own history, and the true sense of its own acts and documents.

The Crown of England would make short work of those who should scientifically interpret the unwritten law, or the acts of Parliament, contrary to judgment.

Do modern critics suppose that the case of Honorious is as new to the Church as it is to them, or that the Church has not a traditional knowledge of the value and bearing of the case upon the doctrines of faith?

This, again, in non-Catholics, would imply no more than the ordinary want of knowledge as to the Divine nature and office of the Church. In Catholics it would imply, if not heresy, at least a heretical animus.

If the Church has prohibited, under pain of excommunication, any appeal from the Holy See to a future General Council, certainly under the same censure it would condemn an appeal from the Council of the Vatican to the Councils of Constantinople interpreted by scientific history.

It is of faith that the Church alone can declare the contents and the limits of revelation, and can alone determine the extent of its own infallibility. And as it alone can judge of the true sense and interpretation of Holy Scripture, it alone can judge of the true sense and interpretation of the acts of its own Pontiffs and Councils.

Under the same head, therefore, and under the same censure, come all appeals from the Divine au-

thority of the Church at this hour, under whatsoever pretext or to whatsoever tribunal; whether to
Councils in the future or the past, or to Scripture
or the Fathers, or to unauthentic interpretations of
the acts of Councils, or to documents of human
history.

This being so, it cannot be said that there exist
grave difficulties from the words and acts of the
Fathers, from the genuine documents of history,
and from the Catholic doctrine itself, which if not
solved, would render it impossible to propose to the
faithful as a doctrine, the infallibility of the Roman
Pontiff; because it was contained before definition,
in the universal and constant teaching of the Church
as a truth of revelation. Who is the competent
judge to declare whether such difficulties really
exist? or, if they exist, what is the value of them;
whether they be grave or light, relevant or irrelevant? Surely it belongs to the Church to judge of
these things. They are so inseparably in contact
with dogma, that the deposit of faith cannot be
guarded or expounded without judging of them
and pronouncing on them. And it is passing
strange if the Church should be incompetent to
judge of these things, and the scientific historians
alone competent; that is, if the Church should be
fallible in dogmatic facts, and the scientific historians infallible. What is this but Lutheranism in history? In those that are without, this is consistent:
in Catholics, it would not only be inconsistent but a
heresy.

The Council of the Vatican has with great precision condemned this error in these words:
" Catholics can have no just cause of calling into

doubt the faith they have received from the teaching authority (magisterium) of the Church, and of suspending their assent, until they shall have completed a scientific demonstration of the truth of their faith.*

Again, the Council lays down, in respect to sciences properly so called, a principle which *a fortiori* applies to "historical science," with signal impropriety so called, by declaring "that every assertion contrary to the truth of enlightened faith is false . . . Wherefore all faithful Christians are not only forbidden to defend as legitimate conclusions of science all such opinions as are known to be contrary to the doctrine of faith, especially if they have been condemned by the Church, but are altogether bound to hold them to be errors, which put on the fallacious appearance of truth."*

I have said that the treatment of history can only be called science with signal impropriety; and for the following reasons:

According to both philosophers and theologians, science is the habit of the mind conversant with necessary truth; that is, truth which admits of demonstration, and of the certainty which excludes the possibility of its contradictory being true.

According to the scholastic philosophy, science is defined as follows:

Viewed *subjectively*, it is "the certain and evident knowledge of the ultimate reasons or principles of truth attained by reasoning."

Viewed *objectively*, it is "the system of known

---

* Constitutio De Fide Catholica. Appendix, p. 206.

truths belonging to the same order as a whole, and depending only upon one principle."

This is founded on the definitions of Aristotle. In the sixth book of the Ethics, chapter iii. he says: "From this it is evident what science is: to speak accurately, and not to follow mere similitudes; for we all understand that what we know cannot be otherwise than we know it. For whatsoever may or may not be, as a practical question, is not known to be, or not to be."

Such also is the definition of St. Thomas. He says: "Whatsoever truths are truly known as by certain knowledge (ut certa scientia) are known by resolution into their first principles, which of themselves are immediately present to the intellect . . . So that it is impossible that the same thing should be the object both of faith and of science, that is, because of the obscurity of the principles of faith." He nevertheless calls theology a science. But Vasquez shows from Cajetan that this is to be understood not simply but relatively, *non simpliciter, sed secundum quid.* The Thomists generally hold theology to be a science; but *imperfect in its kind.*

Gregory of Valentia sums up the opinions of the Schools, and concludes as follows: "That theology is not science is taught by Durandus, Ocham, Gabriel, and others, whose opinions I hold to be the truest." He adds: "Though it be not a proper science, it is a habit absolutely more perfect than any science;" and again: "Yet, nevertheless, by the best of rights, it may be called a science because absolutely it is a habit more perfect than any science described by philosophers."*

---

* Temporal Mission of the Holy Ghost, p. 107–112.

Theology then may be called, though *improprie*, a science. First, because it is a science, if not as to its principles, at least as to its form, method, process, development, and transmission. And secondly, because though its *principles are not evident*, they are, in all the higher regions of it, infallibly certain; and because many of them are the necessary, eternal, and incorruptible truths, which according to Aristotle, generate science.

If then theology, which in certainty is next to science, properly so called, is to be called science only *improprie*, notwithstanding the infallible certainty and immutable nature of its ultimate principles, how can human history, written by uninspired human authors, transmitted by documents open to corruption, change, and mutilation, without custody or security, except the casual tradition of human testimony and human criticism, open to perversion by infirmity and passion of every kind, —how can such subject-matter yield principles of certainty which excludes contradiction, and ultimate truths immediate to the intellect and evident in themselves?

If by historical science be meant an increased precision in examining evidence and in testing documents, and in comparing narratives together, we will gladly use the word by courtesy; but if more than this be meant, if a claim be set up for history, which is not admitted even for theology, then in the name of truth, both Divine and human, let the pretence be exposed. And yet for many years these pretensions have been steadily advancing. Many people have been partly deceived, and partly intimidated by them. The confident and compassionate tone in which certain writers have treated all who differ from them, has won the reward which often follows upon any signal audacity. But when Catholics once understand that this school among us elevates the certainty of history above the certainty of faith, and appeals from the traditional doctrine of the Church to its own historical science, their instincts will recoil from it as irreconcilable with faith.

There is something happily inimitable in the conceit of the words with which Janus opens his preface :

" The immediate object of this work is to investigate by the *light of history* those questions which we are credibly informed are to be decided at the Œcumenical Council already announced. And as we have endeavored to fulfil this task by *direct reference to original authorities*, it is not, perhaps, too much to hope that our labors will attract attention in *scientific circles ;* and serve as a contribution to ecclesiastical history."

Janus goes on to say, " But this work aims also at something more than the mere *calm* and *aimless* exhibition of historical events : the reader will readily perceive that it has a far wider scope, and deals with ecclesiastical politics ; and in one word, that it is a pleading for very life, an appeal to the *thinkers* among believing Christians," &c.*

We have here an unconscious confession. " Janus" strictly is an appeal from the light of faith to the light of history, that is, from the supernatural

---

* The Pope and the Council, by Janus. Preface, p. xiii. London, 1869.

to the natural order; a process, as I have said again and again, consistent in Protestants and Rationalists: in Catholics, simply heretical.

The direct reference to original authorities is, of course, a prerogative of Janus. Who else but he ever could, or would, or did, refer to the original authorities?

Again, it is a work addressed to *scientific circles.* Lord Bacon describes a school of philosophers who, when they come abroad, lift their hand in the attitude of benediction, " with the look of those who pity men." Is science in the Catholic Church confined to " circles?" Is it an esoteric perfection which belongs to the favored and to the few who assemble in chambers and secret places? Our Lord has warned us that the science of God has a wider expanse of light. In truth, this science is a modern Gnosticism, superior to the Church, contemptuous of faith, and profoundly egotistical. It appeals to *thinkers* among believing Christians: that is, to the intellectual few among the herd of mere believers.

But finally the truth escapes: the aim of the book is not merely *calm* and *aimless.* It deals with *ecclesiastical politics* ; that is, it was an organized, combined, and deliberate attempt to hinder the Vatican Council in its liberty of action, and in the same breath, before the Council had assembled, to deny its Œcumenicity on the ground that it would not be free.

The book concludes as follows:

" That is quite enough—it means this, that whatsoever course the Synod may take, one quality can never be predicated of it, namely, that it has been a really free Council. Theologians and canonists declare that without complete freedom, the decisions of the Council are not binding, and the assembly is only a pseudo-synod."*

This was written in Germany during the summer of last year. The English translation was published by a Protestant bookseller in London in the month of November. I bought the Italian translation in the same month in Florence, on my way to the opening of the Council. French and Spanish bishops told me, on arriving, that they had translations in their own language. And in Spain and Italy copies were sent to the bishops through the channels of those Governments.

We have here the latest example of passionless science.

Of the literary merits of the book, I will only say first, that for its accuracy a fair account has been taken in a pamphlet entitled " A few Specimens of Scientific History from Janus;" and for profoundness that it is simply shallow, compared with Jewell's " Defence of the Apology," Barrow " On the Pope's Supremacy," Crackenthorp's " Vigilius Dormitans," Bramhall's " Schism Guarded," Thorndike's " Epilogue," Brown's " Fasciculus Rerum," &c., to say nothing of the Magdeburg Centuriators, or even Mosheim's or Gieseler's Histories.

The old Protestant and especially the Anglican anticatholic writers are solid, learned, and ponderous, compared with Janus. They have also the force of visible sincerity. Used against the Church from without, their arguments are consistent and

---

* Ibid. p. 425.

weighty; used by professing Catholics within the
unity of the Church, they are powerless in controversy, and heretical in their effects and consequences.

I speak thus plainly, Reverend and dear Brethren, because you are charged with the cure of
souls; and in this country, where reading, speaking, writing has no rule or limit, those committed
to your charge will be in daily temptation. They
cannot close their eyes; and if they could, they
cannot close their ears. What they refuse to read
they cannot fail to hear. It is the trial permitted
for the purity and confirmation of their faith. By
your vigilant care they will be what the Catholics
of England, in the judgment often expressed to me
in other countries, already are—and I would we
were so in the degree in which others believe—
that is, firm, fearless, intelligent in faith, and not
ashamed to confess it before men. Nevertheless
the trial is severe for many. And, as I have said
before, the Council will be "in ruinam et in resurrectionem multorem." Some who think themselves to stand will fall; and some, of whom we
perhaps have no hope, will rise to fill their place.
Therefore we must be faithful and fearless for the
truth.

The book "Janus" warns us of two duties. The
one, to watch against this Gnostic inflation of
scientific conceit which is the animus of heresy;
the other, to warn all Catholics that to deny the
Œcumenicity or the freedom of the Council which
the Vicar of Christ has already confirmed in all its
acts hitherto complete, or the obligation imposed
upon the faithful by those acts, is implicitly to

deny the Infallibility of the Church: and that to doubt, or to propagate doubts, of its Œcumenicity and freedom, or of the obligàtions of its acts, is at least the first step to that denial.

CHAPTER V.

CONCLUSION.—TRADITION OF ENGLAND.—GREATER
UNITY OF FAITH RESULTING FROM THE DEFINI-
TION.

IN an Œcumenical Council, Bishops are witnesses
of the Faith of their respective Churches. Not indeed as if they were representatives or delegates of
their flocks ; a theory strangely advanced by some
writers who counted up the population of what
they were pleased to call the greater cities, in order to give weight to the testimony of their Bishops as against that of others. In this they simply
betrayed the fact that they were resting upon the
natural order, and arguing, not on principles of
faith, but of the political world.

Bishops are witnesses, primarily and chiefly, not
of the subjective faith of their flocks, which may
vary or be obscured, but of the objective faith of
the Church committed to their trust, when by
consecration they became witnesses, doctors, and
judges. They were by consecration admitted to
the *Ecclesia docens*, and the Divine Tradition of
the Faith was entrusted to their custody. But
this is one and the same in the humblest Vicar
Apostolic, and in the Bishop of the most populous
and imperial city in Christendom.

In the course of the discussions, testimony was given to the unbroken tradition of the doctrine of Papal Infallibility in Italy, Spain, Ireland, and many other countries. It will not therefore be without its use and interest, if I add briefly a few evidences of the unbroken tradition of England as to the infallibility of the Roman Pontiff. It would be out of place in this Pastoral to do more than offer to you a few passages; but I would wish to stir up some one who has time for such research, to collect and publish a complete *catena* of evidence from the writers before and since the Reformation; which will show that the Gallicanism, or worse than Gallicanism, of Cisalpine Clubs and Political Emancipationists was no more than the momentary aberration of a few minds under the stress of penal laws. They are abnormal instances in the noble fidelity of the Catholics of England.

As to the Bishops and Doctors of the English Church before the Reformation, I may first remind you of the words of St. Anselm, St. Thomas of Canterbury, and Bradwardine, three primates of England, given in the Pastoral of last year. To these may be added St. Ælred of Rivaulx,* John of Salisbury,† Robert Pullen,‡ Thomas of Evesham,§ Robert Grostete,‖ Roger Bacon,¶ Scotus,**

---

* Bibl. Max. Patrum, tom. xxiii. pp. 57, 58. Ed. Lugd. 1677.

† Polycrates, lib. vi. c. 24, p. 61. Ed. Giles.

‡ In Sentent. b. viii. c. iii.

§ In Vita Sti. Egwini, sect. vi.

‖ Epp. 72 and 127.

¶ Opus. c. xiv.

** In Sent. iv. dist. vi. 9, 8

Bachon,* Holcot,† Richard Ralph,‡ and Walden-
sis.§ In these writers the Primacy of the Pontiff, and the obligation, under pain of sin, to obey
his judgments and doctrines, is laid down with a
perfect unconsciousness that any Catholic could
dispute the Divine certainty of his guidance. The
Vatican definition has defined the reason of this
implicit faith, by declaring that in the primacy
there is a *charisma* which preserves the supreme
doctrinal authority of the Pontiff from error in faith
or morals.

But I leave to others to complete this part of the
subject. I will go on to the period of the Reformation.

The controversy against the authority of Rome
drew out more explicit statements from Sir Thomas More and Cardinal Fisher.

More, writing against Luther, says, "Judge, I
pray thee, reader, with what sincerity Father Tippler treats this place of Jerome, when he (Jerome)
says it is enough for him if the Pope of Rome approve his faith; that is, openly declaring that it
cannot be doubted that he is sound in faith who
agrees with that See; than which what could he
more splendidly say? Yet Father Tippler, Luther
and others so dissemble about this as to try to
cloud the reader also with darkness, and to lead
away the minds of men elsewhere, that they may
not remember anything." ‖

---

* Proleg. in Lib. iv. Sentent.
† In Lib. iv. Sentent.
‡ Summa in quæstionibus Armenorum, lib. vii. c. 5.
§ Doctrina Fidei, lib. ii. capp. 47, 48.
‖ "Quæso lector judica quam sincere pater Potator hunc locum

Cardinal Fisher also, writing against Luther, says: "One thing I know, that Augustine everywhere makes Peter first and Prince of the Apostles, and Teacher and Head of the rest, in whom also he says the rest are contained, as in the head of any family the multitude (of the family) are all contained." * And further he adds, "Where else dost thou believe the faith to abide, save in the Church of Christ? 'I,' said Christ to Peter, 'have prayed for thee that thy faith fail not.' The faith of Peter, do not doubt it, will always abide in the succession of Peter, which is the Church." † This is precisely the Vatican definition, "Romanum Pontificem ea infallibilitate pollere, qua divinus Redemptor Ecclesiam suam instructam esse voluit."

Cardinal Pole, after describing the conduct of Peter in the Council at Jerusalem, goes on to say, "The same also the successors of Peter, following his faith, have done in all other Councils; in which

---

Hieronymi tractet: cum ille dicat, satis esse sibi si suam fidem comprobaret papa Romanus: nimirum aperte significans, non dubitandum esse illum recte sentire de fide, qui, cum illa sede consentiat: quo quid potuisset dicere magnificentius? istud adeo dissimulat pater Potator Lutherus ut etiam tenebras lectori conetur offundere et animos hominum verbis alio, ne quid recordentur, abducere."—Morus, *In Lutherum*, lib. ii. cap. iv. p. 87. Louvain, 1566.

* "Unum scio, quod Augustinus ubique Petrum facit Primum et Principem Apostolorum ac Magistrum et Caput cæterorum, in quo et cæteros contineri dicit, sicut in capite cujusvis familiæ reliqua comprehenditur multitudo."—Joannis Roffensis *Confutatio Errorum Lutheri*, art. xxv. ad finem, in Rocaberti *Biblioth. Pontif.* tom. xiv. p. 582.

† "Ubi credis alibi manere fidem quam in Ecclesia Christi? Ego, inquit Christus ad Petrum, rogavi pro te ut non deficiat fides tua. Petri fides ne dubita semper in successione Petri manebit, quæ est Ecclesia."—Id. art. xxvii. ad fin. in Rocaberto, tom. xiv. p. 587.

is found much more signally than in Peter's life-
time, of what kind are the efforts of Satan, who desires to shift the Church of God, and how great is
the efficacy of this special remedy in repressing
them; namely, that which Christ declared when
he turned to Peter, in these words, 'And thou,
being once converted, strengthen thy brethren.'
For let all remedies be found which at any time
the Church has tried against the malice of Satan,
who at all times assails it with all kinds of tempta-
tions; none certainly will be ever found to be compared with this, which is wont to be used in General Councils; namely, that all the Bishops of all
the Churches, as the brethren of Peter, be confirmed by his successors, professors of the same
faith." *

In like manner, Harding, Jewel's antagonist,
writes: " The Pope succeedeth Peter in authority
and power. For whereas the sheep of Christ continue to the world's end, he is not wise that think-
eth Christ to have made a shepherd temporary or
for a time over His perpetual flock. To Peter He

---

* "Idem etiam Petri successores, fidem ejus secuti, fecere in reli-
quis omnibus conciliis, in quibus multo illustrius quam vivo Petro
compertum est, et cujusmodi esset Satanæ conatus Ecclesiam Dei
cribrare expetentis, et quanta ad eos reprimendos extiterit vis hujus
singularis remedii, quod Christus ad Petrum sermonem convertens
verbis illis indicavit: Et tu aliquando conversus confirma fratres
tuos. Ut enim omnia remedia quærantur quæ ullo tempore Ecclesia
est experta contra Satanæ malitiam nunquam non omni tentationis
genere eam aggredientis: nullum certe reperietur quod cum hac
comparari possit, quod in conciliis generalibus adhiberi est solitum,
ut singuli singularum Ecclesiarum episcopi, tanquam Petri fratres,
confirmarentur per ejus successores eandem fidem profitentes."—
Card. Polus, *De Summo Pontifice*, cap. iv. (Rocaberti, *Biblioth. Pontif.* tom. xviii. p. 146.)

gave that He obtained by His prayer made to the
Father, that his faith should not fail. Again, to
him he gave grace thus to perform, the performance
whereof at him He required, to wit, that he confirmed and strengthened his brethren, wherefore
the grace of steadfastness of faith, and of confirming
the wavering and doubtful in faith, every Pope
obtaineth of the Holy Ghost for the benefit of the
Church. And so the Pope, although he may err
by personal error in his own private judgment as a
man, and as a particular doctor in his own opinion,
yet as he is Pope, the successor of Peter, the Vicar
of Christ in earth, the shepherd of the Universal
Church, in public judgment, in deliberation and
definitive sentence, he never erreth, nor never
erred. For whensoever he ordaineth or determin-
eth anything by his high bishoply authority, in-
tending to bind Christian men to perform or believe the same, he is always governed and holpen
with the grace and favor of the Holy Ghost. This
is to Catholic doctors a very certainty, though to
such doughty clerks as ye are it is but a matter of
nothing and a very trifling tale."*

‛ Campian, answering Whitaker, says, " Nor, as
you slander us, do we depend on the voice of one
man, but rather on the Divine promise of Christ
made to Peter and his successors, for the stability
of whose faith He prayed to the Father. . . .
‛ I have prayed for thee, Peter,' He said, ‛ that thy
faith fail not.' The fruit of which prayer, what follows plainly enough shows, belongs not to Peter

---

* Confutation of a Book entitled " An Apology of the Church of
England," by Thomas Harding, D. D., page 335 a. Dedicated to
the Queen. Antwerp, 1565.

alone, but to his successors also. . . . For since the Church was not to become extinct with Peter, but to endure unto the end of the world, the same stability in faith was even more necessary to Peter's successors, the Roman Pontiffs, in proportion as they were weaker than he, and were to be assailed with mightier engines by tyrants, heretics, and other impious men. As, therefore, Peter when converted, confirmed the Apostles his brethren, the Pontiffs also must confirm their brethren the rest of the Bishops." Afterwards, he says, " Under his guidance they cannot err from the right path of the faith."*

These evidences are more than enough to show what was the faith of the Church in England in the sixteenth century, that is, in the controversies of the Reformation. They show what was the faith, for which the Catholics of England at that day stood, and suffered.

In the seventeenth century, we may take Nicholas Sanders as our first witness. He writes in his work " De Clavi David": "But we freely declare, and what in words we declare we prove by fact, that the successor of Peter, the Bishop of Rome, in expounding to the Bishops the faith of Christ, has never erred, nor has either been the author of any heresy, or has lent his authority to any heretic for the promulgation of heresy."†

---

* Confutatio Responsionis G. Whitakeri, p. 44. Parisiis 1582.

† " At vero nos libere dicimus, et quod verbo dicimus re ipsa comprobamus, Petri successorem Episcopum Romanum in exponenda Episcopis fide Christi nunquam errasse, nunquam aut ullius hæresis auctorem fuisse, aut alii hæretico ad promulgandum hæresim suam præbuisse auctoritatem."—Nicolas Sanderus, de Clavi David, lib. v. cap. iv.

Kellison, President of the College at Douai in 1605, writes as follows: " For in two senses Peter may be sayd to be the rocke of the Church: first, as he is a particular man, and so if the Church had been built upon him, it must have fallen with him; secondly, as upon a publique person and supreme Pastor, who is to have successors, to whom constancie in faith is promised, by which they shal uphold the Church: and so the Church dyeth not with Peter, but keepeth her standing upon successors.   And because Peter and his successors, by their indeficient faith, in which as supreme pastors they shal never erre, do uphold the Church, therefore the Fathers alleaged sometimes say that the Church is builded on Peter, sometimes on his faith, as it is the faith of the supreme head: which in effect is al one.   For if Peter upholde the Church by his indeficient faith which he teacheth, then Peter upholdeth the Church, as he hath assured faith, and his faith upholdeth the Church, not howsoever but as it is the faith of Peter, and the supreme head, whose faith especially which he teacheth out of his chaire (that is, not as a particular man only, proposing his opinion; but as a publique Doctor and chiefe Pastor) defineth and commandeth what al Christians ought to beleeve, shal never faile; and consequently the Church which relyeth on his definition, though she may be shaken, yet shal never be overthrowne."*

In a work published by S. N., Doctor of Divinity, 1634, we read: "The same is proved by all such texts as convince that the head or chief Bishop of

* A Survey of the New Religion, set forth by Matthew Kellison, first book, chap. vi. p. 74. Doway, 1605.

the Church cannot err in defining matters of faith. 'Simon, Simon, Satan hath desired you that he might winnow you as wheat, but I have prayed for thee that thy faith may not fail.' Here Christ prayed not for all the Church, but in particular for Peter, as all the words show: *Simon—for thee—thy faith—thy brethren:* also, whereas our Saviour began to speak in the plural number, 'Satan hath desired to have you,' etc., forthwith He changeth His manner of speaking and saith, 'but I have prayed for thee.' Further, He prayeth for him to whom He saith, 'and thou sometimes converted,' which cannot agree to the whole Church, except we will say the whole Church to have been first perverted, which is many ways untrue. But now that which Christ prayed for is expressly that his faith should not fail, and then seeing this prayer for Peter was for the good of the Church, the Devil still desiring to winnow the faithful, it thereof followeth that she never wanteth one whose faith may not fail, by whom she may be confirmed."*

Southwell, or Bacon, who wrote in 1638, affirms: "That the Roman Pontiff, out of Council, is infallible in his definitions." He adds: "It is clearly proved from what is already said, he who is the foundation-stone of the Church, actually and always infusing into it firmness against the gates of hell and heresies: he who is Pastor not of this or that place, but of the whole fold: and therefore in all things necessary to salvation is bound to feed, govern, and direct, cannot err in judgment of faith. . . But the Supreme Pontiff is such a Rock and

---

* The Triple Cord. p. 72. 1634.

7*

Pastor, as has been manifestly proved; therefore he cannot err in judgment of faith." This he proves, among other evidence, by the promise of our Lord: "I have prayed for thee," etc., and adds, "What was said to Peter as pastor was said also to the Roman Pontiffs, as has been abundantly proved."*

Nor was this tradition broken, though the depression which followed the Revolution of 1688 reduced the Catholics to silence. In the eighteenth century, the following testimonies will suffice. More might, no doubt, with ease be found.; but for our present purpose no more are needed. First, of Alban Butler, who assuredly represents the English Catholics of his times, we read as follows: "It is evident from his *Epitome de sex prioribus conciliis œcumenicis in calce tractatus de Incarnatione*, that he had the highest veneration for the Holy See, and for him who sits in the chair of St. Peter; that he constantly held and maintained the rights and singular prerogatives of St. Peter and his successors in calling, presiding over, and confirming, general or œcumenical councils; the Pope's superiority over the whole church and over the whole college of bishops, and over a general council; *the irreformability of his doctrinal decisions in point of faith and morals;* his supreme power to dispense (when there is cause) in the canons of general councils; in short, the plenitude of his authority over the whole Church without exception or limitation. *Nihil excipitur ubi distinguitur nihil.* S. Bernard, l. ii. de Consid. c. 8."† What gives additional

---

* Regula viva, seu Analysis Fidei, p. 41. Antwerpiæ, 1638.

† An Account of the Life and Writings of the Rev. Alban Butler, p. 16. London, 1799.

force to this is, that Alban Butler not only held but taught these doctrines in his theological treatises : and that we receive this testimony from the pen of Charles Butler, who of all men is least to be suspected of ultramontanism.

In the year 1790, when a certain number of Catholics, weary of penal laws, fascinated by Parliment, and perhaps intimidated by the Protestant ascendancy, began to explain away Catholic doctrines, and to describe themselves by a nomenclature which I will not here repeat, the Rev. Charles Plowden published a work, the very title of which is a witness and an argument. It is called " Considerations on the *Modern Opinion* of the *Fallibility* of the Holy See in the Decision of Dogmatical Questions." He opens his first chapter with these words: " Before the Declaration of the Gallican Clergy in 1682, it was the general persuasion of Roman Catholics that the solemn decisions of the Holy See on matters of dogmatical and moral import are infallible. Since that epoch the contrary opinion is asserted in many schools in France, it has been imported with other French rarities into this kingdom, and it now appears to be the prevailing system, especially among those members of our Catholic clergy and laity who have studied little of either." He then most solidly proves what in these Pastorals has been so often asserted, that, with the exception of the modern opinion of the local and transient Gallican School, the universal and traditionary faith of the Church in the infallibility of the Roman Pontiff has never been obscured. Plowden then proceeds to censure the oath which certain Catholics were at that time proposing to themselves and others. He says:—

"The clause which regards Papal Infallibility is a demonstration that the oath was not calculated to accommodate the bulk of Roman Catholics, since the very respectable number who believe the solemn and canonical decrees of the Pope on matters of faith to be irreformable can never conscientiously pronounce it. If the interpreters of the oath tell us that the framers of it did not intend to exclude the belief of infallibility in dogmatical decisions, we must answer them that the admission of such a tacit distinction would justly lay us open to swearing to what we do not believe. *No infallibility* and *some infallibility* will always be contradictories. The Catholic public may already know that I think the modern opinion of papal fallibility in decisions of faith to be ill grounded and dangerous, and it appears to me that the doctrine of infallibility in these matters, though not decided, might easily be proved to be that of the Catholic Church and therefore true. It must not then be renounced. The addition of *personal* in the address does not remove the difficulty. For if the Supreme Head of the Church be infallible in his solemn dogmatical decisions, this infallibility attaches to his person. It was promised and given to St. Peter, and it subsists in his lawful successors. It does not belong *in solidum* to the particular Church of Rome as an aggregate of many individuals; it does not belong to the *chair* or *see* of Rome as a thing distinct from the Pope. The distinction between the *sedes* and the *sedens* is a modern subterfuge of the Jansenists, unknown to antiquity, which always understood the person of the chief Bishop, whether in words they attribute inerrancy directly to him or metaphorically to his see. If the Pope be then infallible, he is *personally* infallible."*

I will now add only two more witnesses who bore their testimony in the last century, but lived on into the present, Bishop Hay, who died in 1811, and Bishop Milner, who died in 1826.

Bishop Hay, in his "Sincere Christian," writes as follows:—

"*Q.* 27. On what grounds do these divines found their opinion, who believe that the Pope himself, when he speaks to all the faithful as head of the Church, is infallible in what he teaches?

"*A.* On several very strong reasons, both from scripture, tradition and reason."

He then draws out these three fully and abundantly; and this done, he asks:—

"*Q.* 31. But what proofs do the others bring for their opinion that the head of the Church is not infallible?

"*A.* They bring not one text of Scripture to prove it," &c.

Lastly, Bishop Milner in his book called "Ecclesiastical Democracy detected," published in 1793, after saying in the text, "The controversy of the Pope's inerrancy is here entirely out of the question," adds the following note: "It is true I was educated in the belief of this inerrancy; nor have I yet seen sufficient argument to change my opinion. . . . But if the layman, who never fails to ridicule

---

* Observations on the Oath proposed to the English Roman Catholics, by Charles Plowden, p. 43. London, 1790.

the doctrine in question, is willing fairly to contest it, he knows where to meet with an antagonist ready to engage with him. Against one assertion however of this writer, which insinuates the political danger arising from the doctrine of Papal Infallibility, I will hurl defiance at him; nothing being more easy to show, than that no greater danger can result to the State from admitting the inerrancy of the Pope than from admitting that of the Church itself."*

I only hope we shall now hear no more that the Catholics of England have not believed, or have not been taught this doctrine; nor that the " Old Catholics" of England refuse to believe the new opinions, and the like. We have heard too much of this: and the honored name of those who through three hundred years of persecution have kept the faith, has been too much dishonored by imputing to them that they are not faithful to the Martyrs, Confessors and Doctors of England. The faith of St. Anselm and St. Thomas, of Thomas More and Cardinal Fisher, of Hay and Milner, is the faith of the Catholics of England. Whoso departs from it forfeits his share in the inheritance of fidelity they have handed down.

I will now add a few words on the disastrous consequences predicted from the Definition.

We were told that the Definition of the Infallibility would alienate the fairest provinces of the Catholic Church, divide the Church into parties, drive the scientific and independent into separation, and set the reason of mankind against the supersti-

---

* Ecclesiastical Democracy detected, p. 98. London, 1793.

tions of Rome. We were told of learned professors, theological faculties, entire universities, multitudes of laity, hundreds of clergy, the flower of the episcopate, who were prepared to protest as a body, and to secede. There was to be a secession in France, in Germany, in Austria, in Hungary. The "Old Catholics" of England would never hear of this new dogma, and with difficulty could be made to hold their peace. Day by day, these illusions have been sharply dispelled; but not a word of acknowledgment is to be heard. A professor is suspended *a divinis* in Germany; a score or two of lay professors, led by a handful whose names are already notorious, and a hundred or so of laymen who, before the Council met, began to protest against its acts, convoke a Congress, which ends in a gathering of some twenty persons. These, with the alleged opposition of one Bishop, whose name out of respect I do not write, as the allegation has never yet been confirmed by his own word or act, these are hitherto the adverse consequences of the Definition.

On the other hand, the Bishops who, because they opposed the Definition as inopportune, were calumniously paraded as opposed to the doctrine of Infallibility, at once began to publish their submission to the acts of the Council. The greater part of the French Bishops who were once in opposition, have explicitly declared their adhesion. The German Bishops, meeting again at Fulda, issued a Pastoral Letter, so valuable in itself, that I have reprinted it in the Appendix.* It was signed by

* See Appendix, p. 247.

seventeen, including all the Chief Bishops of Germany. The others, if silent, cannot be doubted. The leading Bishops of Austria and Hungary, who may be taken as representing the Episcopates of these countries, have in like manner declared themselves. The Clergy and the faithful of these kingdoms, with the rarest exceptions of an individual here and there, are, as they have always been, of one mind in accepting the definition with joy. Ireland has spoken for itself, not only in many dioceses, and by its Bishops, but by the Triduum, or Thanksgiving of three days, held in Dublin with great solemnity and with a concourse, as I am informed by direct correspondence, such as was never seen before. Of England I need say little. The Clergy of this diocese have twice spoken for themselves; and the Clergy of England and Scotland have given unequivocal witness to their faith. As we hear so much and so often of those among us who are called "the Old Catholics," that is, the sons of our martyrs and confessors; and as their name is so lightly and officiously taken in vain by those who desire to find or to make divisions among us, you will not need, but nevertheless be glad, to know, that both by word and by letter I have received from the chief and foremost among them, express assurance that what the Council has defined they have always believed. It is but their old faith in an explicit formula. Among the disappointments to which our adversaries, I regret so to call them, but truth must be spoken, have doomed themse.ves, none is greater than this. They have labored to believe and to make others believe that the Catholic Church is internally divided; that the Council has revealed this division; and that it is nowhere more patent than in England. It is, I know, useless to contradict this illusion. It is not founded in reason, and cannot by reason be corrected. Prejudice and passion are deaf and blind. Time and facts will dispel illusions, and expose falsehoods. And to this slow but inexorable cure we must leave them. It is no evidence of division among us, if here and there a few individuals should fall away. I said before, the Council will be *in ruinam et in ressurrectionem multorum.* It is a time of spiritual danger to many; especially to those who live perpetually among adversaries, hearing diatribes all day long against the Church, the Council, and the Holy Father, reading anti-Catholic accounts and comments upon Catholic doctrines, and upon the words and acts of Catholic Bishops, and always breathing, till they are unconscious of it, an anti-Catholic atmosphere.

St. Paul has foretold that "In the last days shall come dangerous times," * and "in the last times some shall depart from the faith." † Those days seem now to be upon us; and individuals perhaps may fall. But the fall of leaves and sprays and boughs does not divide the Tree. You will know how to deal with them in charity, patience, and firmness, before you act on the Apostolic precept, "A man that is a heretic, after the first and second admonition, avoid." ‡ You will use all the patience of charity, but you will use also, if need be so, its just severity. In these days, laxity is mistaken for charity, and indifference to truth for love of souls.

---

* 2 Tim. iii. 1.   † 1 Tim. iv. 1.

‡ Tit. iii. 10.

This is not the spirit of the Apostle, who in the excess of charity declared that he could desire " to be anathema from Christ " for his brethren according to the flesh, and yet, for the love of souls could say, " I would they were even cut off, who trouble you ; " * because the purity of the faith is vital to the salvation of souls, and the salvation of the flock must be preferred to the salvation of a few.

I will touch but one other topic, and then make an end. The same prophets who foretold disastrous consequences from the definition, are now foretelling the downfall of the Temporal Power. Day by day, we hear and read contemptuous censures of the obstinacy of Pius the Ninth, who has ruined himself by his *Non possumus*, and sealed his downfall by the definition of his own infallibility. I do not hesitate to say, that if what is now happening had been caused by the definition, which is not the fact, yet any external trials would be better than an internal conflict arising from a contradiction of revealed truth. Gold may be bought too dear ; but truth cannot.

Perhaps we ought not to wonder that the Protestant and anti-Catholic world should persist in declaring that Rome, by the definition of the Infallibility, has altered its relations to the world ; or, as I have lately read, " disgusted all the civil governments of Europe." They do not know, or are willingly ignorant, that the doctrine of the Infallibility was as much the doctrine of the Church before as after the definition. The definition only declares

---

* Gal. v. 12.

it to be revealed by God. The relations of Rome
to the Civil Powers are therefore precisely what
they were before. If the Civil Powers 'are disgusted, it is only because the Œcumenical Council
declined to swerve from its duty in compliance to
their dictation; or because they can no longer
affect to disbelieve that the Infallibility of the Roman Pontiff is the true and traditional doctrine of
the Catholic Church. We are called superstitious,
because we do not believe in the downfall of the
Temporal Power; and obstinate, because we will
not recognize the right of Italy to invade the Pa-
trimony of the Church. Our superstition consists
in this. In the history of the Church the Temporal
Power has been suppressed, as the phrase is, over
and over again. The first Napoleon suppressed it
twice. The Triumvirate suppressed it in 1848.
There is nothing new under the sun. The thing
that has been, is the thing that shall be. We do
not believe in the perpetuity of anything but the
Church; nor in the finality of anything but justice.
Sacrilege carries the seeds of its own dissolution.
A robbery so unjust cannot endure. When or how
it shall be chastised we know not; but the day of
reckoning is not less sure for that. Of one thing
there can be no doubt: the nations which have
conspired to dethrone the Vicar of Christ will, for
that sin, be scourged. They will, moreover, scourge
one another and themselves. The people that has
the chief share in the sin, will have the heaviest
share in the punishment. We are therefore in no
way moved. If it be God's will that His Church
should suffer persecution, it will be thereby puri-
fied; but the persecutors will fall one by one.

Rome has seen the map of Europe made over and over again; but Rome remains changeless. It will see out the present dynasties of conquered and conqueror; suffering, it may be, but indefectible.

I have already said, that the definition was made on the eighteenth of July, and war on the nineteenth. Since that date, a crowd of events have hurried to their fulfillment. The French Empire has passed away. Rome is occupied by the armies of Italy. The peace of Europe is broken; never again, it may be, to be restored, till the scourges of war have gone their circuit among the nations. A period of storm has set in, and the rising waters of a flood may be seen approaching. If a time of trial for the Church is at hand, a time of ruin and desolation to all countries in Europe will come with it. The Church may suffer, but cannot die; the dynasties and civil societies of Europe may not only suffer, but be swept away. The Head of the Church, be he where he may, in Rome or in exile, free or in bondage, will be all that the Council of the Vatican has defined, supreme in jurisdiction, infallible in faith. Go where he may, the faithful throughout the world will see in him the likeness of His Divine Master, both in authority and in doctrine. The Council has thus made provision for the Church in its time of trial, when, it may be, not only Œcumenical Councils cannot be held, but even the ordinary administration of ecclesiastical government and consultation may be hardly possible.

Peter's bark is ready for the storm. All that is needful is already on board. Past ages were wild and perilous, but the future bids fair to exceed them in violence, as a hurricane exceeds an ordinary storm. The times of the Council of Trent were tempestuous; but for these three hundred years the licence and the violence of free thought, free speech, and a free press, which spares nothing human or divine, have been accumulating in volume and intensity. All this burst upon the Council of the Vatican. And in the midst of this, the Vicar of Jesus Christ, abandoned by all powers of the once Christian world, stands alone, weak but invincible, the supreme judge and infallible teacher of men. The Church has, therefore, its provision for faith and truth, unity and order. The floods may come, the rain descend, and the winds blow and beat upon it, but it cannot fall, because it is founded upon Peter. But what security has the Christian world? Without helm, chart, or light, it has launched itself into the falls of revolution. There is not a monarchy that is not threatened. In Spain and France, monarchy is already overthrown. The hated Syllabus will have its justification. The Syllabus which condemned Atheism and revolution would have saved society. But men would not. They are dissolving the temporal power of the Vicar of Christ. And why do they dissolve it? Because governments are no longer Christian. The temporal power had no sphere, and therefore no manifestation, before the world was Christian. What matter will it have for its temporal power, when the world has ceased to be Christian? For what is the temporal power, but the condition of peaceful independence and supreme direction over all Christians, and all Christian societies, inherent in the office of Vicar of Christ, and head of the Christian Church? When the Civil powers became Christian, faith and obedience restrained them from casting so much as a shadow of human sovereignty over the Vicar of the Son of God. They who attempt it now will do it at their peril.

The Church of God cannot be bound, and its liberty is in its head. The liberty of conscience and of faith, since the Church entered into peace, have been secured in his independence.

For a thousand years his independence, which is sovereignty, has been secured by the providence of God in the temporal power over Rome; the narrow sphere of his exemption from all civil subjection. But men are nowadays wiser than God, and would unmake and mend His works. They are therefore dissolving the temporal power as He has fashioned it; and in so doing, they are striking out the keystone of the arch which hangs over their own heads. This done, the natural society of the world will still subsist, but the Christian world will be no more. One thing is certain: let all the Civil powers of this world in turn, or all together, claim the Vicar of Jesus Christ as their subject, a subject he will never be. The *Non possumus* is not only immutable, but invincible. The infallible head of an infallible Church cannot depend on the sovereignty of man. The Council of the Vatican has brought out this truth with the evidence of light. The world may despise and fight against it, but the Church of God will believe and act upon this law of divine faith.

The peoples of the world will hear him gladly; but the rulers see in him a superior, and will not brook it. They cannot subdue him, and they will not be subject to his voice. They are therefore in perpetual conflict with him. But who ever fought against him, and has prospered? Kings have carried him captive, and princes have betrayed him; but, one by one, they have passed away, and he still abides. Their end has been so tragically explicit that all men may read its meaning. And yet kings and princes will not learn, nor be wise. They rush against the rock, and perish. The world sees their ruin, but will not see the reason. The faithful read in the ruin of all who lay hands on the Vicar of Christ the warning of the Psalmist, " Nolite tangere Christos meos;" and of our Lord Himself, " Whosoever shall fall on this stone, shall be broken, but on whomsoever it shall fall, it will grind him to powder." *

I remain, reverend and dear Brethren,

Your affectionate Servant in Christ,

✠ HENRY EDWARD,

Archbishop of Westminster.

Feast of S. Edward, the Confessor.

---

* St. Matth. xxi. 44.

APPENDIX.

.

I.

POSTULATUM OF THE BISHOPS FOR THE DEFINITION OF THE INFALLIBILITY

SACRO CONCILIO OECUMENICO VATICANO.

A Sacra Oecumenica Synodo Vaticana infrascripti Patres humillime instanterque flagitant, ut apertis, omnemque dubitandi locum excludentibus verbis sancire velit supremam, ideoque ab errore immunem esse Romani Pontificis auctoritatem, quum in rebus fidei et morum ea statuit ac praecipit, quae ab omnibus christifidelibus credenda et tenenda, quaeve reiicienda et damnanda sint.

RATIONES OB QUAS HAEC PROPOSITIO OPPORTUNA ET NECESSARIA CENSETUR.

Romani Pontificis, beati Petri Apostoli successoris, in universam Christi Ecclesiam iurisdictionis, adeoque etiam supremi magisterii primatis in sacris Scripturis aperte docetur.

Universalis et constans Ecclesiae traditio tum factis tum sanctorum Patrum effatis, tum plurimorum Conciliorum, etiam oecumenicorum, et agendi et loquendi ratione docet, Romani Pontificis iudicia de fidei morumque doctrina irreformabilia esse.

Consentientibus Graecis et Latinis, in Concilio II Lugdunensi admissa professio fidei est, in qua declaratur : "Subortas de fide controversias debere Romani Pontificis iudicio definiri." In Florentina itidem oecumenica Synodo definitum est : "Romanum Pontificem esse verum Christi Vicarium, totiusque Ecclesiae caput, et omnium christianorum patrem et doctorem ; et ipsi in beato Petro pascendi, regendi ac gubernandi universalem Ecclesiam a Domino nostro Iesu Christo plenam potestatem traditam esse." Ipsa quoque sana ratio docet, neminem stare posse in fidei communione cum Ecclesia catholica, qui eius capiti non consentiat, quum ne cogitatione quidem Ecclesiam a suo capite separare liceat.

Attamen fuerunt atque adhucdum sunt, qui, catholicorum nomine gloriantes, eoque etiam ad infirmorum in fide perniciem abutentes, docere praesumant, eam sufficere submissionem erga Romani Pontificis auctoritatem, qua eius de fide moribusque decreta obsequioso, ut aiunt, silentio, sine interno mentis assensu, vel provisorie tantum, usquedum de Ecclesiae assensu vel dissensu constiterit, suscipiantur.

Hacce porro perversa doctrina Romani Pontificis auctoritatem subverti, fidei unitatem dissipari, erroribus campum amplissimum aperiri, tempusque late serpendi tribui, nemo, non videt.

Quare Episcopi, catholicae veritatis custodes et vindices, his potissimum temporibus connisi sunt, ut supremam Apostolicae Sedis docendi auctoritatem synodalibus praesertim decretis et communibus testimoniis tuerentur.*

Quo evidentius vero catholica veritas praedicabutur, eo

---

* 1. Concilium provinciale *Coloniense*, anno 1860 celebratum, cui, praeter eminentissimum Cardinalem et Archiepiscopum Coloniensem, Ioannem de Geissel, quinque subscripcrunt Episcopi, diserte docet: "Ipse

vehementius, tam libellis quam ephemeridibus, nuperrime impugnata est, ut catholicus populus contra sanam doctrinam commoveretur, ipsaque Vaticana Synodus ab ea proclamanda absterreretur.

Quare, si antea de opportunitate istius doctrinae in hoc Oecumenico Concilio pronuntiandae a pluribus dubitari adhuc potuit, nunc eam definire necessarium prorsus videtur. Catholica enim doctrina iisdem plane argumentis denuo impetitur, quibus olim homines, proprio iudicio condemnati, adversus eam utebantur; quibus, si urgeantur, ipse Romani Pontificis primatus, Ecclesiaeque infallibilitas pessumdatur; et quibus saepe deterrima convicia contra Apostolicam Sedem admiscentur. Immo acerbissimi catholicae doctrinae impugnatores, licet catholicos se dicant,

---

(Romanus Pontifex) est omnium Christianorum pater et doctor, *cuius in fidei quaestionibus per se irreformabile est iudicium.*"

2. Episcopi in Concilio provinciali *Ultraiectensi* anno 1865 congregati apertissime edicunt: "(Romani Pontificis) iudicium in iis, quae ad fidem moresque spectant, *infallibile* esse, indubitanter retinemus."

3. Concilium provinciale *Colocense*, anno 1860 celebratum, haec statuit: "Quemadmodum Petrus erat . . . doctrinae fidei magister irrefragabilis, pro quo ipse Dominus rogavit, ut non deficeret fides eius . . .; pari modo legitimi eius in cathedrae Romanae culmine successores . . . depositum fidei summo et irrefragabili oraculo custodiunt . . . Unde propositiones cleri gallicani anno 1682 editas, quas iam piae memoriae Georgius Archiepiscopus Strigoniensis una cum ceteris Hungariae Praesulibus eodem adhuc anno publice proscripsit, itidem reiicimus, proscribimus, atque cunctis Provinciae huius fidelibus interdicimus, ne eas legere vel tenere, multo minus docere auderent."

4. Concilium plenarium *Baltimorense*, anno 1866 coactum, in decretis, quibus 44 Archiepiscopi et Episcopi subscripserunt, inter alia haec docet: "Viva et infallibilis auctoritas in ea tantum viget Ecclesia, quae a Christo Domino supra Petrum, totius Ecclesiae caput, principem et pastorem, cuius fidem nunquam defecturam promisit, aedificata, suos legitimos semper habet Pontifices, sine intermissione ab ipso Petro ducentes originem, in eius cathedra collocatos, et eiusdem etiam doctrinae, dignitatis, honoris et potestatis haeredes et vindices. Et quoniam ubi Petrus, ibi Ecclesia, ac Petrus per Romanum Pontificem loquitur et semper in suis successoribus vivit et iudicium exercet, ac praestat quaerentibus fidei veritatem; *idcirco divina eloquia eo plane sensu sunt accipienda, quae tenuit ac tenet haec Romana beatissimi Petri cathedra,* quae omnium Ecclesiarum mater et magistra, fidem a Christo Domino traditam integram inviolatamque

blaterare non erubescunt, Florentinam Synodum, supremam Romani Pontificis auctoritatem luculentissime profitentem, oecumenicam non fuisse.

Si igitur Concilium Vaticanum, adeo provocatum, taceret et catholicae doctrinae testimonium dare negligeret, tunc catholicus populus de vera doctrina reapse dubitare inciperet, neoterici autem gloriantes assererent, Concilium ob argumenta ab ipsis allata siluisse. Quinimmo silentio hoc semper abuterentur, ut Apostolicae Sedis iudiciis et decretis circa fidem et mores palam obedientiam negarent, sub praetextu quod Romanus Pontifex in eiusmodi iudiciis falli potuerit.

Publicum itaque rei christianae bonum postulare videtur, ut Sacrosanctum Concilium Vaticanum, Florentinum de-

---

semper servavit, *eamque fideles edocuit, omnibus ostendens salutis semitam et incoruptae* veritatis doctrinam.

5. Concilium primum provinciale Westmonasteriense, anno 1852 habitum, profitetur: "Cum Dominus noster adhortetur dicens: Attendite ad petram, unde excisi estis; attendite ad Abraham, patrem vestrum: aequum est, nos, qui immediate ab Apostolica Sede fidem, sacerdotium, veramque religionem accepimus, eidem plus ceteris amoris et observantiae vinculis adstringi. *Fundamentum igitur verae et orthodoxae fidei ponimus, quod Dominus noster Iesus Christus ponere voluit inconcussum, scilicet Petri cathedram, totius orbis magistram et matrem, S. Romanam Ecclesiam. Quidquid ab ipsa semel definitum est, eo ipso ratum et certum tenemus;* ipsius traditiones, ritus, pios usus et omnes apostolicas constitutiones, disciplinam respicientes, toto corde amplectimur et veneramur. Summo denique Pontifici obedientiam et reverentiam, ut Christi Vicario, ex animo profitemur, eique arctissime in catholica communione adhaeremus."

6. Quingenti prope Episcopi, ex toto terrarum orbe ad agenda *solemnia saecularia* Martyrii Sanctorum Petri et Pauli anno 1867 in hac alma Urbe congregati, minime dubitarunt, Supremum Pontificem Pium IX hisce alloqui verbis: "Petrum per os Pii locutum fuisse credentes, quae ad custodiendum depositum a Te dicta, confirmata, prolata sunt, nos quoque dicimus, confirmamus, annunciamus, unoque ore atque animo reiicimus omnia, quae divinae fidei, saluti animarum, ipsi societatis humanae bono adversa, Tu ipse reprobanda ac reiicienda iudicasti. Firmum enim menti nostrae est, atque defixum, quod Patres Florentini in decreto unionis definierunt: Romanum Pontificem Christi Vicarium, totius Ecclesiae caput et omnium Christianorum Patrem et Doctorem exsistere."

cretum de Romano Pontifice denuo profitens et uberius
explicans, apertis, omnemque dubitandi locum praecluden-
tibus verbis sancire velit supremam, ideoque ab errore immunem esse eiusdem Romani Pontificis auctoritatem, quum
in rebus fidei et morum ea statuit ac praecipit, quae ab omnibus christifidelibus credenda et tenenda, quaeve reiicienda
et damnanda sint.

Non desunt quidem qui existiment, a catholica hac veritate sancienda abstinendum esse, ne schismatici atque
haeretici longius ab Ecclesia arceantur. Sed in primis
catholicus populus ius habet, ut ab Oecumenica Synodo
doceatur, quid in re tam gravi, et tam improbe nuper impugnata, credendum sit, ne simplices et incautos multorum
animos perniciosus error tandem corrumpat. Idcirco etiam
Lugdunenses et Tridentini Patres rectam doctrinam stabi-
liendam esse censuerunt, etsi schismatici et haeretici offen-
derentur. Qui si sincera mente veritatem quaerant, non
absterrebuntur sed allicientur, dum ipsis ostenditur, quo
potissimum fundamento catholicae Ecclesiae unitas et firmitas nitatur. Si qui autem, vera doctrina ab Ocumenico
Concilio definita, ab Ecclesia deficerent, hi numero pauci
et iamdudum in fide naufragi sunt, praetextum solummodo
quaerentes, quo externa etiam actione ab Ecclesia se ex-
imant, quam interno sensu iam deseruisse palam ostendunt.
Hi sunt, qui catholicum populum continuo turbare non ab-
horruerunt, et a quorum insidiis Vaticana Synodus fideles
Ecclesiae filios tueri debebit. Catholicus enimvero populus,
semper edoctus et assuetus, Apostolicis Romani Pontificis
decretis plenissimum mentis et oris obsequium exhibere,
Vaticani Concilii sententiam de eiusdem suprema et ab
errore immuni auctoritate laeto fidelique animo excipiet.

TRANSLATION OF THE POSTULATUM FOR THE DEFINITION.

TO THE HOLY ŒCUMENICAL VATICAN COUNCIL.

The undersigned Fathers humbly and earnestly beg the holy Œcumenical Council of the Vatican to define clearly, and in words that cannot be mistaken, that the authority of the Roman Pontiff is supreme, and, therefore, exempt from error, when in matters of faith and morals he declares and defines what is to be believed and held, and what to be rejected and condemned, by all the faithful.

REASONS FOR WHICH THIS DEFINITION IS THOUGHT OPPORTUNE AND NECESSARY.

The Sacred Scriptures plainly teach the Primacy of jurisdiction of the Roman Pontiff, the Successor of St. Peter, over the whole Church of Christ, and, therefore, also his Primacy of supreme teaching authority.

The universal and constant tradition of the Church, as seen both in facts and in the teaching of the Fathers, as well as in the manner of acting and speaking adopted by many Councils, some of which were Œcumenical, teaches us that the judgments of the Roman Pontiff in matters of faith and morals are irreformable.

In the Second Council of Lyons, with the consent of both Greeks and Latins, a profession of faith was agreed upon, which declares : " When controversies in matters of faith arise, they must be settled by the decision of the Roman Pontiff." Moreover, in the Œcumenical Synod of Florence, it was defined that "the Roman Pontiff is Christ's true Vicar, the Head of the whole Church, and Father and Teacher of all Christians ; and that to him, in blessed Peter, was given by Jesus Christ the plenitude of power to rule and govern the universal Church." Sound reason, too, teaches us that no one can remain in communion of faith with the Catholic Church who is not of one mind with its head, since the Church cannot be separated from its head even in thought.

Yet some have been found, and are even now to be found, who, boasting of the name of Catholic, and using that name to the ruin of those weak in faith, are bold enough to teach, that sufficient submission is yielded to the authority of the Roman Pontiff, if we receive his decrees in matters of faith and morals with an obsequious silence, as it is termed, without yielding internal assent, or, at most, with a provisional assent, until the approval or disapproval of the Church has been made known. Any one can see that by this perverse doctrine the authority of the Roman Pontiff is overturned, all unity of faith dissolved, a wide field open to errors, and leisure afforded for spreading them far and wide.

Wherefore the Bishops, the guardians and protectors of Catholic truth, have endeavored, especially now-a-days, to defend in their Synodal decrees, and by their united testimony, the supreme authority of the Apostolic See.*

But the more clearly Catholic truth has been declared, the more vehemently has it been attacked both in books and in newspapers, for the purpose of exciting Catholics against sound doctrine, and preventing the Council of the Vatican from defining it.

Though, then, in times past many might have doubted the opportuneness of declaring this doctrine in the present Œcumenical Council, it would seem now to be absolutely necessary to define it. For Catholic doctrine is now once more assailed by those same arguments which men, condemned by their own conscience, used against it in old times ; arguments which, if carried to their ultimate con-

---

* Many specimens of this testimony are collected in the following Appendix to the Postulatum.

sequences, would bring to the ground the very Primacy of the Roman Pontiff and the infallibility of the Church itself; and to which, also, is frequently added the most violent abuse of the Apostolic See. Nay, more; the most bitter assailants of Catholic doctrine, though calling themselves Catholics, are not ashamed to assert that the Synod of Florence, which so clearly declares the supreme authority of the Roman Pontif, was not Œcumenical.

If, then, the Council of the Vatican, being thus challenged, were to be silent, and omit to give testimony to the Catholic doctrine on this point, then Catholics would, in fact, begin to doubt the true doctrine, and the novelty-mongers would triumphantly assert that the Council had been silenced by the arguments brought forward by them. They would, moreover, abuse this silence on every occasion, and openly deny the obedience due to the judgments and decrees of the Apostolic See in matters of faith and morals, under pretext that the judgment of the Roman Pontiff is fallible on such points.

Wherefore the public good of Christianity seems to require that the holy Council of the Vatican, professing once again, and explaining more fully, the Florentine decree, should define clearly, and in words that can admit of no doubt, that the authority of the Roman Pontiff is supreme, and, therefore, exempt from error, when in matters of faith and morals he decrees and ordains what is to be believed and held by all the faithful of Christ, and what to be rejected and condemned by them.

There are, indeed, some who think that this Catholic truth should not be defined, lest schismatics and heretics should be repelled yet further from the Church. But, above all other considerations, Catholics have a right to be taught by the Œcumenical Council what they are to believe in so weighty a matter, and one which has been of late so iniquitously attacked; lest this pernicious error should in the end infect simple minds, and the masses of people unawares. Hence it was that the Fathers of Lyons and of Trent deemed themselves bound to establish the doctrine of the truth, notwithstanding the offence that might be taken by schismatics and heretics. For if these seek the truth in sincerity, they will not be repelled, but, on the contrary, drawn towards us, when they see on what foundations the unity and strength of the Catholic Church chiefly repose. But, should any leave the Church in consequence of the true doctrine being defined by the Œcumenical Council, these will be few in number, and such as have already suffered shipwreck in the faith ; such as are only seeking a pretext to abandon that Church by an overt act, which they plainly show they have deserted already in heart. These are they who have never shrunk from disturbing our Catholic people ; and from the snares of such men the Council of the Vatican ought to protect the faithful children of the Church. For all true Catholics, taught and accustomed to render the fullest obedience both of thought and word to the Apostolic decrees of the Roman Pontiff, will receive with joyful and devoted hearts the definition of the Council of the Vatican concerning his supreme and infallible authority.

APPENDIX.

DECISIONS OF PROVISIONAL SYNODS RECENTLY HELD, SHOWING THE COMMON OPINION OF BISHOPS CONCERNING THE SUPREME AND INFALLIBLE AUTHORITY OF THE ROMAN PONTIFF IN MATTERS OF FAITH AND MORALS.

1. The Provincial Council held at Cologne in 1860, to which, in addition to his Eminence Cardinal Geissel, Archbishop of Cologne, five Bishops subscribed, expressly declared : " He (the Roman Pontiff) is the father and teacher of all Christians, *whose judgment in questions of faith is 'per se' unalterable.*"

2. The Bishops assembled in the Provincial Council,

8*

held at Utrecht in 1865, most openly assert : "We unhesitatingly hold that the judgment of the Roman Pontiff in matters which refer to faith and morals is *infallible*."

3. The Provincial Council of Prague,* in 1860, to which his Eminence Cardinal Archbishop Frederic de Schwarzenberg and four other Bishops subscribed, under the heading, "On the Primacy of the Roman Pontiff," decreed as follows : "We reject, moreover, the error of those who pretend that the Church can exist anywhere without being joined in bonds of union with the Church of Rome, in which the tradition which has been handed down by the Apostles, has been preserved by those who are in every part." (S. Irenæus, *Adv. Hær.* 1. 3, c. 3, n. 2.)

" We know that no one who is not joined to the Head can be considered as a member of the Body of the Church which Christ founded on Peter, and established on his authority. Let all then prefer to confess with us and with the multitude of orthodox believers spread over the whole world, the Headship of the Roman Church and the Primacy of the Roman Pontiff ; let them, as is fitting, with us, reverence and honor with dutiful affection our Most Holy Father Pius IX., by God's Providence Pope, the lawful Successor of the Prince of the Apostles, the Vicar of Christ on earth, the Chief Teacher of Faith, and Pilot of the Ship of Christ, to whom *the most exact obedience and internal assent is due from all who wish to belong to the fold of Christ.* We declare and teach, that this authority of the Roman Pontiff comes from Christ our Lord, and that consequently it is dependent upon no power or favor of men, and remains unimpaired in all times, even in the most bitter persecutions which the Church of Rome has suffered, as was the case during the imprisonment and martyrdom of blessed Peter.".

4. The Provincial Council of Kalocza, held in 1860, de-

---

* This Council was not included in the original draught from which the Latin is taken.

clared : " That as Peter was . . . the irrefutable teacher
of the doctrines of faith, for whom the Lord Himself
prayed that his faith might not fail ; so his legitimate successors seated aloft on the Chair of Rome . . . preserve
the deposit of faith with supreme and irrefutable powers
of declaring the truth. . . . Wherefore we also reject, proscribe, and forbid all the faithful of this Province, to read
or maintain, and much more to teach, the propositions
published by the Gallican Clergy in 1682, which have already been censured this same year by the Archbishop of
Gran, of pious memory, and by the other Bishops of Hungary."

5. The Plenary Council of Baltimore, which met in 1866,
and to which 44 Archbishops and Bishops subscribed,
says : " The living and infallible authority flourishes in
that Church alone which was built by Christ upon Peter,
who is the Head, Leader, and Pastor of the whole Church,
whose faith Christ promised should never fail ; which ever
had legitimate Pontiffs, dating their origin in unbroken
line from Peter himself, being seated in his Chair, and being the inheritors and defenders of the like doctrine, dignity, office, and power. And because, where Peter is,
there also is the Church, and because Peter speaks in the
person of the Roman Pontiff, ever lives in his successors,
passes judgment, and makes known the truths of faith to
those who seek them ; *therefore are the Divine declarations
to be received in that sense in which they have been and are
held by this Roman See of blessed Peter*, that mother and
teacher of all Churches, which has ever preserved whole
and entire the teaching delivered by Christ, *and which has
taught it to the faithful, showing to all men the paths of salvation and the doctrine of everlasting truth.*"

6. The first Provincial Council of Westminster, held in
1852, states : " When our Blessed Lord exhorts us, saying,
Look to the rock whence you are hewn ; look to Abraham
your father, it is fitting that we who have received our

faith, our priesthood, and the true religion, directly from the Apostolic See, should more than others be attached to it by the bonds of love and fidelity. *Therefore do we maintain that foundation of truth and orthodoxy which Jesus Christ willed should be maintained unshaken ; namely, the See of Peter, the teacher and mother of the whole world, the Holy Roman Church. Whatever is once defined by it, for that very reason alone we consider to be fixed and certain ;* when we look at its traditions, rites, pious customs, discipline, and all its Apostolic Constitutions, we follow and cherish them with all the affection of our hearts. In. fine, we of set purpose publicly declare our obedience and respect for the Pope as Christ's Vicar, and we remain united to him in the closest bonds of Catholic unity."

7. Nearly five hundred of the Bishops assembled in Rome to celebrate the Centenary of the Martyrdom of SS. Peter and Paul, in the year 1867, had no hesitation in addressing Pius IX. in the following terms : " Believing that Peter has spoken by the mouth of Pius, whatever has been said, confirmed, and decreed by You to preserve the deposit of faith, we also repeat, confirm, and profess, and with one mind and heart we reject all that You have judged it necessary to reprove and condemn as contrary to Divine faith, to the salvation of souls, and to the good of society. For what the Fathers of Florence defined in their Decree of Union, is firmly and deeply impressed in our minds ; that the Roman Pontiff is the Vicar of Christ, the Head of the whole Church, the Father and Teacher of all Christians."

II.

LETTER OF H. E. CARDINAL ANTONELLI TO THE NUNCIO AT PARIS.

ROME, March 19th, 1870.

MY LORD :—The Marquis de Banneville, ambassador of his Majesty, read me, a few days ago, a despatch forwarded to him under date February 20, last, from Count Daru, Minister of Foreign Affairs, relative to the affairs of the Council. In this communication, of which the ambassador was kind enough to leave me a copy, the aforesaid minister, referring to the resolution come to by the French Government not to take part in the deliberations of the General Council, desiring at the same time its liberty to be guaranteed fully and absolutely, states that such resolution was based on the supposition that that venerable assembly would occupy itself solely about the sacred interests of the Faith, and would abstain from touching questions of a purely political order. But the publication (he says) by the "Augsburg Gazette" of the canons appertaining to the draft of constitution on the Church and on the Roman Pontiff, showing that there is question of deciding whether the power of the Church and of her Head extends to the whole aggregate of political rights ; the government, keeping firmly to the resolution of leaving, upon this point also, entire liberty to the deliberations of the august assembly, intends to exercise the rights given it by the Concordat of making known to the Council its opinion on questions of such nature.

Passing to the examination of the said canons, the minister sums up their contents (on which he wishes to comment) in the two following propositions :—First, " the Infallibility of the Church extends not only to the Deposit of Faith, but to all that is necessary for the preservation of such deposit ;" and secondly, " the Church is a society divine and perfect ; its power is exercised at once *in foro interno et externo* ; is absolute in the legislative, judicial, and coercive order, and is to be exercised by her with full liberty and independence from any civil power whatever." Hence, as corollaries of these two propositions, he deduces the extension of infallibility to all that is thought necessary for the defence of revealed truths, and consequently to facts, whether historical, philosophical, or scientific, external to revelation ; as also the absolute subordination to the supreme authority of the Church of the constituent principles of civil society ; of the rights and duties of Government; of the political rights and duties of citizens, whether electoral or municipal ; of all that relates to the judicial and legislative order, as well in respect of persons as of things ; of the rules of public administration ; of the rights and duties of corporations, and, in general, of all the rights of the State, not excluding the rights of conquest, peace, and war.

Next the minister passes on to note the profound impression which the simple enunciation of such doctrines must produce in.the entire world ; and asks at the same time how it could be possible for the Bishops to consent to abdicate their episcopal authority, concentrating it in the hands of one alone ; and how it could have been imagined that princes would lower their sovereignty before the supremacy of the Court of Rome.

Lastly, concluding, from all that has been set forth, that political and not religious interests are being discussed in the Council, Count Daru demands that the Governments be heard, or at least admitted to bear testimony to the characters, dispositions, and spirit (disposizioni di spirito)

of the people they represent; and in particular that since
France, by reason of the special protection which for
twenty years she has exercised over the Pontifical State,
has quite special duties to perform, he demands that the
Government of that nation be permitted to exercise its
right of receiving communication of projected decisions
touching politics, and of requesting the delay necessary
for bringing its observations before the Council, before any
resolution be adopted by the same.

This is an abstract of the dispatch communicated to me
by the Marquis de Banneville. I have thought proper to
inform your Lordship of it ; with the view, moreover, of
communicating to you some short considerations which I
think necessary to put in a clearer light the points touched
upon by the minister, and to reply to the deductions made
by him with respect to the points submitted to the deliberations of the Council.

And first, I cannot dispense myself from manifesting to
your Lordship the satisfaction with which the Holy Father
received the declaration expressed at the beginning of
Count Daru's despatch, and repeated in the sequel, of the
fixed intention of the French Government to respect, and
cause to be respected, in any event, the full liberty of the
Council, as well in the discussion of the constitution referred to as of all others which shall hereafter come to be
proposed to the examination of the venerable assembly.
This declaration, which does great honor to the Government of a Catholic nation, is considered by the Holy See
as the natural consequence of that protection which, for
more than twenty years, France has exercised towards it ;
a protection which has called forth several times public
demonstrations of gratitude on the part of the Supreme
Pontiff, who always, but especially at the present moment,
cannot do less than recognize and appreciate all its importance.

But, coming closer to the object of Count Daru's de-

spatch, I must say frankly that I am quite unable to understand (non mi è dato di comprendere) how the declarations contained in the draft of Constitution on the Church,
and the respective canons—published in the "Augsburg
Gazette" by a breach of the Pontifical secret—could have
produced so grave and profound an impression on the
mind of the French Cabinet, as to induce it to change the
line of conduct which it had properly traced out for itself
in regard to the discussions of the Vatican Council.   The
subjects treated in that draft of constitution, and in the
canons appertaining to it, whatever modification they may
undergo in the sequel from the judgment and decision of
the Episcopate, are no more than the exposition of the
maxims and fundamental principles of the Church ; principles repeated over and over again in the Acts of former
General Councils, proclaimed and developed in several
Pontifical Constitutions, published in all Catholic states,
and particularly in the celebrated dogmatic Bulls beginning
" Unigenitus," and " Auctorem Fidei," where all the aforesaid doctrines are generally confirmed and sanctioned ;
principles, finally, which have constantly formed the basis
of teaching in all periods of the Church, and in all Catholic
schools, and have been defended by an innumerable host
of ecclesiastical writers, whose works have served for text
in public schools and colleges, as well Government schools
as others, without any contradiction on the part of the
civil authority, but rather, for the most part, with the approbation and encouragement of the same.

Much less would it be possible for me to agree upon the
character and extent given by the minister to the doctrines
contained in the aforesaid canon.   In virtue of them there
is not attributed, either to the Church or the Roman Pontiff, that direct and absolute power over the whole aggregate of political rights, of which the despatch speaks ; nor
is the subordination of the civil to the religious power to

be understood in the sense set forth by him, but in another order of quite different bearing.

And in truth the Church has never intended, nor now intends, to exercise any direct and absolute power over the political rights of the State. Having received from God the lofty mission of guiding men, whether individually or as congregated in society, to a supernatural end, she has by that very fact the authority and the duty to judge concerning the morality and justice of all acts, internal and external, in relation to their conformity with the natural and divine law. And as no action, whether it be ordained by a supreme power, or be freely elicited by an individual, can be exempt from this character of morality and justice, so it happens that the judgment of the Church, though falling directly on the morality of the acts, indirectly reaches over everything with which that morality is conjoined. But this is not the same thing as to interfere directly in political affairs, which, by the order established by God and by the teaching of the Church herself, appertains to the temporal power without dependence on any other authority. The subordination, also, of the civil to the religious power is in the sense of the pre-eminence of the sacerdotium over the imperium, because of the superiority of the end of the one over that of the other.* Hence, the authority of the imperium depends on that of the sacerdotium, as human things on divine, temporal on spiritual. And if temporal happiness, which is the end of the civil power, is subordinate to eternal beatitude, which is the spiritual end of the sacerdotium, it follows that in order to reach the end to which it has pleased God to direct them, the one power is subordinate to the other. Their powers (I say) are respectively subordinate in the same way as the ends to which they are directed.

---

* We have no exact English equivalents for the abstract terms—*sacerdozio, impero.* "Sacerdozio" means the priestly office, and "imporo" civil authority in the most general sense.—Note of Tr.]

It results from these principles that, if the infallibility of the Church extends also (not, however, in the sense indicated by the French despatch) to all that is necessary to preserve intact the Deposit of Faith, no harm is thereby · done to science, history, or politics. The prerogative of infallibility is not an unknown fact in the Catholic world; the supreme *magisterium* of the Church has dictated in every age rules of faith, without the internal order of States being thereby affected (risentirsene), or princes being disquieted thereat ; rather, wisely appreciating the influence which such rules have on the good order of civil society, these have been themselves, from time to time, the vindicators and defenders of the doctrines defined, and have promoted, by the concurrence of the royal power, their full and respectful observance.

It follows, moreover, that if the Church was instituted by its Divine Founder as a true and perfect society, distinct from the civil power and independent of it, with full authority in the triple order, legislative, judicial and coercive, no confusion springs therefrom in the march of human society, and in the exercise of the rights of the two powers. The competence of the one and the other is clearly distinct and determined, according to the end to which they are respectively directed. The Church does not, in virtue of her authority, intervene directly and absolutely in the constitutive principles of governments, in the forms of civil regulations, in the political rights of citizens, in the duties of the State, and in the other points indicated in the minister's note. But, whereas no civil society can subsist without a supreme principle regulating the morality of its acts and laws, the Church has received from God this lofty mission, which tends to the happiness of the people, while she in no way embarrasses, by the exercise of this her ministry, the free and prompt action of governments. She, in fact, by inculcating the principle of rendering to God that which is God's, and to Cæsar that which is

Cæsar's, imposes at the same time upon her children the obligation of obeying the authority of princes for conscience sake. But these should also recognize that if anywhere a law is made opposed to the principles of eternal justice, to obey would not be a giving to Cæsar that which is Cæsar's, but a taking from God that which is God's.

I proceed now to say a word on the profound impression which the minister expects will be made throughout the world by the mere enunciation of the principles developed in the draft of constitution which forms the object of his despatch. In truth it is not easy to persuade oneself how the doctrines contained in that draft, and understood in the sense above pointed out, can produce the profound impression of which the minister speaks; unless indeed their spirit and character be wrested, or that he speaks of those who, professing principles different from those professed by the Catholic Church, cannot of course approve of such principles being inculcated and sanctioned afresh. I say afresh; because the doctrines contained in that document, as I have already remarked, far from being new and unheard of, embrace no more (non sono nel loro complesso) than the reproduction of the Catholic teaching professed in every age and in every Church, as will be solemnly proved by all the pastors of the Catholic name, called by the head of the hierarchy to bear authentic witness, in the midst of the Council, to the faith and traditions of the Church Universal. It is to be hoped rather that the Catholic doctrine, once more solemnly confirmed by the Fathers of the Vatican Council, will be greeted by the faithful people as the rainbow of peace and the dawn of a brighter future. The object of confirming those doctrines is no other than to recall to modern society the maxims of justice and virtue, and thus to restore to the world that peace and prosperity which can only be found in the perfect keeping of the divine law. This is the firm hope of all honest men, who received with joy the announcement of the Council; this is the conviction of the Fathers of the Church, who have assembled with alacrity in such numbers at the voice of the Chief Pastor; this is the prayer which the Vicar of Jesus Christ is always sending up to God in the midst of the grievous troubles which surround his Pontificate.

For the rest, I do not understand why the bishops should have to renounce their episcopal authority in consequence of the definition of Pontifical authority. This prerogative is not only as ancient as the Church herself, but has been, moreover, always exercised in the Roman Church, without the divine authority and the rights conferred by God on the pastors of the Church being thereby altered in the least degree. Its definition therefore would in no way go to change the relations between the bishops and their head. The rights of the one and the prerogatives of the other are well defined in the Church's divine constitution; and the confirmation of the Roman Pontiff's supreme authority and magisterium, far from being prejudicial to the rights of bishops, will furnish a new support to their authority and magisterium, since the strength and vigor of the members is just so much as comes to them from the head.

By parity of reason—the authority of the pastors of the Church being strengthened anew by the solemn confirmation of Pontifical Infallibility—that of princes, especially Catholic princes, will be no less strengthened. The prosperity of the Church and the peace of the State depend upon the close and intimate union of the two supreme powers. Who does not see then that the authority of princes not only will not receive any blow from the pontifical supremacy, but will instead find therein its strongest support? As sons of the Church they owe obedience, respect, and protection to the authority placed on earth by God to guide princes and peoples to the last end of eternal salvation; nor can they refuse to recognize that royal power has been granted them for the defence also and guardianship of Christian society. But by the very fact of the principle of authority receiving new vigor in the Church and in its head, the sovereign power must necessarily receive a new impulse, since it has from God a common origin, and consequently common interests also. And so, if the wickedness of the age, by separating the one from the other, has placed both in troublesome and painful conditions, to the great injury of human society, closer relations will unite both in indissoluble bonds for the defence of the grand interests of religion and society, and will prepare for them the way to a brighter and more prosperous future.

From what has been said up to this point it results clearly that the Council has not been called to discuss political interests, as the despatch of Count Daru seems to indicate. We may conclude, therefore, that the French Government, finding no longer a sufficient reason for departing from the line of conduct it had set itself to follow in respect of the Council, will not desire to insist on the request for communication of the Decrees which will be submitted to the examination and discussion of the venerable assembly of Bishops. On which point indeed it occurs to me to observe that the right claimed for this purpose by the minister on the ground of the Concordat in force between the Holy See and France, cannot, in my opinion, find any support in that act. In the first place, no special mention of this particular point is found in the articles of that convention. Then, further, the relations of Church and State on points belonging to both Powers (punto di mista competenza) having been regulated by the Concordat, the decisions, which may be come to by the Vatican Council on such matters will in no way alter the special stipulations made by the Holy See, as well with France as with other governments, as long as these place no obstacles in the way of the full keeping of the conditions agreed upon. I may also add that if the Holy See has not thought fit to invite Catholic princes to the Council, as it did on other occasions, every one will easily understand that this is chiefly to be attributed to the changed circumstances of the times. The altered state of the relations between the Church and the Civil Governments has made more difficult their mutual action in the regulation of things religious.

I desire however to hope that the Government of his Majesty the Emperor, fully satisfied with the explanations given by me in the name of the Holy See to the various points of Count Daru's despatch; and recognizing at the same time the difficulties in which the Holy Father might find himself, will not insist further on the demand of communication beforehand of the drafts of constitutions to be examined by the Fathers of the Council. Were such demand conceded, there would be question of things tending to embarrass the free action of the Council. Moreover, since the Church is keeping within the limits assigned to her by her Divine Founder, no anxiety need remain to the Government of his Majesty on account of the deliberations which may come to be adopted by the Episcopal assembly. Finally the French Government will thus give, by the very fact, a new proof of those dispositions of good will which it has manifested in respect of the full liberty of the Conciliar deliberations, and of the confidence which it declares it reposes in the wisdom and prudence of the Apostolic See.

Your Lordship will please read this despatch to Count Daru, as also leave him a copy.

Meanwhile receive, &c., &c.,

(Signed) G. Card. Antonelli.

III.

ACT OF CONDEMNATION BY THE COUNCIL OF CERTAIN PAMPHLETS, &c.

REVERENDISSIMI PATRES,—Ex quo Sacrosancta Synodus Vaticana, opitulante Deo, congregata est, acerrimum statim contra eam bellum exarsit ; atque ad venerandam, eius auctoritatem penes fidelem populum imminuendam, ac si fieri posset, penitus labefactandam, contumeliose de illa detrahere, eamque putidissimis calumniis oppetere plures scriptores certatim aggressi sunt non modo inter heterodoxos et apertos Crucis Christi inimicos, sed etiam inter eos qui Catholicae Ecclesiae filios sese dictitant, et quod maxime dolendum est inter ipsos eius sacros ministros.

Quae in publicis cuiusque idiomatis ephemeridibus, quaeque in libellis absque auctoris nomine passim editis et furtive distributis, congesta hac de re fuerint probrosa mendacia, omnes apprime norunt, quin nobis necesse sit illa singillatim edicere. Verum inter anonymos istiusmodi libellos duo praesertim extant, gallice conscripti sub titulis: *Ce qui se passe au Concile* et *La dernière heure du Concile,* qui ob suam calumniandi artem, obtrectandique licentiam ceteris palmam praeripuisse videntur. In his enim nedum huius Concilii dignitas ac plena libertas turpissimis oppugnantur mendaciis, iuraque Apostolicae Sedis evertuntur; sed ipsa quoque SSmi Dñi Nostri augusta persona gravibus lacessitur iniuriis. Iam vero Nos officii nostri memores, ne silentium nostrum, si diutius protraheretur, sinistre a malevolis hominibus interpretari valeat, contra tot tantasque obtrectationes vocem extollere cogimur, atque in conspectu omnium vestrum, Rmi Patres, protestari ac declarare : falsa omnino esse et calumniosa quaecumque in praedictis ephemeridibus et libellis effutiuntur, sive in spretum et contumeliam SSmi Dñi Nostri et Apostolicae Sedis, sive in dedecus huius Sacrosanctae Synodi, et contra assertum defectum in illa legitimae libertatis.

Datum ex Aula Concilii Vaticani, die 16 Iulii 1870.

PHILIPPUS Card. DE ANGELIS *Praeses.*
ANTONINUS Card. DE LUCA *Praeses.*
ANDREAS Card. BIZZARRI *Praeses.*
ALOYSIUS Card. BILIO *Praeses.*
HANNIBAL Card. CAPALTI *Praeses.*

IOSEPHUS *Ep. S. Hippolyti, Secretarius.*

IV.

TEXT OF THE CONSTITUTIONS.

CONSTITUTIO DOGMATICA DE FIDE CATHOLICA.

PIUS EPISCOPUS, SERVUS SERVORUM DEI, SACRO APPROBANTE CONCILIO, AD PERPETUAM REI MEMORIAM.

DEI Filius et generis humani Redemptor Dominus Noster Jesus Christus, ad Patrem coelestem rediturus, cum Ecclesiâ suâ in terris militante, omnibus diebus usque ad consummationem saeculi futurum se esse promisit. Quare dilectae

Sponsæ præsto esse, adsistere docenti, operanti benedicere, periclitanti opem ferre nullo unquam tempore destitit. Hæc vero salutaris ejus providentia, cum ex aliis beneficiis innumeris continenter apparuit, tum iis manifestissime comperta est fructibus, qui orbi christiano e Conciliis œcumenicis ac nominatim e Tridentino, iniquis licet temporibus celebrato, amplissimi provenerunt. Hinc enim sanctissima religionis dogmata pressius definita, uberiusque exposita, errores damnati atque cohibiti ; hinc ecclesiastica disciplina restituta firmiusque sancita, promotum in Clero scientiæ et pietatis studium, parata adolescentibus ad sacram militiam educandis collegia, christiani denique populi mores et accuratiore fidelium eruditione et frequentiore sacramentorum usu instaurati. Hinc præterea arctior membrorum cum visibili capite communio, universoque corpori Christi mystico additus vigor ; hinc religiosæ multiplicatæ familiæ, aliaque christianæ pietatis instituta, hinc ille etiam assiduus et usque ad sanguinis effusionem constans ardor in Christi regno late per orbem propagando.

Verumtamen hæc aliaque insignia emolumenta, quæ per ultimam maxime œcumenicam Synodum divinâ clementiâ Ecclesiae largita est, dum grato, quo par est, animo recolimus, acerbum compescere haud possumus dolorem ob mala gravissima, inde potissimum orta, quod ejusdem sacrosanctæ Synodi apud permultos vel auctoritas contempta, vel sapientissima neglecta fuere decreta.

Nemo enim ignorat hæreses quas Tridentini Patres proscripserunt, dum, rejecto divino Ecclesiæ magisterio, res ad religionem spectantes privati cujusvis judicio ·permitterentur, in sectas paulatim dissolutas esse multiplices, quibus inter se dissentientibus et concertantibus, omnis tandem in Christum fides apud non paucos labefacta est. Itaque ipsa sacra Biblia, quæ antea christianæ doctrinæ unicus fons et judex asserebantur, jam non pro divinis haberi, imo mythicis commentis accenseri cœperunt.

Tum nata est et late nimis per orbem vagata illa rationalismi seu naturalismi doctrina, quæ religioni christianæ utpote supernaturali instituto per omnia adversans, summo studio molitur, ut Christo, qui solus Dominus et Salvator noster est, a mentibus humanis, a vitâ et moribus populorum excluso, meræ quod vocant rationis vel naturæ regnum stabiliatur. Relictâ autem projectâque christianâ religione, negato vero Deo et Christo ejus, prolapsa tandem est multorem mens in pantheismi materialismi atheismi barathrum, ut jam ipsam rationalem naturam, omnemque justi rectique normam negantes, ima humanæ societatis fundamenta diruere connitantur.

Hâc porro impietate circumquaque grassante, infeliciter contigit, ut plures etiam e catholicæ Ecclesiæ filiis a viâ veræ pietatis aberrarent, in iisque, diminutis paullatim veritatibus, sensus catholicus attenuaretur. Variis enim ac peregrinis doctrinis abducti, naturam et gratiam, scientiam humanam et fidem divinam perperàm commiscentes, genuinum sensum dogmatum, quem tenet ac docet Sancta Mater Ecclesia, depravare, integritatemque et sinceritatem fidei in periculum adducere comperiuntur.

Quibus omnibus perspectis, fieri qui potest, ut non commoveantur intima Ecclesiæ viscera? Quemadmodum enim Deus vult omnes homines salvos fieri, et ad agnitionem veritatis venire; quemadmodum Christus venit, ut salvum faceret, quod perierat, et filios Dei, qui erant dispersi, congregaret in unum: ita Ecclesia, a Deo populorum mater et magistra constituta, omnibus debitricem se novit, ac lapsos erigere, labantes sustinere, revertentes amplecti, confirmare bonos et ad meliora provehere parata semper et intenta est. Quapropter nullo tempore a Dei veritate, quæ sanat omnia, testanda et prædicanda quiescere potest, sibi dictum esse non ignorans: "Spiritus meus, qui est in te, et verba mea, quæ posui in ore tuo, non recedent de ore tuo amodo et usque in sempiternum." *

* Isal. lix. 21.

Nos itaque, inhærentes Prædecessorum Nostrorum vestigiis, pro supremo Nostro Apostolico munere veritatem catholicam docere ac tueri, perversasque doctrinas reprobare nunquam intermisimus. Nunc autem sedentibus Nobiscum et judicantibus universi orbis Episcopis, in hanc œcumenicam Synodum auctoritate Nostrâ in Spiritu Sancto congregatis, innixi Dei verbo scripto et tradito, prout ab Ecclesiâ catholicâ sancte custoditum et genuine expositum accepimus, ex hâc Petri Cathedrâ in conspectu omnium salutarem Christi doctrinam profiteri et declarare constituimus, adversis erroribus potestate nobis a Deo traditâ proscriptis atque damnatis.

CAPUT I.

DE DEO RERUM OMNIUM CREATORE.

Sancta Catholica Apostolica Romana Ecclesia credit et confitetur, unum esse Deum verum et vivum, Creatorem ac Dominum cœli et terræ, omnipotentem, æternum, immensum incomprehensibilem, intellectu ac voluntate omnique perfectione infinitum ; qui cum sit una singularis, simplex omnino et incommutabilis substantia spiritualis, prædicandus est re et essentiâ a mundo distinctus, in se et ex se beatissimus, et super omnia, quæ præter ipsum sunt et concipi possunt, ineffabiliter excelsus.

Hic solus verus Deus bonitate suâ et omnipotenti virtute non ad augendam suam beatitudinem, nec ad acquirendam, sed ad manifestandam perfectionem suam per bona, quæ creaturis impertitur, liberrimo consilio simul ab initio temporis utramque de nihilo condidit creaturam, spiritualem et corporalem, angelicam videlicet et mundanam, ac deinde

humanam quasi communem ex spiritu et corpore constitutam.*

Universa vero, quæ condidit, Deus providentiâ suâ tuetur
atque gubernat, attingens a fine usque ad finem fortiter, et
disponens omnia suaviter.† Omnia enim nuda et aperta
sunt oculis ejus,‡ ea etiam, quæ liberâ creaturarum actione
futura sunt.

CAPUT II.

DE REVELATIONE.

Eadem sancta Mater Ecclesia tenet et docet, Deum,
rerum omnium principium et finem, naturali humanæ
rationis lumine e rebus creatis certo cognosci posse ; in-
visibilia enim ipsius, a creaturâ mundi, per ea quæ facta
sunt, intellecta, conspiciuntur : § attamen placuisse ejus
sapientiæ et bonitati, aliâ, eâque supernaturali viâ se ipsum
ac æterna voluntatis suæ decreta humano generi revelare,
dicente Apostolo : "Multifariàm, multisque modis olim
Deus loquens patribus in Prophetis : novissime, diebus
istis locutus est nobis in Filio." ‖

Huic divinæ revelationi tribuendum quidem est, ut ea,
quæ in rebus divinis humanæ rationi per se impervia non
sunt, in præsenti quoque generis humani conditione ab
omnibus expedite, firmâ certitudine et nullo admixto errore
cognosci possint. Non hâc tamen de causâ revelatio absolute necessaria dicenda est, sed quia Deus ex infinitâ bonitate suâ ordinavit hominem ad finem supernaturalem, ad
participanda scilicet bona divina, quæ humanæ mentis in-

---

* Concil. Lateran. IV. cap. 1. De fide Catholica.
† Sap. viii. 1.   ‡ Cf. Hebr. iv. 18.
§ Rom. i. 20.   ‖ Hebr. i. 1, 2.

telligentiam omnino superant ; siquidem oculus non vidit, nec auris audivit, nec in cor hominis ascendit, quæ præparavit Deus iis, qui diligunt illum.*

Hæc porro supernaturalis revelatio, secundum universalis Ecclesiæ fidem, a sanctâ Tridentinâ Synodo declaratam, continetur in libris scriptis et sine scripto traditionibus, quæ ipsius Christi ore ab Apostolis acceptæ, aut ab ipsis Apostolis Spiritu Sancto dictante quasi per manus traditæ, ad nos usque pervenerunt.† Qui quidem veteris et novi Testamenti libri integri cum omnibus suis partibus, prout in ejusdem Concilii decreto recensentur, et in veteri vulgatâ latinâ editione habentur, pro sacris et canonicis suscipiendi sunt. Eos vero Ecclesia pro sacris et canonicis habet, non ideo quod solâ humanâ industriâ concinnati, suâ deinde auctoritate sint approbati ; nec ideo dumtaxat, quod revelationem sine errore contineant; sed propterea quod Spiritu Sancto inspirante conscripti Deum habent auctorem, atque ut tales ipsi Ecclesiæ traditi sunt.

Quoniam verò, quæ sancta Tridentina Synodus de interpretatione divinæ Scripturæ ad coercenda petulantia ingenia salubriter decrevit, a quibusdam hominibus pravè exponuntur, Nos, idem decretum renovantes, hanc illius mentem esse declaramus, ut in rebus fidei et morum, ad ædificationem doctrinæ Christianæ, pertinentium, is pro vero sensu sacræ Scripturæ habendus sit, quem tenuit ac tenet Sancta Mater Ecclesia, cujus est judicare de vero sensu et interpretatione Scripturarum sanctarum ; atque ideo nemini licere contra hunc sensum, aut etiam contra unanimem consensum Patrum ipsam Scripturam sacram interpretari.

---

* 1 Cor. ii. 9.
† Concil. Trid. Sess. IV. de Can. Script.

CAPUT III.

DE FIDE.

Quum homo a Deo tanquam Creatore et Domino suo totus dependeat, et ratio creata increatæ Veritati penitùs subjecta sit, plenum revelanti Deo intellectùs et voluntatis obsequium fide præstare tenemur. Hanc vero fidem, quæ humanæ salutis initium est, Ecclesia catholica profitetur, virtutem esse supernaturalem, quâ, Dei aspirante et adjuvante gratiâ, ab eo revelata vera esse credimus, non propter intrinsecam rerum veritatem naturali rationis lumine perspectam, sed propter auctoritatem ipsius Dei revelantis, qui nec falli nec fallere potest. Est enim fides, testante Apostolo, sperandarum substantia rerum, argumentum non apparentium.*

Ut nihilominus fidei nostræ obsequium rationi consentaneum esset, voluit Deus cum internis Spiritûs Sancti auxiliis externa jungi revelationis suæ argumenta, facta scilicet divina, atque imprimis miracula et prophetias, quæ cum Dei omnipotentiam et infinitam scientiam luculenter commonstrent, divinæ revelationis signa sunt certissima et omnium intelligentiæ accommodata. Quare tum Moyses et Prophetæ, tum ipse maxime Christus Dominus multa et manifestissima miracula et prophetias ediderunt, et de Apostolis legimus: "Illi autem profecti prædicaverunt ubique, Domino cooperante, et sermonem confirmante, sequentibus signis."† Et rursum scriptum est: "Habemus firmiorem propheticum sermonem, cui bene facitis attendentes quasi lucernæ lucenti in caliginoso loco."‡

Licet autem fidei assensus nequaquam sit motus animi cæcus: nemo tamen evangelicæ prædicationi consentire

---

* Hebr. xi. 1.   † Marc. xvi. 20.
‡ 2 Petr. i. 19.

potest, sicut oportet ad salutem consequendam, absque illuminatione et inspiratione Spiritûs Sancti, qui dat omnibus suavitatem in consentiendo et credendo veritati.* Quare fides ipsa in se, etiamsi per charitatem non operetur, donum Dei est, et actus ejus est opus ad salutem pertinens, quo homo liberam praestat ipsi Deo obedientiam gratiae ejus, cui resistere posset, consentiendo et cooperando.

Porro fide divinâ et catholicâ ea omnia credenda sunt, quae in verbo Dei scripto vel tradito continentur, et ab Ecclesiâ sive solemni judicio sive ordinario et universali magisterio tamquam divinitùs revelata credenda proponuntur.

Quoniam vero sine fide impossibile est placere Deo, et ad filiorum ejus consortium pervenire ; ideo nemini unquam sine illâ contigit justificatio, nec ullus, nisi in eâ perseveraverit usque in finem, vitam aeternam assequetur. Ut autem officio veram fidem amplectendi, in eâque constanter perseverandi satisfacere possemus, Deus per Filium suum unigenitum Ecclesiam instituit, suaeque institutionis manifestis notis instruxit, ut ea tamquam custos et magistra verbi revelati ab omnibus posset agnosci. Ad solam enim catholicam Ecclesiam ea pertinent omnia, quae ad evidentem fidei christianae credibilitatem tam multa et tam mira divinitùs sunt disposita. Quin etiam Ecclesia per se ipsa, ob suam nempe admirabilem propagationem, eximiam sanctitatem et inexhaustam in omnibus bonis fœcunditatem, ob catholicam unitatem, invictamque stabilitatem, magnum quoddam et perpetuum est motivum credibilitatis et divinae suae legationis testimonium irrefragabile.

Quo fit, ut ipsa veluti signum levatum in nationes,† et ad se invitet, qui nondum crediderunt, et filios suos certiores faciat, firmissimo niti fundamento fidem, quam profitentur. Cui quidem testimonio efficax subsidium accedit ex supernâ virtute. Etenim benignissimus Dominus et errantes gratiâ

---

* Syn. Araus. ii. can. 7.　　　　† Isai. xl. 12.

suâ excitat atque adjuvat, ut ad agnitionem veritatis venire possint ; et eos, quos de tenebris transtulit in admirabile lumen suum, in hoc eodem lumine ut perseverent, gratiâ suâ confirmat, non deserens, nisi deseratur. Quocirca minime par est conditio eorum, qui per cœleste fidei donum catholicæ veritati adhæserunt, atque eorum, qui ducti opinionibus humanis, falsam religionem sectantur ; illi enim, qui fidem sub Ecclesiæ magisterio susceperunt, nullam unquam habere possunt justam causam mutandi, aut in dubium fidem eamden revocandi. Quæ cum ita sint, gratias agentes Deo Patri, qui dignos nos fecit in partem sortis sanctorum in lumine, tantam ne negligamus salutem, sed aspicientes in auctorem fidei et consummatorem Jesum, teneamus spei nostræ confessionem indeclinabilem.

CAPUT IV.

DE FIDE ET RATIONE.

Hoc quoque perpetuus Ecclesiæ catholicæ consensus tenuit et tenet, duplicem esse ordinem cognitionis, non solùm principio, sed objecto etiam distinctum : principio quidem, quia in altero naturali ratione, in altero fide divinâ cognoscimus ; objecto autem, quia præter ea, ad quæ naturalis ratio pertingere potest, credenda nobis proponuntur mysteria in Deo abscondita, quæ, nisi revelata divinitus, innotescere non possunt. Quocirca Apostolus, qui a gentibus Deum per ea, quæ facta sunt, cognitum esse testatur, disserens tamen de gratiâ et veritate, quæ per Jesum Christum facta est,* pronuntiat : "Loquimur Dei sapientiam in mysterio, quæ abscondita est, quam prædestinavit Deus ante sæcula in gloriam nostram, quam nemo principum

---

* Joan. 1. 17.

hujus sæculi cognovit : nobis autem revelavit Deus per Spiritum suum : Spiritus enim omnia scrutatur, etiam profunda Dei.* Et ipse Unigenitas confitetur Patri, quia abscondit hæc a sapientibus, et prudentibus, et revelavit ea parvulis.†

Ac ratio quidem, fide illustrata, cum sedulò, piè et sobriè quærit, aliquam, Deo dante, mysteriorum intelligentiam eamque fructuosissimam assequitur, tum ex eorum, quæ naturaliter cognoscit, analogià, tum e mysteriorum ipsorum nexu inter se et cum fine hominis ultimo; numquam tamen idonea redditur ad ea perspicienda instar veritatum, quæ proprium ipsius objectum constituunt. Divina enim mysteria suâpte naturâ intellectum creatum sic excedunt, ut etiam revelatione tradita et fide suscepta, ipsius tamen fidei velamine contecta et quâdam quasi caligine obvoluta maneant, quamdiu in hâc mortali vitâ peregrinamur a Domino: per fidem enim ambulamus, et non per speciem.‡

Verum etsi fides sit supra rationem, nulla tamen unquam inter fidem et rationem vera dissensio esse potest ; cum idem Deus, qui mysteria revelat et fidem infundit, animo humano rationis lumen indiderit ; Deus autem negare seipsum non possit, nec verum vero unquam contradicere. Inanis autem hujus contradictionis species inde potissimum oritur, quod vel fidei dogmata ad mentem Ecclesiæ intellecta et exposita non fuerint, vel opinionum commenta pro rationis effatis habeantur. Omnem igitur assertionem veritati illuminatæ fidei contrariam omnino falsam esse definimus.§ Porro Ecclesia, quæ una cum apostolico munere docendi, mandatum accepit, fidei depositum custodiendi, jus etiam et officium divinitùs habet falsi nominis scientiam proscribendi, ne quis decipiatur per philosophiam, et inanem fallaciam.‖ Quapropter omnes christiani fideles hujusmodi opiniones, quæ fidei doctrinæ contrariæ esse cognoscuntur,

---

* 1 Cor. ll. 7, 9.   † Matth. xi. 25.   ‡ 2 Cor. v. 7.
§ Concil. Lateran. V. Bulla *Apostolici regiminis.*   ‖ Coloss. ll. 8.

maxime si ab Ecclesiâ reprobatæ fuerint, non solum prohibentur tanquam legitimas scientiæ conclusiones defendere, sed pro erroribus potius, qui fallacem veritatis speciem præ se ferant, habere tenentur omnino.

Neque solùm fides et ratio inter se dissidere nunquam possunt, sed opem quoque sibi mutuam ferunt, cum recta ratio fidei fundamenta demonstret, ejusque lumine illustrata rerum divinarum scientiam excolat; fides vero rationem ab erroribus liberet ac tueatur, eamque multiplici cognitione instruat. Quapropter tantum abest, ut Ecclesia humanarum artium et disciplinarum culturæ obsistat, ut hanc multis modis juvet atque promoveat. Non enim commoda ab iis ad hominum vitam dimanantia aut ignorat aut despicit; fatetur imo, eas, quemadmodum a Deo, scientiarum Domino, profectæ sunt, ita si rite pertractentur, ad Deum, juvante ejus gratiâ, perducere. Nec sane ipsa vetat, ne hujusmodi disciplinæ in suo quæque ambitu propriis utantur principiis et propriâ methodo; sed justam hanc libertatem agnoscens, id sedulò cavet, ne divinæ doctrinæ repugnando errores in se suscipiant, aut fines proprios trangressæ, ea, quæ sunt fidei, occupent et perturbent.

Neque· enim fidei doctrina, quam Deus revelavit, velut philosophicum inventum proposita est humanis ingeniis perficienda, sed tanquam divinum depositum Christi Sponsæ tradita, fideliter custodiendo et infallibiliter declaranda. Hinc sacrorum quoque dogmatum is sensus perpetuo est retinendus, quem semel declaravit Sancta Mater Ecclesia, nec unquam ab eo sensu, altioris intelligentiæ specie et nomine, recedendum. Crescat igitur et multum vehementerque proficiat, tam singulorum, quam omnium, tam unius hominis, quam totius Ecclesiæ, ætatum ac sæculorum gradibus, intelligentia, scientia, sapientia: sed in suo dumtaxat genere, in eodem scilicet dogmate, eodem sensu, eâdemque sententiâ.*

---

* Vincent. Lirin. *Common.* n. 28.

CANONES.

I.

De Deo rerum omnium Creatore.

1. Si quis unum verum Deum visibilium et invisibilium Creatorum et Dominum negaverit; anathema sit.

2. Si quis præter materiam nihil esse affirmare non erubuerit; anathema sit.

3. Si quis dixerit, unam eamdemque esse Dei et rerum. omnium substantiam vel essentiam ; anathema sit.

4. Si quis dixerit, res finitas, tum corporeas tum spirituales, aut saltem spirituales, e divinâ substantiâ emanasse;

aut divinam essentiam sui manifestatione vel evolutione fieri omnia;

aut denique Deum esse ens universale seu indefinitum, quod sese determinando constituat rerum universitatem in genera, species et individua distinctam; anathema sit.

5. Si quis non confiteatur, mundum, resque omnes, quæ in eo continentur, et spirituales et materiales, secundum totam suam substantiam a Deo ex nihilo esse productas;

aut Deum dixerit non voluntate ab omni necessitate liberâ, sed tam necessario creasse, quam necessario amat seipsum;

aut mundum ad Dei gloriam conditum esse negaverit; anathema sit.

II.

De Revelatione.

1. Si quis dixerit, Deum unum et verum, Creatorem et Dominum nostrum, per ea, quæ facta sunt, naturali rationis humanæ lumine certo cognosci non posse; anathema sit.

2. Si quis dixerit, fieri non posse, aut non expedire, ut

per revelationem divinam homo de Deo, cultuque ei exhibendo edoceatur; anathema sit.

3. Si quis dixerit, hominem ad cognitionem et perfectionem, quæ naturalem superet, divinitùs evehi non posse, sed ex seipso ad omnis tandem veri et boni possessionem jugi profectu pertingere posse et debere; anathema sit.

4. Si quis sacræ Scripturæ libros integros cum omnibus suis partibus, prout illos sancta Tridentina Synodus recensuit, pro sacris et canonicis non susceperit, aut eos divinitùs inspiratos esse negaverit; anathema sit.

III.

De Fide.

1. Si quis dixerit, rationem humanam ita independentem esse, ut fides ei a Deo imperari non possit; anathema sit.

2. Si quis dixerit, fidem divinam a naturali de Deo et rebus moralibus scientiâ non distingui, ac propterea ad fidem divinam non requiri, ut revelata veritas propter auctoritatem Dei revelantis credatur; anathema sit.

3. Si quis dixerit, revelationem divinam externis signis credibilem fieri non posse, ideoque solâ internâ cujusque experientiâ aut inspiratione privatâ homines ad fidem moveri debere; anathema sit.

4. Si quis dixerit, miracula nulla fieri posse, proindeque omnes de iis narrationes, etiam in sacrâ Scripturâ contentas, inter fabulas vel mythos ablegandas esse: aut miracula certo cognosci numquam posse, nec iis divinam religionis christianæ originem ritè probari; anathema sit.

5. Si quis dixerit, assensum fidei christianæ non esse liberum, sed argumentis humanæ rationis necessario produci; aut ad solam fidem vivam, quæ per charitatem operatur, gratiam Dei necessariam esse; anathema sit.

6. Si quis dixerit, parem esse conditionem fidelium atque eorum, qui ad fidem unice veram nondum pervenerunt, ita

ut catholici justam causam habere possint, fidem, quam sub Ecclesiæ magisterio jam susceperunt, assensu suspenso in dubium vocandi, donec demonstrationem scientificam credibilitatis et veritatis fidei suæ absolverint; anathema sit.

IV.

De Fide et Ratione.

1. Si quis dixerit, in revelatione divinâ nulla vera et proprie dicta mysteria contineri, sed universa fidei dogmata posse per rationem rite excultam e naturalibus principiis intelligi et demonstrari; anathema sit.

2. Si quis dixerit, disciplinas humanas eâ cum libertate tractandas esse, ut earum assertiones, etsi doctrinæ revelatæ adversentur, tanquam veræ retineri, neque ab Ecclesiâ proscribi possint; anathema sit.

3. Si quis dixerit, fieri posse, ut dogmatibus ab Ecclesiâ propositis aliquando secundum progressum scientiæ sensus tribuendus sit alius ab eo, quem intellexit et intelligit Ecclesia; anathema sit.

Itaque supremi pastoralis Nostri officii debitum exequentes, omnes Christi fideles, maxime vere eos, qui præsunt vel docendi munere funguntur, per viscera Jesu Christi obtestamur, nec non ejusdem Dei et Salvatoris nostri auctoritate jubemus, ut ad hos errores a Sanctâ Ecclesiâ arcendos et eliminandos, atque purissimæ fidei lucem pandendam studium et operam conferant.

Quoniam vero satis non est, hæreticam pravitatem devitare, nisi ii quoque errores diligenter fugiantur, qui ad illam plus minusve accedunt; omnes officii monemus, servandi etiam Constitutiones et Decreta, quibus pravæ ejus-modi opiniones, quæ isthic diserte non enumerantur, ab hâc Sanctâ Sede proscriptæ et prohibitæ sunt.

Datum Romanæ in publicâ Sessione in Vaticanâ Basilicâ

solemniter celebratâ anno Incarnationis Dominicæ mille-
simo octingentesimo septuagesimo, die vigesimâ quartâ
Aprilis.

Pontificatûs Nostri anno vigesimo, quarto.

Ita est.

JOSEPHUS,
Episcopus S. Hippolyti,
Secretarius Concilii Vaticani.

DOGMATIC CONSTITUTION ON THE CATHOLIC FAITH.

PIUS, BISHOP, SERVANT OF THE SERVANTS OF GOD, WITH THE
APPROVAL OF THE SACRED COUNCIL, FOR PERPETUAL RE-
MEMBRANCE.

OUR LORD JESUS CHRIST, the Son of God, and Redeemer
of Mankind, before returning to his heavenly Father, promised that He would be with the Church Militant on earth
all days, even to the consummation of the world. Therefore, He has never ceased to be present with His beloved
Spouse, to assist her when teaching, to bless her when at
work, and to aid her when in danger. And this His salutary providence, which has been constantly displayed by
other innumerable benefits, has been most manifestly
proved by the abundant good results which Christendom
has derived from Œcumenical Councils, and particularly
from that of Trent, although it was held in evil times.
For, as a consequence, the sacred doctrines of the faith
have been defined more closely, and set forth more fully,
errors have been condemned and restrained, ecclesiatical

discipline has been restored and more firmly secured, the love of learning and of piety has been promoted among the clergy, colleges have been established to educate youth for the sacred warfare, and the morals of the Christian world have been renewed by the more accurate training of the faithful, and by the more frequent use of the sacraments. Moreover, there has resulted a closer communion of the members with the visible head, an increase of vigor in the whole mystical body of Christ, the multiplication of religious congregations and of other institutions of Christian piety, and such ardor in extending the kingdom of Christ throughout the world, as constantly endures, even to the sacrifice of life itself.

But while we recall with due thankfulness these and other signal benefits which the divine mercy has bestowed on the Church, especially by the last Œcumenical Council, we cannot restrain our bitter sorrow for the grave evils, which are principally due to the fact that the authority of that sacred Synod has been contemned, or its wise decrees neglected, by many.

No one is ignorant that the heresies proscribed by the Fathers of Trent, by which the divine magisterium of the Church was rejected, and all matters regarding religion were surrendered to the judgment of each individual, gradually became dissolved into many sects, which disagreed and contended with one another, until at length not a few lost all faith in Christ. Even the Holy Scriptures, which had previously been declared the sole source and judge of Christian doctrine, began to be held no longer as divine, but to be ranked among the fictions of mythology.

Then there arose, and too widely overspread the world, that doctrine of rationalism, or naturalism, which opposes itself in every way to the Christian religion as a supernatural institution, and works with the utmost zeal in order that, after Christ, our sole Lord and Saviour, has been excluded from the minds of men, and from the life and moral acts of nations, the reign of what they call pure reason or nature may be established. And after forsaking and rejecting the Christian religion, and denying the true God and His Christ, the minds of many have sunk into the abyss of Pantheism, Materialism, and Atheism, until, denying rational nature itself, and every sound rule of right, they labor to destroy the deepest foundations of human society.

Unhappily, it has yet further come to pass that, while this impiety prevailed on every side, many even of the children of the Catholic Church have strayed from the path of true piety, and by the gradual diminution of the truths they held, the Catholic sense became weakened in them. For, led away by various and strange doctrines, utterly confusing nature and grace, human science and divine faith, they are found to deprave the true sense of the doctrines which our Holy Mother Church holds and teaches, and endanger the integrity and the soundness of the faith.

Considering these things, how can the Church fail to be deeply stirred? For, even as God wills all men to be saved, and to arrive at the knowledge of the truth ; even as Christ came to save what had perished, and to gather together the children of God who had been dispersed, so the Church, constituted by God the mother and teacher of nations, knows its own office as debtor to all, and is ever ready and watchful to raise the fallen, to support those who are falling, to embrace those who return, to confirm the good and to carry them on to better things. Hence, it can never forbear from witnessing to and proclaiming the truth of God, which heals all things, knowing the words addressed to it : " My Spirit that is in thee, and my words that I have put in thy mouth, shall not depart out of thy mouth, from henceforth and forever " (Isaias lix. 21).

We, therefore, following the footsteps of our predecessors, have never ceased, as becomes our supreme Apostolic office, from teaching and defending Catholic truth, and condemning doctrines of error. And now, with the Bishops of the whole world assembled round us, and judging with us, congregated by our authority, and in the Holy Spirit, in this Œcumenical Council, we, supported by the Word of God written and handed down as we received it from the Catholic Church, preserved with sacredness and set forth according to truth,—have determined to profess and declare the salutary teaching of Christ from this Chair of Peter, and in sight of all, proscribing and condemning, by the power given to us of God, all errors contrary thereto.

CHAPTER I.

OF GOD, THE CREATOR OF ALL THINGS.

THE Holy Catholic Apostolic Roman Church believes and confesses that there is one true and living God, Creator and Lord of heaven and earth, Almighty, Eternal, Immense, Incomprehensible, Infinite in intelligence, in will, and in all perfection, who, as being one, sole, absolutely simple and immutable spiritual substance, is to be declared as really and essentially distinct from the world, of supreme beatitude in and from Himself, and ineffably exalted above all things which exist, or are conceivable, except Himself.

This one only true God, of His own goodness and almighty power, not for the increase or acquirement of His own happiness, but to manifest His perfection by the blessings which He bestows on creatures, and with absolute freedom of Counsel, created out of nothing, from the very first beginning of time, both the spiritual and the corporeal creature, to wit, the angelical and the mundane, and afterwards the human creature, as partaking, in a sense, of both, consisting of spirit and of body.

God protects and governs by His Providence all things

which He hath made, "reaching from end to end mightily,
and ordering all things sweetly" (Wisdom viii. 1). For
"all things are bare and open to His eyes" (Heb. iv. 13),
even those which are yet to be by the free action of creatures.

CHAPTER II.

OF REVELATION.

The same Holy Mother Church holds and teaches that
God, the beginning and end of all things, may be certainly
known by the natural light of human reason, by means of
created things; "for the invisible things of Him from the
creation of the world are clearly seen, being understood
by the things that are made" (Romans i. 20), but that it
pleased His wisdom and bounty to reveal Himself, and the
eternal decrees of His will, to mankind by another and a
supernatural way: as the Apostle says, "God, having spok-
en on divers occasions, and many ways, in times past, to
the fathers by the prophets; last of all, in these days, hath
spoken to us by His Son" (Hebrews i. 1, 2).

It is to be ascribed to this divine revelation, that such
truths among things divine as of themselves are not beyond human reason, can, even in the present condition of
mankind, be known by every one with facility, with firm
assurance, and with no admixture of error. This, however, is not the reason why revelation is to be called absolutely necessary; but because God of His infinite goodness
has ordained man to a supernatural end, viz., to be a
sharer of divine blessings which utterly exceed the intelligence of the human mind; for "eye hath not seen, nor
ear heard, neither hath it entered into the heart of man,
what things God hath prepared for them that love Him"
(1 Cor. ii. 9).

Further, this supernatural revelation, according to the universal belief of the Church, declared by the Sacred Synod of Trent, is contained in the written books and unwritten traditions which have come down to us, having been received by the Apostles from the mouth of Christ himself, or from the Apostles themselves, by the dictation of the Holy Spirit, have been transmitted, as it were, from hand to hand.* And these books of the Old and New Testament are to be received as sacred and canonical, in their integrity, with all their parts, as they are enumerated in the decree of the said Council, and are contained in the ancient Latin edition of the Vulgate. These the Church holds to be sacred and canonical, not because, having been carefully composed by mere human industry, they were afterwards approved by her authority, nor merely because they contain revelation, with no admixture of error, but because, having been written by the inspiration of the Holy Ghost, they have God for their author, and have been delivered as such to the Church herself.

And as the things which the Holy Synod of Trent decreed for the good of souls concerning the interpretation of Divine Scripture, in order to curb rebellious spirits, have been wrongly explained by some, We, renewing the said decree, declare this to be their sense, that, in matters of faith and morals, appertaining to the building up of Christian doctrine, that is to be held as the true sense of Holy Scripture which our Holy Mother Church hath held and holds, to whom it belongs to judge of the true sense and interpretation of the Holy Scripture; and therefore that it is permitted to no one to interpret the Sacred Scripture contrary to this sense, nor, likewise, contrary to the unanimous consent of the Fathers.

---

* Canons and Decrees of the Council of Trent, Session the Fourth. Decree concerning the Canonical Scriptures.

CHAPTER III.

ON FAITH.

Man being wholly dependent upon God, as upon his Creator and Lord, and created reason being absolutely subject to uncreated truth, we are bound to yield to God, by faith in His revelation, the full obedience of our intelligence and will. And the Catholic Church teaches that this faith, which is the beginning of man's salvation, is a supernatural virtue, whereby, inspired and assisted by the grace of God, we believe that the things which He has revealed are true ; not because of the intrinsic truth of the things, viewed by the natural light of reason, but because of the authority of God Himself who reveals them, and Who can neither be deceived nor deceive. For faith, as the Apostle testifies, is "the substance of things hoped for, the conviction of things that appear not" (Hebrews i. 11).

Nevertheless, in order that the obedience of our faith might be in harmony with reason, God willed that to the interior help of the Holy Spirit, there should be joined exterior proofs of His revelation; to wit, divine facts, and especially miracles and prophecies, which, as they manifestly display the omnipotence and infinite knowledge of God, are most certain proofs of His divine revelation, adapted to the intelligence of all men. Wherefore, both Moses and the Prophets, and most especially, Christ our Lord Himself, showed forth many and most evident miracles and prophecies; and of the Apostles we read: "But they going forth preached everywhere, the Lord working withal, and confirming the word with signs that followed" (Mark xvi. 20). And again, it is written: "We have the more firm prophetical word, whereunto you do well to attend, as to a light shining in a dark place" (2 St. Peter i. 19).

But though the assent of faith is by no means a blind action of the mind, still no man can assent to the Gospel teaching, as is necessary to obtain salvation, without the illumination and inspiration of the Holy Spirit, who gives to all men sweetness in assenting to and believing in the truth.* Wherefore, Faith itself, even when it does not work by charity, is in itself a gift of God, and the act of faith is a work appertaining to salvation, by which man yields voluntary obedience to God Himself, by assenting to and co-operating with His grace, which he is able to resist.

Further, all those things are to be believed with divine and Catholic faith which are contained in the word of God, written or handed down, and which the Church, either by a solemn judgment, or by her ordinary and universal magisterium, proposes for belief as having been divinely revealed.

And since, without faith, it is impossible to please God, and to attain to the fellowship of His children, therefore without faith no one has ever attained justification, nor will any one obtain eternal life, unless he shall have persevered in faith unto the end. And, that we may be able to satisfy the obligation of embracing the true faith and of constantly persevering in it, God has instituted the Church through His only begotten Son, and has bestowed on it manifest notes of that institution, that it may be recognized by all men as the guardian and teacher of the revealed Word; for to the Catholic Church alone belong all those many and admirable tokens which have been divinely established for the evident credibility of the Christian Faith. Nay, more, the Church by itself, with its marvellous extension, its eminent holiness, and its inhexhaustible fruitfulness in every good thing, with its Catholic unity and its

---

* Canons of the Second Council of Orange, confirmed by Pope Boniface II., A.D. 529, against the Semipelagians, can. vii. See Denzinger's *Enchiridion Symbolorum*, p. 50. Würzburg, 1854.

invincible stability, is a great and perpetual motive of credibility, and an irrefutable witness of its own divine mission.

And thus, like a standard set up unto the nations (Isaias xi. 12), it both invites to itself those who do not yet believe, and assures its children that the faith which they profess rests on the most firm foundation. And its testimony is efficaciously supported by a power from on high. For our most merciful Lord gives His grace to stir up and to aid those who are astray, that they may come to a knowledge of the truth; and to those whom He has brought out of darkness into His own admirable light He gives His grace to strengthen them to persevere in that light, deserting none who desert not Him. Therefore there is no parity between the condition of those who have adhered to the Catholic truth by the heavenly gift of faith, and of those who, led by human opinions, follow a false religion; for those who have received the faith under the magisterium of the Church can never have any just cause for changing or doubting that faith. Therefore, giving thanks to God the Father who has made us worthy to be partakers of the lot of the Saints in light, let us not neglect so great salvation, but with our eyes fixed on Jesus, the author and finisher of our Faith, let us hold fast the confession of our hope without wavering. (Hebr. xii. 2, and x. 23.)

CHAPTER IV.

OF FAITH AND REASON.

The Catholic Church, with one consent has also ever held and does hold that there is a two-fold order of knowledge distinct both in principle and also in object; in principle, because our knowledge in the one is by natural reason, and in the other by divine faith; in object, because, besides those things to which natural reason can attain, there are proposed to our belief mysteries hidden in God, which, unless divinely revealed, cannot be known. Wherefore the Apostle, who testifies that God is known by the gentiles through created things, still, when discoursing of the grace and truth which come by Jesus Christ (John i. 17) says : "We speak the wisdom of God in a mystery, a wisdom which is hidden, which God ordained before the world unto our glory; which none of the princes of this world knew . . . but to us God hath revealed them by His Spirit. For the Spirit searcheth all things, yea, the deep things of God " (1 Cor. ii. 7–9). And the only-begotten Son himself gives thanks to the Father, because He has hid these things from the wise and prudent, and has revealed them to little ones (Matt. xi. 25).

Reason, indeed, enlightened by faith, when it seeks earnestly, piously, and calmly, attains by a gift from God some, and that a very fruitful, understanding of mysteries; partly from the analogy of those things which it naturally knows, partly from the relations which the mysteries bear to one another and to the last end of man; but reason never becomes capable of apprehending mysteries as it does those truths which constitute its proper object. For the divine mysteries by their own nature so far transcend the created intelligence that, even when delivered by revelation and received by faith, they remain covered with the veil of faith itself, and shrouded in a certain degree of darkness, so long as we are pilgrims in this mortal life, not yet with God; "for we walk by faith and not by sight" (2 Cor. v. 7).

But although faith is above reason, there can never be any real discrepancy between faith and reason, since the same God who reveals mysteries and infuses faith has bestowed the light of reason on the human mind, and God cannot deny Himself, nor can truth ever contradict truth.

The false appearance of such a contradiction is mainly due, either to the dogmas of faith not having been understood and expounded according to the mind of the Church, or to the inventions of opinion having been taken for the verdicts of reason. We define, therefore, that every assertion contrary to a truth of enlightened faith is utterly false.* Further, the Church, which, together with the Apostolic office of teaching, has received a charge to guard the deposit of faith, derives from God the right and the duty of proscribing false science, lest any should be deceived by philosophy and vain fallacy (Coloss. ii. 8). Therefore all faithful Christians are not only forbidden to defend, as legitimate conclusions of science, such opinions as are known to be contrary to the doctrines of faith, especially if they have been condemned by the Church, but are altogether bound to account them as errors which put on the fallacious appearance of truth.

And not only can faith and reason never be opposed to one another, but they are of mutual aid one to the other; for right reason demonstrates the foundations of faith, and enlightened by its light, cultivates the science of things divine; while faith frees and guards reason from errors, and furnishes it with manifold knowledge. So far, therefore, is the Church from opposing the cultivation of human arts and sciences, that it in many ways helps and promotes it. For the Church neither ignores nor despises the benefits of human life which result from the arts and sciences, but confesses that, as they came from God, the Lord of all science, so, if they be rightly used, they lead to God by the help of His grace. Nor does the Church forbid that each of these sciences in its sphere should make use of its own principles and its own method; but, while recognizing this just liberty, it stands watchfully on guard, lest sciences,

---

* From the Bull of Pope Leo X., *Apostolici regiminis*, read in the VIII. Session of the Fifth Lateran Council, A.D. 1513. See Labbe's Councils, vol. xix. p. 842. Venice, 1732.

setting themselves against the divine teaching, or transgressing their own limits, should invade and disturb the domain of faith.

For the doctrine of faith which God hath revealed has not been proposed, like a philosophical invention, to be perfected by human ingenuity, but has been delivered as a divine deposit to the Spouse of Christ, to be faithfully kept and infallibly declared. Hence also, that meaning of the sacred dogmas is perpetually to be retained which our Holy Mother the Church has once declared; nor is that meaning ever to be departed from, under the pretence or pretext of a deeper comprehension of them. Let, then, the intelligence, science, and wisdom of each and all, of individuals and of the whole Church, in all ages and all times, increase and flourish in abundance and vigor; but simply in its own proper kind, that is to say, in one and the same doctrine, one and the same sense, one and the same judgment (Vincent. of Lerins, *Common.* n. 28).

CANONS.

I.

Of God, the Creator of all things.

1. If any one shall deny One true God, Creator and Lord of things visible and invisible; let him be anathema.

2. If any one shall not be ashamed to affirm that, except matter, nothing exists; let him be anathema.

3. If any one shall say that the substance and essence of God and of all things is one and the same; let him be anathema.

4. If any one shall say that finite things, both corporeal and spiritual, or at least spiritual, have emanated from the divine substance; or that the divine essence by the mani-

festation and evolution of itself becomes all things; or, lastly, that God is universal or indefinite being, which by determining itself constitutes the universality of things, distinct according to genera, species and individuals; let him be anathema.

5. If any one confess not that the world, and all things which are contained in it, both spiritual and material, have been, in their whole substance, produced by God out of nothing; or shall say that God created, not by His will, free from all necessity, but by a necessity equal to the necessity whereby He loves Himself; or shall deny that the world was made for the glory of God; let him be anathema.

II.

Of Revelation.

1. If any one shall say that the One true God, our Creator and Lord, cannot be certainly known by the natural light of human reason through created things; let him be anathema.

2. If any one shall say that it is impossible or inexpedient that man should be taught, by divine revelation, concerning God and the worship to be paid to Him; let him be anathema.

3. If any one shall say that man cannot be raised by divine power to a higher than natural knowledge and perfection, but can and ought, by a continuous progress, to arrive at length, of himself, to the possession of all that is true and good; let him be anathema.

4. If any one shall not receive as sacred and canonical the Books of Holy Scripture, entire with all their parts, as the Holy Synod of Trent has enumerated them, or shall deny that they have been divinely inspired; let him be anathema

III.

Of Faith.

1. If any one shall say that human reason is so independent that faith cannot be enjoined upon it by God; let him be anathema.

2. If any one shall say that divine faith is not distinguished from natural knowledge of God and of moral truths, and therefore that it is not requisite for divine faith that revealed truth be believed because of the authority of God, Who reveals it ; let him be anathema.

3. If any one shall say that divine revelation cannot be made credible by outward signs, and therefore that men ought to be moved to faith solely by the internal experience of each, or by private inspiration ; let him be anathema.

4. If any one shall say that miracles are impossible, and therefore that all the accounts regarding them, even those contained in Holy Scripture, are to be dismissed as fabulous or mythical ; or that miracles can never be known with certainty, and that the divine origin of Christianity cannot be proved by them ; let him be anathema.

5. If any one shall say that the assent of Christian faith is not a free act, but inevitably produced by the arguments of human reason ; or that the grace of God is necessary for that living faith only which worketh by charity; let him be anathema.

6. If any one shall say that the condition of the faithful, and of those who have not yet attained to the only true faith, is on a par, so that Catholics may have just cause for doubting, with suspended assent, the faith which they have already received under the magisterium of the Church, until they shall have obtained a scientific demonstration of the credibility and truth of their faith ; let him be anathema.

IV.

Of Faith and Reason.

1. If any one shall say that in divine revelation there are no mysteries, truly and properly so called, but that all the doctrines of faith can be understood and demonstrated from natural principles, by properly cultivated reason ; let him be anathema.

2. If any one shall say that human sciences are to be so freely treated, that their assertions, although opposed to revealed doctrine, are to be held as true, and cannot be condemned by the Church ; let him be anathema.

3. If any one shall assert it to be possible that sometimes, according to the progress of science, a sense is to be given to doctrines propounded by the Church different from that which the Church has understood and understands ; let him be anathema.

Therefore We, fulfilling the duty of our supreme pastoral office, entreat, by the mercies of Jesus Christ, and, by the authority of the same our God and Saviour, We command, all the faithful of Christ, and especially those who are set over others, or are charged with the office of instruction, that they earnestly and diligently apply themselves to ward off, and eliminate, these errors from Holy Church, and to spread the light of pure faith.

And since it is not sufficient to shun heretical pravity, unless those errors also be diligently avoided which more or less nearly approach it, We admonish all men of the further duty of observing those constitutions and decrees by which such erroneous opinions as are not here specifically enumerated, have been proscribed and condemned by this Holy See.

Given at Rome in public Session solemnly held in the Vatican Basilica in the year of our Lord, one thousand

eight hundred and seventy, on the twenty-fourth day of
April, in the twenty-fourth year of our Pontificate.

In conformity with the original.

JOSEPH, *Bishop of S. Polten,*
Secretary of the Vatican Council.

TEXT OF THE CONSTITUTIONS

CONSTITVTIO DOGMATICA PRIMA DE ECCLESIA CHRISTI.

PIVS EPISCOPVS SERVVS SERVORVM DEI SACRO APPROBANTE
CONCILIO AD PERPETVAM REI MEMORIAM.

PASTOR aeternus et episcopus animarum nostrarum, ut
salutiferum redemptionis opus perenne redderet, sanctam
aedificare Ecclesiam decrevit, in qua veluti in domo Dei
viventis fideles omnes unius fidei et charitatis vinculo con-
tinerentur. Quapropter, priusquam clarificaretur, rogavit
Patrem non pro Apostolis tantum, sed et pro eis, qui cre-
dituri erant per verbum eorum in ipsum, ut omnes unum
essent, sicut ipse Filius et Pater unum sunt. Quemadmodum igitur Apostolos, quos sibi de mundo elegerat,
misit sicut ipse missus erat a Patre: ita in Ecclesia sua
Pastores et Doctores usque ad consummationem saeculi
esse voluit. Ut vero episcopatus ipse unus et indivisus
esset, et per cohaerentes sibi invicem sacerdotes credentium
multitudo universa in fidei et communionis unitate conservaretur, beatum Petrum caeteris Apostolis praeponens in
ipso instituit perpetuum utriusque unitatis principium ac

visibile fundamentum, super cuius fortitudinem aeternum exstrueretur templum, et Ecclesiae coelo inferenda sublimitas in huius fidei firmitate consurgeret.* Et quoniam portae inferi ad evertendam, si fieri posset, Ecclesiam contra eius fundamentum divinitus positum maiori in dies odio undique insurgunt ; Nos ad catholici gregis custodiam, incolumitatem, augmentum, necessarium esse iudicamus, sacro approbante Concilio, doctrinam de institutione, perpetuitate, ac natura sacri Apostolici primatus, in quo totius Ecclesiae vis ac soliditas consistit, cunctis fidelibus credendam et tenendam, secundum antiquam atque constantem universalis Ecclesiae fidem, proponere, atque contrarios, dominico gregi adeo perniciosos errores proscribere et condemnare.

CAPUT I.

DE APOSTOLICI PRIMATUS IN BEATO PETRO INSTITUTIONE.

Docemus itaque et declaramus, iuxta Evangelii testimonia, primatum iurisdictionis in universam Dei Ecclesiam immediate et directe beato Petro Apostolo promissum atque collatum a Christo Domino fuisse. Unum enim Simonem, cui iam pridem dixerat : Tu vocaberis Cephas.† postquam ille suam edidit confessionem inquiens : Tu es Christus, Filius Dei vivi, solemnibus his verbis allocutus est Dominus : Beatus es Simon Bar-Iona : quia caro et sanguis non revelavit tibi, sed Pater meus, qui in coelis est : et ego dico tibi, quia tu es Petrus, et super hanc petram aedificabo Ecclesiam meam, et portae inferi non praevalebunt adversus eam : et tibi dabo claves regni coelorum : et quodcumque ligaveris super terram, erit ligatum

---

* S. Leo M. Serm. iv. (al. iii.) cap. 2, in diem Natalis sui.
† Ioan. i. 42.

et in coelis: et quodcumque solveris super terram, erit
solutum et in coelis.* Atque uni Simoni Petro contulit
Iesus post suam resurrectionem summi pastoris et rectoris
iurisdictionem in totum suum ovile, dicens : Pasce agnos
meos : Pasce oves meas.† Huic tam manifestae sacrarum
Scripturarum doctrinae, ut ab Ecclesia catholica semper
intellecta est, aperte opponuntur pravae eorum sententiae,
qui constitutam a Christo Domino in sua Ecclesia regiminis
formam pervertentes negant, solum Petrum prae caeteris
Apostolis, sive seorsum singulis sive omnibus simul, vero
proprioque iurisdictionis primatu fuisse a Christo instruc-
tum ; aut qui affirmant, eundem primatum non immediate,
directeque ipsi beato Petro, sed Ecclesiae, et per hanc illi
ut ipsius Ecclesiae ministro delatum fuisse.

Si quis igitur dixerit, beatum Petrum Apostolum non
esse a Christo Domino constitutum Apostolorum omnium
principem et totius Ecclesiae militantis visibile caput ; vel
eundem honoris tantum, non autem verae propriaeque
iurisdictionis primatum ab eodem Domino nostro Iesu
Christo directe et immediate accepisse ; anathema sit.

CAPUT II.

DE PERPETUITATE PRIMATUS BEATI PETRI IN ROMANIS PONTIFICIBUS.

Quod autem in beato Apostolo Petro princeps pastorum
et pastor magnus ovium Dominus Christus Iesus in perpetuam salutem ac perenne bonum Ecclesiae instituit, id
eodem auctore in Ecclesiae, quae fundata super petram ad
finem saeculorum usque firma stabit, iugiter durare necesse
est. Nulli sane dubium, imo saeculis omnibus notum est,

---

* Matth. xvi. 16-19   † Ioan. xxi. 15-17.

quod sanctus beatissimusque Petrus, Apostolorum princeps
et caput, fideique columna et Ecclesiae catholicae fundamentum, a Domino nostro Iesu Christo,·Salvatore humani
generis ac Redemptore, claves regni accepit: qui ad hoc
usque tempus et semper in suis successoribus, episcopis
sanctae Romanae Sedis, ab ipso fundatae, eiusque conse-
cratae sanguine, vivet et praesidet et iudicium exercet.*
Unde quicumque in hac cathedra Petro succedit, is secundum Christi ipsius institutionem primatum Petri in universam Ecclesium obtinet. Manet ergo dispositio veritatis, et
beatus Petrus in accepta fortitudine petraea perseverans
suscepta Ecclesiae gubernacula non reliquit.† Hac de
causa ad Romanam Ecclesiam propter potentiorem princi-
palitatem necesse semper fuit omnem convenire Ecclesiam,
hoc est, eos, qui sunt undique fideles, ut in ea Sede, e qua
venerandae communionis iura in omnes dimanant, tamquam membra in capite consociata, in unam corporis
compagem coalescerent.‡

Si quis ergo dixerit, non esse ex ipsius Christi Domini
institutione seu iure divino, ut beatus Petrus in primatu
super universam Ecclesiam habeat perpetuos successores;
aut Romanum Pontificem non esse beati Petri in eodem
primatu successorem; anathema sit.

CAPUT III.

DE VI ET RATIONE PRIMATUS ROMANI PONTIFICIS.

Quapropter apertis innixi sacrarum litterarum testimoniis, et inhaerentes tum Praedecessorum Nostrorum, Ro-

---

* Cf. Ephesini Concilii Act. iii.
† S. Leo M. Serm. iii. (al. ii.) cap. 3.
‡ S. Iren Adv. Haer. l. iii. c. 3, et Conc. Aquilei. a. 381. inter epp. S.
Ambros. ep. xi.

manorum Pontificum, tum Conciliorum generalium disertis, perspicuisque decretis, innovamus oecumenici Concilii Florentini definitionem, qua credendum ab omnibus Christi fidelibus est, sanctam Apostolicam Sedem, et Romanum Pontificem in universum orbem tenere primatum, et ipsum Pontificem Romanum successorem esse beati Petri Principis Apostolorum, et verum Christi Vicarium, totiusque Ecclesiae caput, et omnium Christianorum patrem ac doctorem existere ; et ipsi in beato Petro pascendi, regendi ac gubernandi universalem Ecclesiam a Domino nostro Iesu Christo plenam potestatem traditam esse ; quemadmodum etiam in gestis oecumenicorum· Conciliorum et in sacris canonibus continetur.

Docemus proinde et declaramus, Ecclesiam Romanam disponente Domino super omnes alias ordinariae potestatis obtinere principatum, et hanc Romani Pontificis iurisdictionis potestatem, quae vere episcopalis est, immediatam esse : erga quam cuiuscumque ritus et dignitatis pastores atque fideles, tam seorsum singuli quam simul omnes, officio hierarchicae subordinationis, veraeque obedientiae obstringuntur, non solum in rebus, quae ad fidem et mores, sed etiam in iis, quae ad disciplinam et regimen Ecclesiae per totum orbem diffusae pertinent ; ita ut custodita cum Romano Pontifice tam communionis, quam eiusdem fidei professionis unitate, Ecclesia Christi sit unus grex sub uno summo pastore. Haec est catholicae veritatis doctrina, a qua deviare salva fide atque salute nemo potest.

Tantum autem abest, ut haec Summi Pontificis potestas officiat ordinariae ac immediatae illi episcopalis iurisdictionis potestati, qua Episcopi, qui positi a Spiritu Sancto in Apostolorum locum successerunt, tamquam veri pastores assignatos sibi greges, singuli singulos, pascunt et regunt, ut eadem a supremo et universali Pastore asseratur, roboretur ac vindicetur, secundum illud sancti Gregorii Magni : Meus honor est honor universalis Ecclesiae. Meus honor est fratrum meorum solidus vigor. Tum ego vere

10*

honoratus sum, cum singulis quibusque honor debitus non negatur.*

Porro ex suprema illa Romani Pontificis protestate gubernandi universam Ecclesiam ius eidem esse consequitur, in huius sui muneris exercitio libere communicandi cum pastoribus et gregibus totius Ecclesiae, ut iidem ab ipso in via salutus doceri ac regi possint. Quare damnamus ac reprobamus illorum sententias, qui hanc supremi capitis cum pastoribus et gregibus communicationem licite impediri posse dicunt, aut eandem reddunt saeculari potestati obnoxiam, ita ut contendant, quae ab Apostolica Sede vel eius auctoritate ad regimen Ecclesiae constituuntur, vim ac valorem non habere, nisi potestatis saecularis placito confirmentur.

Et quoniam divino Apostolici primatus iure Romanus Pontifex universae Ecclesiae praeest, docemus etiam et declaramus, eum esse iudicem supremum fidelium,† et in omnibus causis ad examen ecclesiasticum spectantibus ad ipsius posse iudicium recurri; ‡ Sedis vero Apostolicae, cuius auctoritate maior non est, iudicium a nemine fore retractandum, neque cuiquam de eius licere iudicare iudicio.§ Quare a recto veritatis tramite aberrant, qui affirmant, licere ab iudiciis Romanorum Pontificum ad Oecumenicum Concilium tamquam ad auctoritatem Romano Pontifice superiorem appellare.

Si quis itaque dixerit, Romanum Pontificem habere tantummodo officium inspectionis vel directionis, non autem plenam et supremam potestatem iurisdictionis in universam Ecclesiam, non solum in rebus, quae ad fidem et mores, sed etiam in iis, quae ad disciplinam et regimen Ecclesiae per totum orbem diffusae pertinent ; aut eum habere tantum potiores partes, non vero totam plenitudinem huius su-

---

* Ep. ad. Eulog. Alexandrin. 1. viii. ep. xxx.
† Pii PP. VI. Breve, Super soliditate. d. 28 Nov. 1786.
‡ Concil. Oecum. Lugdun. II.
§ Ep. Nicolai I. ad Michaelem Imperatorem.

premae potestatis; aut hanc eius potestatem non esse
ordinariam et immediatam sive in omnes ac singulas
ecclesias, sive in omnes et singulos pastores et fideles ; anathema sit.

CAPUT IV.

DE ROMANI PONTIFICIS INFALLIBILI MAGISTERIO.

Ipso autem Apostolico primatu, quem Romanus Pontifex
tamquam Petri principis Apostolorum successor in universam Ecclesiam obtinet, supremam quoque magisterii potestatem comprehendi, haec Sancta Sedes semper tenuit,
perpetuus Ecclesiae usus comprobat, ipsaque oecumenica
Concilia, ea imprimis, in quibus Oriens cum Occidente in
fidei charitatisque unionem conveniebat, declaraverunt.
Patres enim Concilii Constantinopolitani quarti, maiorum
vestigiis inhaerentes, hanc solemnem ediderunt professionem : Prima salus est, rectae fidei regulam custodire.
Et quia non potest Domini nostri Iesu Christi praeter-
mitti sententia dicentis : Tu es Petrus, et super hanc petram
aedificabo Ecclesiam meam, haec, quae dicta sunt, rerum
probantur effectibus, quia in Sede Apostolica immaculata
est semper catholica reservato religio, et sancta celebrata
doctrina. Ab huius ergo fide et doctrina separari minime
cupientes, speramus, ut in una cummunione, quam Sedes
Apostolica praedicat, esse mereamur, in qua est integra et
vera Christianae religionis soliditas.* Approbante vero
Lugdunensi Concilio secundo, Graeci professi sunt : Sanctam Romanam Ecclesiam summum et plenum primatum et
principatum super universam Ecclesiam catholicam obtinere,
quem se ab ipso Domino in beato Petro Apostolorum

---

* Ex formula S. Hormisdae Papae, prout ab Hadriano II. Patribus
Concilii Oecumenici VIII., Constantinopolitani IV., proposita et ab
iisdem subscripta est.

principe sive vertice, cuius Romanus Pontifex est successor, cum potestatis plenitudine recepisse veraciter et humiliter recognoscit ; et sicut prae caeteris tenetur fidei veritatem defendere, sic et, si quae de fide subortae fuerint quaestiones, suo debent iudicio definiri. Florentinum denique Concilium definivit: Pontificem Romanum, verum Christi Vicarium, totiusque Ecclesiae caput et omnium Christianorum patrem ac doctorum existere ; et ipsi in beato Petro pascendi, regendi ac gubernandi universalem Ecclesiam a Domino nostro Jesu Christo plenam potestatem traditam esse.

Huic pastorali muneri ut satisfacerent, Praedecessores Nostri indefessam semper operam dederunt, ut salutaris Christi doctrina apud omnes terrae populus propagaretur, parique cura vigilarunt, ut, ubi recepta esset, sincera et pura conservaretur. Quocirca totius orbis Antistites nunc singuli, nunc in Synodis congregati, longam ecclesiarum consuetudinem et antiquae regulae formam sequentes, ea praesertim pericula, quae in negotiis fidei emergebant ad hanc Sedem Apostolicam retulerunt, ut ibi potissimum resarcirentur damna fidei, ubi fides non potest sentire defectum.* Romani autem Pontifices, prout temporum et rerum conditio suadebat, nunc convocatis oecumenicis Conciliis aut explorata Ecclesiae per orbem dispersae sententia, nunc per Synodos particulares, nunc aliis, quae divina suppeditabat providentia, adhibitis auxiliis, ea tenenda definiverunt, quae sacris Scripturis et apostolicis Traditionibus consentanea Deo adiutore cognoverant. Neque enim Petri successoribus Spiritus Sanctus promissus est, ut eo revelante novam doctrinam patefacerent, sed ut eo assistente traditam per Apostolos revelationem seu fidei depositum sancte custodirent et fideliter exponerent. Quorum quidem apostolicam doctrinam omnes venerabiles Patres amplexi et sancti Doctores orthodoxi venerati atque secuti sunt ;

---

* Cf. S. Bern. Epist. exc.

plenissime scientes, hanc sancti Petri Sedem ab omni
semper errore illibatam permanere, secundum Domini
Salvatoris nostri divinam pollicitationem discipulorum
suorum principi factam : Ego rogavi pro te, ut non deficiat
fides tua, et tu aliquando conversus confirma fratres tuos.

Hoc igitur veritatis et fidei numquam deficientis charisma Petro eiusque in hac Cathedra successoribus divinitus
collatum est, ut excelso suo munere in omnium salutem
fungerentur, ut universus Christi grex per eos ab erroris
venenosa esca aversus, coelestis doctrinae pabulo nutrire-
tur, ut sublata schismatis occasione Ecclesia tota una conservaretur, atque suo fundamento innixa firma adversus
inferi portas consisteret.

Atvero cum hac ipsa aetate, qua salutifera Apostolici
muneris efficacia vel maxime requiritur, non pauci invenian-
tur, qui illius auctoritati obtrectant ; necessarium omnino
esse censemus, praerogativam, quam unigenitus Dei Filius
cum summo pastorali officio coniungere dignatus est,
solemniter asserere.

Itaque Nos traditioni a fidei Christianae exordio per-
ceptae fideliter inhaerendo, ad Dei Salvatoris nostri gloriam,
religionis Catholicae exaltationem et Christianorum populorum salutem, sacro approbante Concilio, docemus et
divinitus revelatum dogma esse definimus ; Romanum
Pontificem, cum ex Cathedra loquitur, id est, cum omnium
Christianorum Pastoris et Doctoris munere fungens, pro
suprema sua Apostolica auctoritate doctrinam de fide vel
moribus ab universa Ecclesia tenendam. definit, per assis-
tentiam divinam, ipsi in beato Petro promissam, ea infallibilitate pollere, qua divinus Redemptor Ecclesiam suam
in definienda doctrina de fide vel moribus instructam esse
voluit ; ideoque eiusmodi Romani Pontificis definitiones ex
sese, non autem ex consensu Ecclesiae irreformabiles esse.

Si quis autem huic Nostrae definitioni contradicere, quod
Deus avertat, praesumpserit ; anathema sit.

Datum Romae, in publica Sessione in Vaticana Basilica

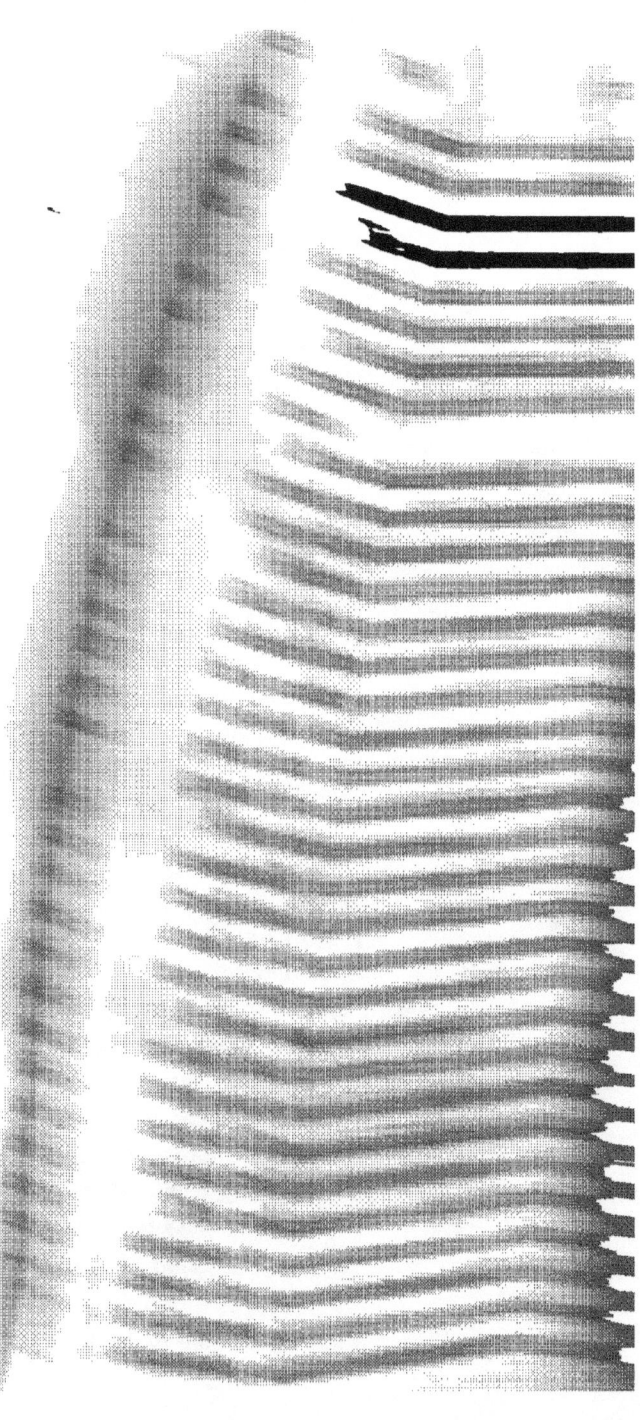

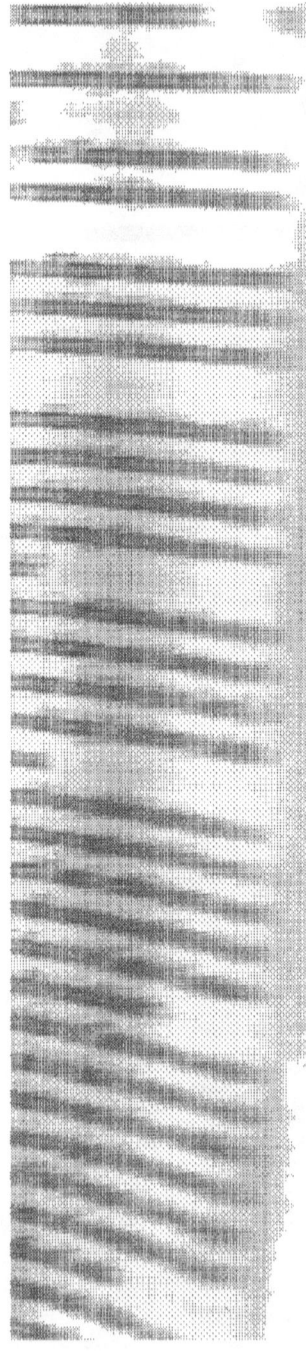

…ancti Petri Sedem **ab omni**
…armanere, secundum Domini
…pollicitationem **discipulorum**
…o rogavi pro te, **ut non deficiat**
…onversus confirma **fratres tuos.**
…ei numquam deficientis **charis-**
…athedra successoribus **divinitus**
…o munere in omnium **salutem**
Christi grex per **eos ab erroris**
…lestis doctrinae **pabulo nutriro-**
…ccasione Ecclesia **tota una con-**
…amento innixa **firma adversus**

…aetate, qua salutifera **Apostolici**
…ne requiritur, non **pauci invenian-**
…obtrectant; necessarium **omnino**
…vam, quam unigenitus **Dei Filius**
…officio coniungere **dignatus est,**

…a fidei Christianae **exordio per-**
…io, ad Dei Salvatoris **nostri gloriam,**
…ltationem et Christianorum **pop-**
…approbante Conciolio, docemus et
…ogma esse definimus; **Romanum**
…hedra loquitur, id est, **cum omnium**
…a et Doctoris munere **fungens,** pro
…a auctoritate doctrinam de fide vel
…cclesia tenendam definit, per omnin
…in beato Petro promissam, ea in-
…a divinus Redemptor Ecclesiam suam
…de fide vel moribus instructam omni
…odi Romani Pontificis definitionem ex
…onsensu Ecclesiae irreformabiles ess.
…Nostrae definitioni contradicere, quod
…mpserit; anathema sit.
…publica Sessione in Vaticana Basilica

solemniter celebrata anno Incarnationis Dominicae mille-
simo octingentesimo septuagesimo, die decima octava Iulii.
Pontificatus Nostri anno vigesimo quinto.

Ita est.

JOSEPHUS,
Episcopus S. Ippolyti,
Secretarius Concilii Vaticani.

TRANSLATION.

FIRST DOGMATIC CONSTITUTION ON THE CHURCH OF CHRIST.

PUBLISHED IN THE FOURTH SESSION OF THE HOLY ŒCUMENICAL
COUNCIL OF THE VATICAN.

PIUS BISHOP, SERVANT OF THE SERVANTS OF GOD, WITH
THE APPROVAL OF THE SACRED COUNCIL, FOR AN
EVERLASTING REMEMBRANCE.

THE Eternal Pastor and Bishop of our souls, in order to
continue for all time the life-giving work of His Redemp-
tion, determined to build up the Holy Church, wherein, as
in the House of the living God, all who believe might be
united in the bond of one faith and one charity. Wherefore, before he entered into His glory, He prayed unto the
Father, not for the apostles only, but for those also who
through their preaching should come to believe in Him,
that all might be one even as He the Son and the Father
are one.* As then He sent the Apostles whom He had
chosen to Himself from the world, as he Himself had been
sent by the Father: so He willed that there should ever
be pastors and teachers in His Church to the end of the

---

* St. John, xvii. 21.

world. And in order that the Episcopate also might be one and undivided, and that by means of a closely united priesthood the multitude of the faithful might be kept secure in the oneness of faith and communion, He set Blessed Peter over the rest of the Apostles, and fixed in him the abiding principle of this two-fold unity, and its visible foundation, in the strength of which the everlasting temple should arise and the Church in the firmness of that faith should lift her majestic front to Heaven.* And seeing that the gates of hell with daily increase of hatred are gathering their strength on every side to upheave the foundation laid by God's own hand, and so, if that might be, to overthrow the Church : We, therefore, for the preservation, safe-keeping, and increase of the Catholic flock, with the approval of the Sacred Council, do judge it to be necessary to propose to the belief and acceptance of all the faithful, in accordance with the ancient and constant faith of the universal Church, the doctrine touching the institution, perpetuity, and nature of the sacred Apostolic Primacy, in which is found the strength and solidity of the entire Church, and at the same time to proscribe and condemn the contrary errors, so hurtful to the flock of Christ.

CHAPTER I.

OF THE INSTITUTION OF THE APOSTOLIC PRIMACY IN BLESSED PETER.

We therefore teach and declare that, according to the testimony of the Gospel, the primacy of jurisdiction over the universal Church of God was immediately and directly promised and given to Blessed Peter the Apostle by Christ the Lord. For it was to Simon alone, to whom he had al-

---

* From Sermon iv. chap. ii. of St. Leo the Great, A. D. 440, vol. I. p. 17 of edition of Ballerini, Venice, 1753 ; read in the eighth lection on the Feast of St. Peter's Chair at Antioch, February 22.

ready said : Thou shalt be called Cephas,* that the Lord
after the confession made by him, saying : Thou art the
Christ, the Son of the living God, addressed these solemn
words : Blessed art thou, Simon Bar-Jona, because flesh
and blood have not revealed it to thee, but my Father who
is in Heaven. And I say to thee that thou art Peter ; and
upon this rock I will build my Church, and the gates of
hell shall not prevail against it. And I will give to thee
the keys of the kingdom of Heaven. And whatsoever thou
shalt bind upon earth, it shall be bound also in Heaven,
and whatsoever thou shalt loose on earth, it shall be
loosed also in heaven.† And it was upon Simon alone
that Jesus after his resurrection bestowed the jurisdiction
of Chief Pastor and Ruler over all His fold in the words :
Feed my lambs: feed my sheep.‡ At open variance with
this clear doctrine of Holy Scripture as it has been ever understood by the Catholic Church are the perverse opinions
of those who, while they distort the form of government
established by Christ the Lord in His Church, deny that
Peter in his single person, preferably to all the other Apostles, whether taken separately or together, was endowed
by Christ with a true and proper primacy of jurisdiction ;
or of those who assert that the same primacy was not bestowed immediately and directly upon Blessed Peter himself, but upon the Church, and through the Church on
Peter as her Minister.

If any one, therefore, shall say that Blessed Peter the
Apostle was not appointed the Prince of all the Apostles
and the visible Head of the whole Church Militant ; or
that the same directly and immediately received from the
same Our Lord Jesus Christ a primacy of honor only, and
not of true and proper jurisdiction ; let him be anathema.

---

* St. John i. 42,   † St. Matthew xvi. 16–19.   ‡ St. John xxi. 15–17

CHAPTER II.

That which the Prince of Shepherds and great Shepherd
of the sheep, Jesus Christ our Lord, established in the
person of the Blessed Apostle Peter to secure the perpetual welfare and lasting good of the Church, must, by the
same institution, necessarily remain unceasingly in the
Church; which, being founded upon the Rock, will stand
firm to the end of the world. For none can doubt, and it
is known to all ages, that the holy and Blessed Peter, the
Prince and Chief of the Apostles, the pillar of the faith
and foundation of the Catholic Church, received the keys
of the kingdom from Our Lord Jesus Christ, the Saviour
and Redeemer of mankind, and lives, presides, and judges,
to this day and always, in his successors the Bishops of the
Holy See of Rome, which was founded by him, and conse-
crated by his blood.* Whence, whosoever succeeds to
Peter in this See, does by the institution of Christ Himself
obtain the Primacy of Peter over the whole Church. The
disposition made by Incarnate Truth therefore remains,
and Blessed Peter, abiding through the strength of the
Rock in the power that he received, has not abandoned
the direction of the Church.† Wherefore it has at all
times been necessary that every particular Church—that is
to say, the faithful throughout the world—should agree
with the Roman Church, on account of the greater authority of the princedom which this has received; that all
being associated in the unity of that See whence the rights

---

* From the Acts (session third) of the Third General Council of Ephesus, A.D. 431, Labbe's Councils, vol. iii. p. 1154, Venice edition of 1728. See
also letter of St. Peter Chrysologus to Eutyches, in life prefixed to his
works, p. 13, Venice, 1750.

† From Sermon iii. chap. iii. of St. Leo the Great, vol. i. p. 12.

of communion spread to all, might grow together as members of one Head in the compact unity of the body.*

If then, any should deny that it is by the institution of Christ the Lord, or by divine right, that Blessed Peter should have a perpetual line of successors in the Primacy over the Universal Church, or that the Roman Pontiff is the successor of Blessed Peter in this primacy ; let him be anathema.

CHAPTER III.

ON THE POWER AND NATURE OF THE PRIMACY OF THE ROMAN PONTIFF.

Wherefore, resting on plain testimonies of the Sacred Writings, and adhering to the plain and express decrees both of our predecessors, the Roman Pontiffs, and of the General Councils, We renew the definition of the Œcumenical Council of Florence, in virtue of which all the faithful of Christ must believe that the Holy Apostolic See and the Roman Pontiff possesses the primacy over the whole world, and that the Roman Pontiff is the successor of Blessed Peter, Prince of the Apostles, and is true Vicar of Christ, and Head of the whole Church, and Father and Teacher of all Christians ; and that full power was given to him in Blessed Peter to rule, feed, and govern the Universal Church by Jesus Christ our Lord ; as is also contained in the acts of the General Councils and in the Sacred Canons.

Hence we teach and declare that by the appointment of our Lord the Roman Church possesses a superiority of ordinary power over all other Churches, and that this power

---

* From St. Irenaeus against Heresies, book iii. cap. iii. p. 175, Benedictine edition, Venice 1734 ; and Acts of Synod of Aquileia, A. D. 381, Labbé's Councils, vol. ii. p. 1185, Venice, 1728.

of jurisdiction of the Roman Pontiff, which is truly episcopal, is immediate; to which all, of whatever rite and dignity, both pastors and faithful, both individually and collectively, are bound, by their duty of hierarchial subordination and true obedience, to submit not only in matters
which belong to faith and morals, but also in those that ap-
pertain to the discipline and government of the Church
throughout the world, so that the Church of Christ may
be one flock under one supreme pastor through the preservation of unity both of communion and of profession of
the same faith with the Roman Pontiff. This is the teaching of Catholic truth, from which no one can deviate without loss of faith and of salvation.

But so far is this power of the Supreme Pontiff from
being any prejudice to the ordinary and immediate power
of episcopal jurisdiction, by which Bishops, who have been
set by the Holy Ghost to succeed and hold the place of
the Apostles,* feed and govern, each his own flock, as true
Pastors, that this their episcopal authority is really
asserted, strengthened, and protected by the supreme and
universal Pastor; in accordance with the words of St.
Gregory the Great; my honor is the honor of the whole
Church. My honor is the firm strength of my brethren.
I am truly honored, when the honor due to each and all
is not withheld.†

Further, from this supreme power possessed by the
Roman Pontiff of governing the Universal Church, it follows that he has the right of free communication with the
Pastors of the whole Church, and with their flocks, that
these may be taught and ruled by him in the way of salvation. Wherefore we condemn and reject the opinions
of those who hold that the communication between this

---

* From chap. iv. of xxiii. session of Council of Trent, "Of the Ecclesiastical Hierarchy."

† From the letters of St. Gregory the Great, book viii. 30, vol. ii. p.
919, Benedictine edition, Paris, 1705.

supreme Head and the Pastors and their flocks can lawfully be impeded; or who make this communication subject to the will of the secular power, so as to maintain that whatever is done by the Apostolic See, or by its authority, for the government of the Church, cannot have force or value unless it be confirmed by the assent of the secular power. And since by the divine right of Apostolic primacy, the Roman Pontiff is placed over the Universal Church, we further teach and declare that he is the supreme judge of the faithful,[*] and that in all causes, the decision of which belongs to the Church, recourse may be had to his tribunal,[†] and that none may re-open the judgment of the Apostolic See, than whose authority there is no greater, nor can any lawfully review its judgment.[‡] Wherefore they err from the right course who assert that it is lawful to appeal from the judgments of the Roman Pontiffs to an Œcumenical Council, as to an authority higher than that of the Roman Pontiff.

If then any shall say that the Roman Pontiff has the office merely of inspection or direction, and not full and supreme power of jurisdiction over the Universal Church, not only in things which belong to faith and morals, but also in those which relate to the discipline and government of the Church spread throughout the world; or assert that he possesses merely the principal part, and not all the fullness of this supreme power; or that this power which he enjoys is not ordinary and immediate, both over each and all the Churches and over each and all the Pastors and the faithful; let him be anathema.

---

* From a Brief of Pius VI. *Super soliditate*, of November 28, 1786.

† From the Acts of the Fourteenth General Council of Lyons, A. D. 1274. Labbé's Councils, vol. xiv. p. 512.

‡ From Letter viii. of Pope Nicholas I., A.D. 858, to the Emperor Michael, in Labbé's Councils, vol. ix. pp. 1339 and 1570.

CHAPTER IV.

CONCERNING THE INFALLIBLE TEACHING OF THE ROMAN PONTIFF.

Moreover, that the supreme power of teaching is also included in the Apostolic primacy, which the Roman Pontiff, as the successor of Peter, Prince of the Apostles, possesses over the whole Church, this Holy See has always held, the perpetual practice of the Church confirms, and Œcumenical Councils also have declared, especially those in which the East with the West met in the union of faith and charity. For the Fathers of the Fourth Council of Constantinople, following in the footsteps of their predecessors, gave forth this solemn profession : The first condition of salvation is to keep the rule of the true faith. And because the sentence of our Lord Jesus Christ cannot be passed by who said : Thou art Peter, and upon this Rock I will build my Church,* these things which have been said are approved by events, because in the Apostolic See the Catholic Religion and her holy and well-known doctrine has always been kept undefiled. Desiring, therefore, not to be in the least degree separated from the faith and doctrine of that See, we hope that we may deserve to be in the one communion, which the Apostolic See preaches, in which is the entire and true solidity of the Christian religion.† And, with the approval of the Second Council of Lyons, the Greeks professed that the Holy Roman Church enjoys supreme and full Primacy and preeminence over the whole Catholic Church, which it truly and humbly acknowledges that it has received with the plenitude of power from our Lord Himself in the person of blessed

---

* St. Matthew xvi. 18.

† From the Formula of St. Hormisdas, subscribed by the Fathers of the Eighth General Council (Fourth of Constantinople), A.D. 869. Labbé's Councils, vol. v. pp. 583, 622.

Peter, Prince or Head of the Apostles, whose successor the Roman Pontiff is; and as the Apostolic See is bound before all others to defend the truth of faith, so also if any questions regarding faith shall arise, they must be defined by its judgment.* Finally, the Council of Florence defined: † That the Roman Pontiff is the true Vicar of Christ, and the Head of the whole Church, and the Father and Teacher of all Christians; and that to him in blessed Peter was delivered by our Lord Jesus Christ the full power of feeding, ruling, and governing the whole Church.‡

To satisfy this pastoral duty our predecessors ever made unwearied efforts that the salutary doctrine of Christ might be propagated among all the nations of the earth, and with equal care watched that it might be preserved genuine and pure where it had been received. Therefore the Bishops of the whole world, now singly, now assembled in synod, following the long-established custom of Churches,§ and the form of the ancient rule,‖ sent word to this Apostolic See of those dangers especially which sprang up in matters of faith, that there the losses of faith might be most effectually repaired where the faith cannot fail.¶ And the Roman Pontiffs, according to the exigencies of times and circumstances, sometimes assembling Œcumenical Councils, or asking for the mind of the Church scattered throughout the world, sometimes by particular Synods, sometimes using other helps which Divine Providence sup-

---

* From the Acts of the Fourteenth General Council (Second of Lyons), A.D. 1274. Labbé, vol xiv. p. 512.

† From the Acts of the Seventeenth General Council of Florence, A.D. 1438. Labbé, vol. xviii. p. 526.

‡ John xxi. 15–17.

§ From a letter of St. Cyril of Alexandria to Pope St. Celestine I., A.D. 422, vol. vi. part ii. p. 36, Paris edition of 1638.

‖ From a Rescript of St. Innocent I. to the Council of Milevis, A.D. 402. Labbé, vol. iii. p. 47.

¶ From a letter of St. Bernard to Pope Innocent II. A.D. 1130. Epist. 191, vol. iv. p. 433, Paris edition of 1742.

plied, defined as to be held those things which with the help of God they had recognized as conformable with the Sacred Scriptures and Apostolic Traditions. For the Holy Spirit was not promised to the successors of Peter that by His revelation they might make known new doctrine, but that by His assistance they might inviolably keep and faithfully expound the revelation or deposit of faith delivered through the Apostles. And indeed all the venerable Fathers have embraced and the holy orthodox Doctors have venerated and followed their Apostolic doctrine; knowing most fully that this See of holy Peter remains ever free from all blemish of error according to the divine promise of the Lord our Saviour made to the Prince of His disciples : I have prayed for thee that thy faith fail not, and, when thou art converted, confirm thy brethren.*

This gift, then, of truth and never-failing faith was conferred by heaven upon Peter and his successors in this Chair, that they might perform their high office for the salvation of all; that the whole flock of Christ kept away by them from the poisonous food of error, might be nourished with the pasture of heavenly doctrine; that the occasion of schism being removed the whole Church might be kept one, and, resting on its foundation, might stand firm against the gates of hell.

But since in this very age, in which the salutary efficacy of the Apostolic office is most of all required, not a few are found who take away from its authority, we judge it altogether necessary solemnly to assert the prerogative which the only-begotten Son of God vouchsafed to join with the supreme pastoral office.

Therefore faithfully adhering to the tradition received from the beginning of the Christian faith, for the glory of God Our Saviour, the exaltation of the Catholic Religion, and the salvation of Christian people, the Sacred Council

---

* St. Luke xxii. 32. See also the Acts of the Sixth General Council, A.D. 680. Labbé vol. vii. p. 659.

approving, We teach and define that it is a dogma divinely revealed : that the Roman Pontiff, when he speaks *ex cathedra*, that is, when in discharge of the office of Pastor and Doctor of all Christians, by virtue of his supreme Apostolic authority he defines a doctrine regarding faith or morals to be held by the Universal Church, by the divine assistance promised to him in blessed Peter, is possessed of that infallibility with which the divine Redeemer willed that His Church should be endowed for defining doctrine regarding faith or morals : and that therefore such definitions of the Roman Pontiff are irreformable * of themselves, and not from the consent of the Church.

But if any one—which may God avert—presume to contradict this Our definition ; let him be anathema.

Given at Rome in Public Session solemnly held in the Vatican Basilica in the year of Our Lord one thousand eight hundred and seventy, on the eighteenth day of July, in the twenty-fifth year of our Pontificate.

In conformity with the original.

JOSEPH, *Bishop of S. Pollen,*
Secretary to the Vatican Council.

V.

RULES LAID DOWN BY THEOLOGIANS FOR DOCTRINAL DEFINITIONS.

Question.—What are the characters and marks whereby we may know whether a proposition can be submitted to the authoritative judgment of the Catholic magisterium, or

---

* *i.e.* in the words used by Pope Nicholas I. note 13, and in the Synod of Quedlinburg, A.D. 1085, "it is allowed to none to revise its judgment, and to sit in judgment upon what it has judged." Labbé, vol. xii. p. 679.

in other words, whether a proposition be definable as *de fide?*

Answer.—In the answer distinction was made between that which was sufficient in order to come to a definition, and that which was not necessary for that purpose.

With respect to that which was not necessary, the following four points were established unanimously.

1. It is not necessary, that antecedently there should not have been a variety of opinions in the Catholic Church, and that all should have agreed in that which is to be defined.

This is manifest from the ancient controversy long ago decided on re-baptism, although many bishops held the opposite opinion. This is also confirmed by the practice of the church, which many times has permitted the profession of opposite opinions, provided there has been a willingness to submit to any decision that might be made. This practice supposes that points may be defined, about which Catholics have been permitted to think and dispute freely.

2. It is not necessary that no writers of authority should be cited for an opinion contrary to that which is to be defined. This is manifest from the history of the dogmas successively defined; and in this place it will be sufficient to observe, that the Council of Trent (sess. vi. can. 23) did not hesitate to affirm as the faith of the church, that the most Holy Virgin Mother of God had never committed any even venial sin, although it is certain that grave doctors and Fathers wrote otherwise.

3. It is not necessary to cite texts, either implicit or explicit, from Holy Scripture, since it is manifest that the extent of revelation is greater than that of Holy Scripture. Thus, it has been defined, for example, that even infants may and ought to be baptized, that Christ our Lord is wholly contained and received under one species of the most Holy Eucharist, that the Holy Ghost proceeds from the Father and the Son as from one

II

principle, although theologians do not produce texts either implicit or explicit from Scripture in which such dogmas are taught.

4. Lastly, it is not necessary to have a series of fathers and testimonies reaching to apostolic times, in order to prove that such a proposition belongs to apostolic tradition. With respect to this, it was observed, that the assertion of such a necessity rests upon false hypotheses, and is refuted by the most palpable facts.

The false hypotheses are,

a. That all doctrine preached from the beginning has been committed to writing by the fathers.

b. That all the monuments of antiquity have come down to us.

c. That the entire object of faith has always been distinctly conceived and formally expressed;

d. That subsequent tradition may differ from the preceding;

e. That it cannot be legitimately concluded from the fact that a doctrine is held in any age, that the same doctrine was never denied by the majority, and that it was at least implicitly believed by the greater number.

The facts that refute such a necessity are manifold, but it suffices to mention the definition of Ephesus, of Chalcedon, of the Lateran Synod under Martin I. or the dogmatical letters of St. Leo and St. Agatho, in which appeal is made to the faith of the fathers and to tradition, and where there appears to be no anxiety to produce testimonies of the first three centuries, on the contrary, authors are quoted, who in those times were of recent date.

Having thus laid down by common agreement that which was not necessary, they passed on to discuss what was sufficient in order that an opinion should be defined as an article of faith.

The five following characters were proposed and decided upon as being sufficient.

I. A certain number of grave testimonies containing the controverted proposition.

This after thorough discussion was unanimously acknowledged to be a sufficient character, and it was said that to deny it would be going against the councils, the dogmatic bulls of pontiffs, and the economy of the church itself. Thus with a certain number of such testimonies referred to in the acts of the councils, it is easily seen how the fathers proceeded to a definition at Ephesus against Nestorius, in the sixth council against the Monothelites, and in the seventh against the Iconoclasts.

II. One or more revealed principles in which is contained the proposition in question.

Upon this also the consultors were unanimous, and they moreover said that the production of such principles would be equivalent to a virtual and immediate revelation. Thus, from the revealed principle that Jesus Christ is perfect God and perfect man, it follows as revealed that Jesus Christ has two wills:. also, in the revealed principle that God is One and the Divine Persons three, and that all in God is one except where the relation of origin intervenes, it is also revealed that the Holy Ghost can only proceed from the Father and the Son as from one principle of spiration.

III. The intimate nexus of the dogmas, or, what is the same thing, that a proposition must be believed to be revealed, from the denial of which the falsity of one or more articles of faith would necessarily and immediately follow.

The consultors were unanimous on this point, agreeing that such a character was equivalent to a virtual and immediate revelation. Thus, when it is established that some sins are mortal, and that not every sin is incompatible with a state of grace, it necessarily follows that the distinction between mortal and venial sins is a revealed doctrine. So also from the fact that the Sacraments produce their effect *ex opere operato* and that Jesus Christ is the primary minister of them, it follows as virtually and immediately revealed, that the effect of the Sacraments does not depend upon the virtue or malice of the secondary minister.

IV. The concordant testimony of the existing episcopate.

The consultors with regard to this were again unanimous, and it was said that to deny the sufficiency of this character was to contradict the promises of our Lord, and the constant practice of the fathers in proving the articles of faith. Thus Irenæus, Tertullian, Augustine, and Fulgentius, in order to put an end to controversies, considered it sufficient to ascertain the faith of the Sees and more especially the chief ones.

V. The practice of the Church.

That this point would afford sufficient evidence to proceed to a definition, was likewise unanimously affirmed by the consultors.

VI.

THE CASE OF HONORIUS.

I HAVE intentionally refrained from treating the historical evidence in the case of Honorius in the text of the fourth chapter, for the following reasons:

1. Because it is sufficient to the argument of that chapter to affirm that the case of Honorius is doubtful. It is in vain for the antagonists of Papal Infallibility to quote this case as if it were certain. Centuries of controversy have established, beyond contradiction, that the accusation against Honorius cannot be raised by his most ardent antagonists to more than a probability. And this probability, at its maximum, is less than that of his defence. I therefore affirm the question to be doubtful; which is abundantly sufficient against the private judgment of his accusers. The

cumulus of evidence for the Infallibility of the Roman Pontiff outweighs all such doubts.

2. Because the argument of the fourth chapter necessarily excludes all 'discussion of detailed facts. Had they been introduced into the text, our antagonists would have evaded the point, and confused the argument by a discussion of details. I will, nevertheless, here affirm, that the following points in the case of Honorius can be abundantly proved from documents :

(1) That Honorius defined no doctrine whatsoever.
(2) That he forbade the making of any new definition.
(3) That his fault was precisely in this omission of Apostolic authority, for which he was justly censured.
(4) That his two epistles are entirely orthodox; though, in the use of language, he wrote as was usual before the condemnation of Monothelitism, and not as it became necessary afterwards. It is an anachronism and an injustice to censure his language, used before that condemnation, as it might be just to censure it after the condemnation had been made.

To this I add the following excellent passage from the recent Pastoral of the Archbishop of Baltimore :

"The case of Honorius forms no exception; for 1st, Honorius expressly says in his letters to Sergius, that he meant to define nothing, and. he was condemned precisely because he temporized and would not define; 2nd, because in his letters he clearly taught the sound Catholic doctrine, only enjoining silence as to the use of certain terms, then new in the Church; and 3rd, because his letters were not addressed to a general council of the whole Church, and were rather private, than public and official; at least they were not published, even in the East, until several years later. The first letter was written to Sergius in 633, and eight years afterwards, in 641, the Emperor Heraclius, in exculpating himself to Pope John II., Honorius' successor, for having published his edict—the *Ecthesis*—which enjoined silence on the disputants, similar to that imposed by Honorius, lays the whole responsibility thereof on Sergius, who he declares, composed the edict. Evidently, Sergius had not communicated the letter to the Emperor, probably because its contents, if published, would not have suited his wily purpose of secretly introducing, under another form, the Eutcyhian heresy. Thus falls to the ground the only case upon which the opponents of Infallibility have continued to insist. This entire subject has been exhausted by many recent learned writers."

On the question of Virgilius, see Cardinal Orsi *De irreformabili Rom. Pont. in definiendis fidei controversiis judicio,* tom. i. p. i. capp. 19, 20; Jeremias a Benetti's *Privileg. S. Petri vindic.* p. ii. tom. v. art. 12, p. 397, ed. Roman. 1759; Ballerini *De vi et ratione primatus,* cap. 15; Lud. Thomassin, *Disp. xix. in Concil.;* Petr. De Marca *Diss. de Vigilio;* Vincenzi in S. Gregorii Nyss. et Origenis scripta cum App. de actis Synodi V. tom. iv. and v.

On the question of Honorius, amongst older writers: Ios. Biner S. J. in *Apparatu eruditionis,* p. iii. iv. and xi.; Orsi, op. cit. capp. 21–28; Bellarm. *De Rom. Pontif.* liv. iv.; Thomassin, op. cit. diss. xx.; Natalis Alex. *Hist. Eccles. Saec. VII.* diss. 2.; Zaccaria *Antifebrom.* p. ii. lib. iv. Amongst later authors, see *Civilta cattolica,* ann. 1864, ser. v. vol. xi. and xii.; Schneeman, *Studia in qu. de Honorio;* Ios. Pennachi *de Honorii I. Romani Pontificis causa in Concilio VI.*

VII.

PASTORAL OF THE GERMAN BISHOPS ASSEMBLEI) AT FULDA.

" The undersigned Bishops to the reverend clergy and faithful, greeting, and peace in the Lord.

" Having returned to our respective Dioceses from the Holy Œcumenical Council of the Vatican, we, in union with other German Bishops who were prevented attending the Council, consider it our duty as your chief pastors to address to you, dearly beloved in the Lord, a few words of instruction and exhortation. The occasion and reason for our doing so, and that unitedly and solemnly, is found in the fact that many erroneous ideas have for several months been disseminated, and still, without any authority, are striving in many places to gain acceptance.

" In order, then, to maintain the divine truths which Christ our Lord hath taught mankind in their entire purity, and to secure them from all change and distortion, He has established in His Holy Church the office of infallible teaching, and has promised and also given to it His protection and the assistance of the Holy Ghost for all times. On this office of infallible teaching of the Church reposes entire the security and joy of our faith.

" As often as in the course of time misunderstandings of or oppositions to, individual points of teaching have sprung up, this office of infallible teaching has in various ways, at one time in greater Councils, at another without them, both exposed and foiled the errors, and declared and established the truth. This has been done in the most solemn manner by the General Councils, that is, by those great assemblies in which the Head and the members of the one teaching body of the Church combined for the deciding of the doubts and controversies in matters of faith which then prevailed.

"These decisions, according to the unanimous and un-doubted tradition of the Church, have always been held to be preserved from error by a supernatural and divine as-sistance. Hence the faithful in all times have submitted themselves to these decisions as to the infallible expres-sions of the Holy Ghost Himself, and, with undoubting faith, have held them to be true. They have done so, not, as persons might suppose, because the Bishops were men of mature and extended experience, not because many of them were versed in all sciences, not because they had come together from all parts of the world, and therefore, in a cer-tain sense, brought together the human knowledge of the whole earth; not, lastly, because through a long life they had studied and taught the Word of God, and hence were trustworthy witnesses of its meaning. All this indeed gives to their declarations a very high, indeed perhaps the highest possible, degree of mere human trustworthiness. Still this is not a sufficient ground on which to rest super-natural faith. For this act, in its last resort, rests not on the testimony of men, even when they are most worthy of confidence, and even if the whole human race by the voice of its best and most noble representatives should bear wit-ness to it; but such an act always rests wholly and alone on the truth of God Himself. When therefore the chil-dren of the Church receive with faith the decrees of a Gen-eral Council, they do it with a conviction that God the Eternal and alone of Himself Infallible Truth co-operates with it in a supernatural manner, and preserves it from error.

"Such a General Council is the present one which our Holy Father Pius IX., as you know, convoked in Rome, and to which the successors of the Apostles, in larger num-bers than ever before, have hastened from all parts of the world, that they might, with the successor of St. Peter and under his guidance, consult for the present urgent interests of the Church. After many and serious debates the Holy

Father, in virtue of his Apostolical authority as teacher, on April 24 and July 18 of this year, with the consent of the holy Council, solemnly published several decrees relating to the true doctrine about faith, the Church, and its supreme head.

"By this means, then, the infallible teaching authority of the Church has decreed, and the Holy Ghost by the vicar of Christ and the Episcopate united with him has spoken: and therefore all, whether Bishops, priests or laymen, are bound to receive their degrees as divinely revealed truths, and with joyful hearts lay hold of them, and confess the same, if they wish to be and remain true members of the one Holy Catholic and Apostolic Church. When, then, beloved in the Lord, objections are raised, and you hear it maintained that the Vatican Council is no true General Council, and that its decisions are of no authority, do not allow yourselves to be led astray thereby, so as to falter in your devotion to the Church and in your belief and acceptance of its decrees; for such objections are wholly unfounded.

"Bound together in the unity of faith and love with the Pope, have the assembled Bishops, both those who in Christian lands administer well-established sees, and also those who are called to extend the Kingdom of God among the heathen in apostolic poverty, Bishops, whether they tend a larger or a smaller flock—these, as legitimate successors of the Apostles, have all with the same right taken part in the Council, and maturely considered everything.

"As long as the discussions lasted, the Bishops, as their consciences demanded, and as became their office, expressed their views plainly and openly, and with all necessary freedom ; and, as was only to be expected in an assembly of nearly 800 Fathers, many differences of opinion were manifested. These differences of opinion can in no way affect the authority of the decrees themselves ; should even we not take into consideration the fact, that almost

II*

the entire body of the Bishops who, at the time of the
Public Session, still maintained an opposite opinion, ab-
stained in the said Session from expressing dissent.

" However, to maintain that either the one or the other
of the doctrines decided by the General Council are not
contained in the Holy Scripture, and in tradition of the
Church—those two sources of the Catholic faith—or that
they are even in opposition to the same, is a first step,
irreconcilable with the primary principles of the Catholic
Church, which leads to separation from her communion.
Wherefore, we hereby declare that the present Vatican
Council is a legitimate General Council; and, moreover,
that this Council, as little as any other General Council,
has propounded or formed a new doctrine at variance with
the ancient teaching; but that it has simply developed and
thrown light upon the old and faithfully-preserved truth
contained in the deposit of faith, and in opposition to the
errors of the day has proposed it expressly to the belief of
all the faithful; and, lastly, that these decrees have received a binding power on all the faithful by the fact of
their final publication by the Supreme Head of the Church
in solemn form at the Public Session.

" While, then, we ourselves with full and unhesitating
faith adhere to the decrees of the Council, we exhort you
as your divinely appointed pastors and teachers, and be-
seech you in love to your souls, to give no ear to any
teaching contrary to this, whencesoever it may come.
Cling all the more unwaveringly, in union so with your
Bishops, to the teaching and faith of the Catholic Church;
let nothing separate you from the Rock on which Jesus
Christ has founded His Church, with the promise that the
' gates of hell shall not prevail against it.' In view of the
excitement which exists in consequence of un-ecclesiastical
manifestations and movements against the decrees of the
Council in several places, and which undoubtedly forms no
small trial and danger to many souls, as well as considering

the tremendous war which has been forced upon our German Fatherland, and which claims at the same time our intense interest and watchfulness, and which has already plunged innumerable families into sorrow and mourning, we cannot forbear from earnestly calling all the faithful to fervent prayer for the present great necessities of Church and State. Lift up, then, your hearts in faith and confidence to our Father in Heaven, Whose wise and loving Providence guides and rules everything, and whose Divine Son has promised most surely to hear us when we ask in His name.

"Pray, also, with faith and trust that this sanguinary war, by a complete triumph of the right cause, and a true and lasting peace, may quickly end. Pray for the wants of Holy Church, especially for all who err or hesitate in their faith, that they may have the grace of a firm, decided, and living faith. Pray for the Supreme Head of the Church, the holy Father, who most likely at this very moment is more than ever before in distress and embarrassment. Pray with confidence in the merits and infinite love of the Divine heart of Jesus Christ, invoking the powerful intercession of the Immaculate Virgin Mother of God.

"And may the blessing of God Almighty descend upon you and remain with you all, in the name of the Father, and of the Son and of the Holy Ghost.—Amen.

"At the end of August, 1870.

✠ GREGORY, Archbishop of Munich.
✠ PAUL, Archbishop of Cologne.
✠ PETER JOSEPH, Bishop of Limburg.
✠ CHRISTOPHER FLORENTIUS, Bishop of Fulda.
✠ WILLIAM EMMANUEL, Bishop of Mayence.
✠ EDWARD JAMES, Bishop of Hildesheim.
✠ CONRAD, Bishop of Paderhorn.
✠ JOHN, Bishop of Kulm.
✠ IGNATIUS, Bishop of Ratisbon.

✠ Pancratius, Bishop of Augsburg.

✠ Francis Leopold, Bishop of Eichstadt.

✠ Matthias, Bishop of Treves.

✠ Philip, Bishop of Ermland.

✠ Lothair, Bishop of Leuka *in partibus*, Administrator of the Archbishopric of Friburg.

✠ Adolphus, Bishop of Agathonopolis *in partibus*, Chaplain-in-Chief of the Forces.

✠ Bernard Brinkmann, Vicar-Capitular and Bishop Elect of Munster

Conrad Reitha, Bishop Elect of Speyer."

• THE END.